HIS
FORGOTTEN
HIGHLAND
BRIDE

CLAN MACPHERSON SERIES

HIS FORGOTTEN HIGHLAND BRIDE

CLAN MACPHERSON SERIES

ALLISON B. HANSON

This book is a work of fiction. Names, characters, places, and incidents are the product of the author's imagination or are used fictitiously. Any resemblance to actual events, locales, or persons, living or dead, is coincidental.

Copyright © 2026 by Allison B. Hanson. All rights reserved, including the right to reproduce, distribute, or transmit in any form or by any means. For information regarding subsidiary rights, please contact the Author.

Edited by Alethea Spiridon
Cover design by Mayhem Cover Creations

Chapter One

Scottish Highlands
May 1690

No word, English or Gaelic, could adequately describe the amount of trouble Brenna Innes was in. Nudging her black warhorse faster, she prayed it wasn't as late as she thought. But even the gray sky could not hide the muted glow of the sun hanging much too low to the western horizon.

This day, of all days, her absence would be noticed, for the man she'd be marrying on the morrow had most certainly already arrived. Had she slept soundly the night before, she might not have dozed off by the loch for what now seemed to be a large part of the day.

She slowed only slightly as she took the gate that stood open for her. Pulling her horse to a stop, Brenna realized it was far worse than she'd expected. The bailey was filled with her parents and their guests staring at her. There'd be no opportunity to sneak in the side door by the kitchens to get to her room to wash and change.

With the sudden absence of wind rushing past her ears, she was struck with deadly silence, interrupted only by her sister's gasp, followed by her mother's whispered, "Good God in heaven," in direct opposition to the handsome, blond man who cursed, "What the devil?"

Brenna was sure he wasn't speaking of her horse, Brimstone, when questioning the devil. He was indeed referring to her. What a horrible impression she'd made on her intended. Her booted feet made a soft thud on the bricks as she slid down unassisted and handed the reins to her colossal stallion off to a gaping groom.

Most of her unruly brown hair had liberated itself from the messy plait she'd had it in. Running a nervous hand over it, she was jabbed in the thumb by a stick she quickly tossed aside. Giving up on straightening her hair, she slid her damp palms over the buttery leather of her braes. Because, of course, she hadn't been riding in a gown. It was so much more humiliating to be seen for the first time by one's betrothed while wearing men's clothing.

Her father, the laird of the Innes clan, would no doubt think this was some stubborn attempt to avoid the marriage he'd hastily arranged for her, but in truth, she was eager for the match. Or, instead, she was eager to leave Innes House.

She'd hoped for the chance to cast aside her former reputation of being the wild, younger daughter of the Innes laird and start anew somewhere no one knew her. Now, it would seem she'd ruined her chance at appearing anything but a hellion in front of her groom. Brenna's sister, Hannah, was the picture of perfection with her silky, russet waves and green eyes. She chuckled endearingly as she rushed forth and snatched a leaf from Brenna's tunic.

"Wherever have you been, sister?" she asked loud enough for everyone to hear. "Did a rival clan capture ye? Mayhap pirates?" Hannah's jest earned a chuckle from the guests. The petite woman could win over any crowd, even one suffering utter shock from Brenna's chaotic entrance.

If they were already put off by this small example of Brenna's recklessness, she worried there was no hope of them ever accepting her—not if they ever found out about her current title as fastest rider or how often she was found running. Brenna disliked anything that happened slowly. She had no patience to sit and read, and her embroidery was nothing but a mess of thread.

She needed to be moving. Except that was not the way of proper ladies. At least, that was what Hannah told her repeatedly.

Brenna wondered if her sister would even care if pirates had taken her. Somehow, such a situation would be twisted to be Brenna's fault for allowing herself to be kidnapped.

Everything was Brenna's fault. She wished she could cast off such an accusation as unfair, but it was best not to lie to oneself, so she owned the truth.

She was a right mess most days and a menace other days. Things always seemed to get worse when she attempted decorum, as if a curse had been placed on her as a babe. Oh, how she wished to believe in such things because then, at least, there would be an excuse. And unlike with most things, this situation *was* completely Brenna's fault.

Her mother, always the proper lady of the keep, clapped her hands to get everyone's attention. "My daughter has just arrived. Shall we venture inside for refreshments while Brenna makes herself presentable?"

Presentable. She would be a happy soul if she could go the rest of her life without hearing that word. In all of Brenna's ten and nine years, she couldn't remember when anyone had used that word to describe her. Instead, it was a state she was constantly unable to achieve. She looked over to the man she assumed was her bridegroom. Two men were standing in formal plaids with brooches. Brenna knew it was the laird of the Grants, and his grandson, her intended. The three men behind them looked like retainers, so she was sure she was looking into her future husband's sharp, brown eyes.

They'd be married to each other by this time tomorrow. Swallowing loudly, she realized she'd not caught his name. She only remembered her father referring to him as "the Grant heir" while her mother called him "a dear soul." At the time, Brenna had assumed he suffered from some impairment. But now she realized *she* was most likely the man's impairment. No matter. She was sure he wouldn't know her name, either.

"Lady Brenna." Her future husband offered a nod of respect in her direction. His lips were pulled up on one side in what she could only describe as a smirk.

Did he find her a person to be smirked at? Did he think her amusing? Her fingers clenched as she refrained from reaching for her dirk and drawing his blood. That behavior wouldn't help her cause; neither would stabbing her intended. It wouldn't be deemed presentable by her mother. Instead, she gazed at the lovely man. His golden, blond locks curled elegantly down to his shoulders, catching the day's remaining sunlight and reflecting it in a high shine. His warm, brown eyes took her in from her scuffed boots up to the messy nest of hair and possibly more twigs.

His stare, thorough as it was, gave no hint as to what he was thinking. When he'd finished his perusal, he looked back to her mother. Hannah, still at Brenna's side, nudged her.

"What?" Brenna asked.

Her sister curtseyed and pulled Brenna along with her. Ah, yes. He must think her a barbarian with no manners. Brenna dropped lower than her sister. Everything between them was a competition, and she'd not be outdone. If there was any advantage to wearing men's clothing, it was to dip the lowest courtesy in all the lands. She wished she'd been able to smirk at herself for such a foolish thought.

"Henry," Hannah whispered as they rose. Bless her for helping Brenna through this devastating display. Hannah was unlikely to help her with anything, but perhaps Brenna was such an embarrassment that she'd even turned Hannah sweet.

"It is very nice to meet you, Henry."

That deafening silence returned, and she heard her sister's soft laughter behind her in the echo of nothingness. Desperation caused Brenna to drop her defenses.

"I say, who is Henry?" the old laird asked.

"I believe I am," her groom said, turning to her parents. "Is the girl daft?" And then, back to his grandfather, he said, "We wouldn't be the first clan tricked into an alliance with a deficient daughter. We should go."

As Brenna stood close to them, ready to beg he not run off, she heard the older man's whispered response.

"Ronan, you know why we must move forward with the match. Think of Ewan."

Her intended, Ronan—not Henry—frowned at his grandsire and then narrowed his gaze on her again.

"Perhaps we may all retire to our chambers to wash and prepare for the last meal," the elderly laird suggested.

Ronan gestured she should follow him into the keep. When he did the same to her sister, Hannah snaked her arm through Ronan's and was now being properly escorted inside like a queen. Why hadn't Brenna thought of this?

The only thing keeping Brenna from shoving Hannah away from her intended was the knowledge Hannah was also betrothed. An elaborate ceremony was being planned for the nuptials between the eldest daughter of Laird Innes and the Laird of the MacIntosh clan in the most important alliance to grace the Highlands in centuries.

Meanwhile, Brenna's offer was made only a few days ago, and she'd be handfasted in the morning without even the benefit of a new dress, for there had been no time. Looking over her shoulder, Brenna saw her sister flirting with her intended. Hannah managed to earn a few low rumbles of laughter from his broad chest. Brenna straightened her shoulders and lifted her chin.

What she should have been doing was watching where she was walking. Her boot found an uneven brick, and she sprawled on her stomach. How was she so adept seated on a beast with four hooves yet unable to master her feet?

A curse left Brenna's lips. She'd thought it had been whispered, but her mother's whimper proved it'd been louder than she'd thought. Hannah snickered behind her as Ronan came forward to offer a hand she didn't need. She was capable of getting up on her own. Another benefit of wearing breeches…covering her arse when she fell.

Frowning at the man, he hastily pulled back his hand as she brushed her scraped hands on her legs. This first meeting could have been better. But what had she expected?

If this man wanted a biddable wife who spent her days sitting in the solar sewing and reading, he would be disappointed and likely frustrated with her.

Should she attempt to hide the less acceptable things about herself? The late-night wandering, the hunting, the racing, the running, the cursing and general disorder? All the things that made her who she was. Her very soul.

It was too late, she thought, as she watched Hannah take his arm yet again.

Besides, it was no matter what happened today, for, in the morning, Brenna would be wed to Ronan and they'd have the rest of their lives, without Hannah's presence, to get to know one another. And maybe, someday, even fall in love. Not that she knew much about falling in love or how one went about making it happen. Her parents, while always respectful in their dealings, weren't overly fond of one another.

But Hannah often spoke of the emotion as if it was the most coveted thing one could hope to acquire. She described it as a partnership where the subjects accept each other through their faults and shortcomings. The idea that someone would take her as she was and choose to be with her above all others sounded divine.

She didn't know how to get her new husband to fall in love with her, but she would stop at nothing to make it happen. She spent all her days feeling as if she didn't belong in her own family, always falling short and disappointing them when she acted herself and failing when she tried to be who they wanted her to be.

Hannah once told her she was most likely a changeling, an inept replacement for the proper sister who fairies had taken. Despite her mother's promise it was untrue, Brenna thought it made a good bit of sense. If the real Brenna Innes lived with the fairies, did she feel as out of place as Brenna felt here among her clan?

This marriage would be a fresh start, a chance to belong.

She could not make a mess of it.

***

As soon as Ronan extricated himself from the green-eyed beauty who'd escorted him to his room, he left his chamber to speak to his grandsire. Having only spent summers with the Grants since his mother married the MacPherson laird when Ronan was ten, he wasn't as close with his grandfather as most heirs would have been. But he felt comfortable enough to complain about the man's plan formally.

"I canna marry the hellion. Did ye see her?"

"Aye. My sight has not abandoned me yet. The lass is feisty."

"*Feisty?* She's a menace. How am I to take such a woman to wife? I believe she was drunk, based on the inability to keep on her feet, calling me the wrong name, and the cursing." He rubbed his forehead. "She was wearing men's clothing, and don't even get me started on the sticks in her nest of hair. Is that the way she greets guests?"

His grandsire offered a wink. "The spirited ones are better in bed. I can think of worse things than having a bride unafraid to get some sticks in her hair."

Ronan rolled his eyes. At twenty summers, he had more on his mind than taking a wife. He'd had no trouble getting women to warm his bed when he'd shown interest. There was much more to life than bed sport. The glory of being a soldier, for one. But if he didn't agree to this ridiculous arrangement, his grandsire would not allow him to go to the war in France with his stepbrother, Shane. They'd entered into this agreement a few days before. But now Ronan felt sure he was getting the worst part of the deal. As an heir, only his grandfather could grant his permission to leave Scotland. The man had refused until, thanks to Ronan's uncle, he'd needed Ronan's help.

The lift of his grandfather's bushy, gray eyebrow proved he knew he had Ronan by the cods. Still, there might be another way…

"The older daughter," he said. "She's quite lovely, and from the way she gripped my arse before leaving me, she'd be agreeable to a match."

Before he'd even finished speaking the words, the laird shook his head.

"The pretty one is already betrothed to the MacIntosh clan. There's no getting her free of it. I'd marry you off to the MacIntosh laird if it could be done." The man chuckled at his jest.

Ronan felt a strange relief at learning the other woman was already spoken for. Despite her being the more acceptable of the sisters, the eldest—dressed in her fine silks and air of entitlement—put him in mind of his mother. Lady Deirdre MacPherson expected all to fawn over her. She'd undoubtedly found a man to do her bidding. But Ronan didn't wish to fall victim to a cunning bride.

Still, while he didn't wish to be manipulated by a woman's beauty, he didn't want such a mess for a wife.

"Why can't Ewan marry the girl? His doing has gotten us into this mess in the first place."

Ewan, only four years Ronan's senior, was Uncle Ewan. They'd grown up more like brothers than uncle and nephew because of their ages. Ronan had followed the older lad across every hill on Grant lands as a boy, wanting to be like him.

When Ronan's father died, and his mother married the MacPherson laird, Ronan begged to stay behind with Ewan and the Grants. For the first week after arriving at Cluny Castle, Ronan had refused to speak to his new stepbrothers and stepsister. Eventually, the walls were broken down, and Shane became the older brother Ronan had once had in Ewan. Now, as adults, Ewan had taken to drinking and carousing, while as heir, Ronan was taught the ways of being the laird in his father's absence.

"You are the heir, not Ewan. My youngest isn't even war chief because he refused the honor. No laird is going to marry his daughter to a second son. We need a strong alliance with the Innes clan. If anyone were to discover what Ewan has done, there'd be war between us. A war we'd not win against the Inneses, especially with the MacIntoshes at their back."

His grandsire rubbed absently at his chest. Ronan wasn't sure if there was pain or if the gesture was to remind Ronan that his grandsire was not a young man. If the laird were to fall ill and die, it would end Ronan's plans to go to France, not to mention Ronan cared for the old buzzard.

"Very well, I'll see it done."

His grandfather clapped him on the back. "Marry the lass, bed her, get an heir on her, and then ye can take as many lemans as ye wish and forget about her."

Ronan swallowed at the thought of doing such a thing. He did not pretend to harbor feelings for Brenna Innes, but he'd never treat a wife in such a way. Perhaps his years of seeing how the MacPherson laird doted on Ronan's mother, Deirdre, had made an impression. He didn't plan to be as obsessed as his stepfather was with his mother, but he'd not betray his vows. What was a man without his word? His grandsire must have seen the disgust on his face, for he softened and patted Ronan on the shoulder.

"Who can say what might come of it? It could work out quite well."

Ronan would marry the lass, bed her to consummate the union, and then go to battle as planned. However, recalling her entrance earlier, he doubted the lass would be easy to forget.

Chapter Two

Brenna pulled back from the door and covered her mouth. She'd been punished more than a few times for eavesdropping, but seeing her future husband enter his grandfather's room and leave the door cracked proved too great a temptation.

"Eavesdroppers never hear good of themselves," her mother always scolded. She had never heard something so wretched as the instructions for Ronan. Bed her and *forget* her? How appalling.

She knew that her prospects were limited as a laird's daughter. To be married off to create an alliance was the only thing waiting for her. But she'd hoped for a kind man, not to become a broodmare while her husband warmed the bed of lasses high and low.

Forget about her.

Was that to be her fate?

She shook her head and returned to her bed chamber. She briefly looked at the window, wondering if she could escape from this height. But what would she do then? Fortunately, there was another way. She could escape this destiny by telling her father what else she'd heard at the door. Something this Ewan had done that would bring the clans to war if it were found out. Surely, that would change her father's mind about shackling her to such a horrid clan.

War wasn't something she'd enjoy starting, but wouldn't it be better than marrying a man who seemed to despise her? Who wouldn't be faithful to his vows? She called for her maid to help her dress in her second-best gown as she considered her options. Brenna still hadn't come up with a solution as she went down to the great hall to sit next to the man who may or may not become her husband.

She presented a curtsey at his bow, not relatively as low as before because of the corset, and directly met his warm, brown eyes. His lips pulled up into a smile. She could only think he was heartened by the lack of flora spilling from her hair.

"I must apologize for earlier," she said quietly when everyone was seated and the food served.

"You do not always rush into the bailey riding Satan's beast in breeches?"

She cleared her throat. To say no would be a lie. While this man held secrets, too, she did not have to stoop to such a level. Telling him the truth would be the easier way to do that rather than spur war between their clans.

"I do. However, I don't often do so in anticipation of visitors. And I'm rarely late."

His smile grew into a full grin. If she thought telling the truth would force him to back down, it appeared she'd need to try harder.

"I see. And as for calling me Henry?"

"In truth, your name was not told to me. I should have thought to ask. I was so excited by the news, I didn't stop to take in the details." This seemed to surprise him.

"You're excited to wed a stranger?"

She swallowed and stuck to her plan to tell him the truth. She granted him a nod. The truth without elaboration. "I take it you are not excited to be marrying me."

He opened his mouth to refute her insinuation, but she put up a hand to stop him.

"Ye don't need to deny it. I know I'm rather plain." Her brown hair was rather dull. Her eyes were the color of green mud. Her stature was without the soft curves other women had. And if all of this wasn't enough, standing next to her sister was so much worse as if in contrast.

"May I ask something?"

He squinted and nodded.

"We do not know each other yet. It won't be easy to learn about the other if we don't speak the truth. Attempting to spare my feelings won't get the job done. Promise me we will at least offer one another honesty."

"Honesty." Ronan's throat bobbed with the word, and he met her eyes. "Aye."

She smiled and held out her hand to shake his. With a laugh and a shake of his head, he took it and gave it a firm shake. When her groom smiled as he did then, he was charming. A dimple pulled along the crease of his cheek, and his white teeth sparkled in the light from the sconces. Those brown eyes became deep pools of warmth, beckoning her closer. Being this close to him, she realized how tall he was. His shoulders, broad with muscle, fit well on his lean body.

When he blinked in what she guessed was confusion, she noticed she'd been leaning closer than was typical for two people during a meal.

Clearing his throat, he pulled away and focused on his food instead. She did the same, realizing she was now even more uncertain about how to proceed than she'd been before.

"Brimstone."

"Excuse me?"

"Ye said my horse was from Satan. His name is Brimstone."

"I see." He frowned. "May I ask, why is your horse so large? Is your father unable to purchase a fitting horse for a lady?"

She tilted her head to the side. "I assure you he is quite fitting for *this* lady."

He looked her over and shook his head. "He is too large for you. And too spirited. You'll be thrown to your death. I'll get you something suitable."

"Might I point out that if I am thrown to my death after the wedding, you'll be free without needing to bother with the effort of forgetting me?" As soon as the words were out, she realized her error. She looked up into his horror-stricken face.

"You were listening?" His whisper was almost too low to make out in the busy hall.

"I—I happened by and overheard…"

"How much did you overhear?"

"Enough." She shrugged. Hadn't she been the one to suggest honesty between them? "I know it's marriage or war with the Innes clan."

"And what do you plan to do with this information?"

It was a fitting question. She'd been weighing her options as she was scrubbed and prodded into the image of a proper lady, and she'd come to no conclusions.

Telling her father would put an end to her marriage before they'd spoken their vows. They could be launched directly into war, and she'd be forced to wait for the next match.

And if none came?

She would stay here, trying to be someone she wasn't and failing miserably.

Or…she could follow through with this marriage and move to the Grants' stronghold where she might have the opportunity to find a home or make a family who'd like her for who she was.

The chances weren't good, having heard how much her betrothed wished to marry Hannah instead of her. But he'd smiled at her moments ago, and she felt warmed by the sincerity in his eyes.

She let out a sigh and shook her head before answering his question. "I'm not sure yet."

***

Ronan was married, though he still wasn't sure why she'd gone through with it. But as Brenna smiled up at him with a wreath of flowers on her head, he felt a silly bit of pride that she had. She'd called herself plain, and while he'd thought of arguing the notion at the time, he had to agree with her. But she'd asked for honesty, so he hadn't offered her flattery.

It wasn't that she was unsightly. She was just

rather ordinary. None of the features of her face stood out as bonny. But now, with the pleased smile lighting her bright, hazel eyes, he found she was not as plain as he'd initially considered. Next to her angelic sister, Brenna was subdued by the brightness of Lady Hannah. But here, next to him, with happiness lighting her from within and flora *purposely* twisted in her wild curls, Brenna was striking. It would be no difficulty to take her to his bed, which would be soon.

After their handfasting, the rest of the morning was spent in the hall celebrating with a moderate feast. Laird and Lady Innes spoke of their eldest daughter's pending nuptials as if they'd be the year's festivities. Ronan wondered how his new wife bore it, having her special day overshadowed by her sister. But there she smiled as if nothing would mar this moment, knowing it was a collection of paupers compared to what would be done for Lady Hannah's wedding.

He marveled at the strength to keep that smile in place, knowing what she'd heard the evening before. Shame brought heat to his cheeks as he recalled his grandsire's recommendation to bed and forget her.

Ronan watched Brenna bubbling over in happy chatter as those closest to her rolled their eyes at her antics. Sympathy spurred defensiveness in his heart, and he reached for her hand.

"Shall we be on our way? We'll want to get to Strathspey before dark," he announced. It was true enough, but he wanted to leave for another reason—to get her away from these people who should have cared for her and so clearly didn't. Not that he'd do much better, but at least he had a reason.

"Aye," his wife answered. "I've already packed my things, and the trunk has been loaded onto the wagon."

Not only had she stood up with him to become his wife, but she was eager to go to his home. He was amazed by her courage and saddened she must be so desperate to leave this place.

Her parents, while not patient, didn't seem cruel. The sister seemed to take great amusement in embarrassing Brenna at every opportunity. Had he initially thought Hannah was bonny? Seeing her as he knew her after this short time, he found her lacking, even possibly lacking a soul. A better man would have encouraged Brenna to tell her father why his grandsire requested the alliance. But Ronan was not a better man.

It wasn't only that a war between the Grants and the Innes clan would delay his plans to go to France with Shane, but that Ronan wanted to take his new bride away from this place that, for whatever reason, she was eager to leave. And then what?

Shaking off any thoughts beyond tonight, he escorted his bride to the bailey, where they'd say their goodbyes to her family. Their horses had been brought around. His large destrier, Merlin, was dwarfed by his wife's Brimstone. Another gelding had been brought around, though Ronan wasn't sure why. A tug on his sleeve pulled his attention from the horses to his wife, who was sheepishly looking up at him.

"You seemed to think Brimstone was too large for me, so I thought I would give him to you as a wedding gift."

His eyes went wide at her generosity. Then his brows pulled together. Hasty as this union had been, he'd not gotten his wife a wedding gift. He'd not even considered it, as opposed to it as he'd been. But now, in light of her gift, he felt unworthy. It wasn't a pleasant feeling.

Digging about in his sporran, he found something that meant a great deal to him. He placed the brooch in her palm. "For ye, wife."

She squinted at the bit of metal in her hand and looked up at him.

"'Tis the MacPherson crest."

"Aye. I was raised half my life with Grants and half with MacPhersons. I think myself both."

She smiled. "Then I shall be both as well. Thank ye."

It didn't pass his notice she hadn't owned to being loyal to *three* clans. The one she'd just spent the last nineteen years with had been tossed aside without further thought. They walked to Brimstone so she could introduce them. When she moved to take the reins of the gelding, he couldn't help but feel like she didn't belong on such a mundane beast.

"Wait." He shook his head. "Perhaps you'd prefer my Merlin. He may not be as wicked as your beast, but he'll keep your ride interesting."

Her smile nearly took over her face as she nodded. Reaching up to pet the red horse between the eyes, she looked back at him. "Thank ye, husband."

With warm cheeks, he nodded and cleared his throat. "Let us go home."

His wife didn't make a single complaint as they pushed to make their return by nightfall. As they crested the final hill, the view took his breath. The sun was deeply rested on the far horizon, coloring the sky in pink and orange. The white stone castle seemed to glow in the last of the day's light.

After the initial feeling of relief, he was overwhelmed with the slithering feeling of dread. He felt as if something was choking him. He couldn't breathe. He knew the thing would never go away, having suffered with it much of his life.

Duty.

Ronan was the laird's heir. He'd known the weight of that since he'd known his father had passed. For all his ten and eight years, he'd been trained and groomed to one day become laird of clan Grant. There was no escape. It mattered not what he might have wanted for his life. His dreams were dismissed, overshadowed by his responsibilities.

Now his duty to his clan had forced him to marry this stranger. But he'd gained a reprieve. He only needed to get through this night, and he'd be free again for at least a while. He'd allow his people their proper feast and bed his new bride, but come morning, his life would be his own once more.

Chapter Three

The ride to Strathspey, the Grant stronghold, was an enlightening one. Brenna observed her new husband when he wasn't looking, which was hardly ever. While he'd seemed rather serious previously, he'd fallen in with the retainers in a bit of joking and fun.

"I grew up making mischief with Will and Hugh, as well as Ewan, though he isn't here," he'd told her. The last part was said quieter.

She'd recognized that name from the night before, the man who'd caused their hurried alliance. Brenna still didn't know what he'd done, and with the other men riding so closely, she didn't dare ask.

Her husband became more serious as they descended the rise that would lead them to the castle. A stern frown had taken the place of the earlier grin. She worried Strathspey might not be the refuge she'd hoped it to be if he wasn't happy to be there. But all the Grants she'd met so far had been kind to her.

Despite his callous words in his chamber, even his grandsire seemed pleased to chat with her along the way.

In the bailey, the people poured out to greet them.

"I see you've all been celebrating without us," the laird said jovially.

A few women came forward to greet her. One placed a laurel wreath on her head, claiming her as their guest of honor. She was pulled into the great hall, filled with laughter and delicious scents that made her stomach growl. She was led to the high table to be seated beside Ronan, to the right of the laird—except a man was already in her seat.

His dark hair hung in straggly clumps past his shoulders and matched his unkempt beard. But it was the icy gaze boring into her that made her blood turn cold. She'd thought him a man, but the longer she remained trapped in his gaze, the more she felt as if she were looking into the eyes of a soulless demon. His eyes held hardly any color, and she shuddered from the chill.

"Make room for the bride, Ewan," Ronan ordered, giving the man a playful shove.

Taking the seat Ronan offered her, she caught the scent of sour whiskey and body odor from her husband's kin, which caused her earlier appetite to retreat. She placed a hand on her face and swallowed deeply to keep from being ill.

This man was a childhood friend and uncle to her husband. But unlike Will and Hugh, who had traveled with them from Innes House, this man didn't look like he'd ever laughed in his entire life.

"She's not much to look at, is she?" the man

said with the slurred speech of drunkenness.

Beside her, Ronan stiffened. "Watch your tongue, man. This is not her fault."

"Nay. 'Tis mine. I'll never forgive myself for this. I should have been the one shackled to her, not ye."

Brenna pressed her lips tightly together to keep from shouting out how that would have never happened. She didn't care if she'd had to start a war with all of Scotland; she would have found a way to free herself from this wretch.

"If ye canna be civil, I'd ask you to leave," the laird said. "Ye've done enough."

The hall fell silent as the man to her right stood and swayed.

"I'll take it to my bed, but first, a toast to the happy couple," he said, grabbing his glass and hoisting it into the air. "To my wee nephew and his new bride. May ye survive the bedding so ye can return to rutting the fairer lassies."

Years of suffering Hannah's comments had hardened Brenna against such taunts and gave her the strength to sit there with her head held high. Nothing irritated her sister more than seeing she couldn't make Brenna cower away in tears. This man was much the same as her sister, and she'd not give him the satisfaction, either.

The man made to leave but tripped and fell with a thud to the stones where he remained, eyes closed as the maids served the meal around him.

"My apologies," Ronan said. "He's angry but shouldn't have said such a horrible thing."

Brenna nodded, though she had noticed he hadn't assured her he didn't plan to take up with other women after their marriage was consummated. She spent much of the rest of the meal wondering about what came next.

Eventually, the maids came to clear their food. Brenna frowned at the meal she hadn't managed to eat. She was never one to let food go to waste, but she was far too nervous.

The laird cleared his throat, and when Brenna looked up, she watched her new husband and his grandfather share a silent conversation. She understood what the laird was implying with his raised white eyebrows. It was time for the bedding.

"Are ye ready to go to my chamber?" Ronan asked, quiet enough that only she would hear.

She swallowed and answered. "Yes. If you are."

He offered her his arm with a stiff nod and led her from the hall. They'd nearly made it to the door when someone noticed their departure and howled a crude suggestion. Others joined in, but Ronan kept her hand and hurried their pace out of the hall.

"My apologies," he said again.

"No matter, they're just having a bit of fun." She was nevertheless glad to be away from the teasing.

"At our expense," he said with a scowl.

"You've got broad shoulders, and it doesn't bother me overmuch. I've endured my share of name-calling. This was not so bad."

His brows creased even more. "No one will call you names now that you're my wife. I won't stand for it. You'll let me know right away, and I will handle it." The fierceness in his eyes tempered quickly. "Or if I'm not nearby, speak to my grandsire.

He'll address it."

Her initial flush of warmth at his concern withered. So quickly he wriggled out of taking care of her.

"Aye," she murmured.

He pushed open the door to his chamber and nodded for her to go in before him. Everything was as she'd expected. Thick, dark fabrics were everywhere, and nothing was out of place. A pitcher holding a few fresh flowers sat on a table in the corner. Perhaps a maid's kind welcome.

"If you feel you're not ready to do this, we can put it off," he said, briefly meeting her eyes.

"But the marriage isn't official until we've consummated it." There was still a chance he could change his mind until their marriage was legitimate. Despite everything, she didn't want that.

"Aye, but no one would know what happens in our bed but us."

"Are you suggesting a lie, husband?"

"I am suggesting I don't like forcing myself on a lass who's not willing."

"But I am willing," she nearly shouted in exasperation. *Was* she ready to lie with him? She had many questions and worries about the act. Hannah had given her more advice than Brenna expected a virgin to have, but she wasn't sure how much of it was true. No doubt Hannah had embellished the truth to frighten her.

She'd never been so nervous, not when she'd jumped from the cliff into the loch, nor when she'd stood up on Brimstone's back for the first time. Those things had frightened her initially, but they'd also brought her much joy.

This was sure to be the same. At least, she hoped so. She knew she would do what was needed to make this marriage work. This was her chance to start fresh, to cast off the reckless reputation that made her a laughingstock at Innes House.

To earn her husband's approval and, perhaps, one day, his heart.

***

Ronan's bride stood before the hearth, looking at the floor instead of at him. Despite Brenna's outburst about being ready, he could see the truth in her worried greenish eyes and the stiff set of her shoulders. She seemed determined to have this happen tonight, which fit his plans nicely, so he persevered. "Please don't be afraid," he said as gently as he would to soothe a newborn colt.

"I'm not afraid," she said so quickly and firmly that he had no choice but to believe her.

"Do you understand what is to happen between us now?" he asked, his nerves getting the best of him. Maybe he should have had more ale before bringing her to his chamber. He was not a green lad, but he'd never taken a lass's virginity before, either, and it seemed a great responsibility.

"Aye," she said crisply. "I will lie on the bed. You will lie atop of me and put your—" She waved in the direction of his groin as her cheeks turned pink. "There will be some pain, but I'm not to whimper or cry out, for it might disconcert you and impede your enjoyment."

Impede his enjoyment? God's balls. Who had taught her about relations between men and women? It sounded like torture. No wonder the lass was terrified. "I'll try my best to be gentle. If you do cry out, don't fret. I'll not be angry or…disconcerted."

She nodded and reached around the back of her gown. She undid her own laces, and her gown dropped in a pile at her feet.

"You don't require help to undress?"

She blinked. "Oh, no. I learned to do it myself so I could go swimming whenever I wanted. I couldn't take a maid with me. She might have told my mother, and I would have been scolded for being unladylike."

Ronan wondered how often she'd been scolded for such a thing and was oddly proud that it hadn't changed her. His bride was many things, but she was true to herself, and he admired that quality considerably in a man, so why not a woman?

She stepped out of her dress and removed her shoes and stockings as if it were a race.

"Slow down. We have all night."

She bit her lip. "I'm sorry I'm not more to your liking," she whispered, covering herself with her thin arms. "Hannah said men sometimes wish to put out the candles so as not to have to look at their partner if she is not to his taste. She told me to expect such a thing tonight."

He frowned at both his doubts and her sister's questionable tutelage. "You're lovely," he said, wanting to compliment her as a husband should. In truth, she was more enticing than he'd expected. Her brown hair rippled over the pale skin of her bare shoulders, with strands of copper glowing in the firelight. The slight slope of her hips enticed him. "I would like to see you, wife."

Her hazel eyes glittered in the candlelight. As he removed his shirt, she watched with blatant curiosity. She stood before him in nothing but her shift and bravely reached down to loosen the tie, but he stopped her. Because something had stopped him. The way her hands trembled made his breath catch. He would be a gentleman and wait until she was ready and not rush her, despite the need growing under his kilt. "If you would rather wait…"

"Nay. We would know it wasn't a proper marriage," she said more steadily than she'd seemed.

"Aye, we would." He gazed at her for a long moment, watching the emotions play out in her eyes. Under everything else—the fear, the worry, and the doubt—he saw something else. Something that had him reaching for her shift and pull it over her head.

Excitement.

She wanted him. She might not know why or for what, but she had a womanly desire for him.

Having tried to delay her twice to no avail, the only option was to move forward. He stepped closer and bent to press his lips to hers. It took only a moment for her to respond in a way only Brenna Innes—make that Brenna *Grant*—would.

She wrapped both arms around his neck and hauled him to her. She didn't seem to do anything gently or in a ladylike fashion. And yet he found that in this particular activity, he was grateful for her fire, though he still worried about hurting her.

"I've never taken a maidenhead or been with anyone inexperienced before," he admitted as they moved to the bed.

She bit her lip again as she looked down at herself nervously.

"I think it best to be done with it so the pain is quick. What do you think?" he asked, feeling like a dolt. He might have asked one of his grandfather's men for advice. He'd have to deal with their jests, but at least he would know the easiest way to remove someone's virginity.

She nodded. "Aye. When I needed to be stitched last fall, I wished they'd hurry it up so the pain would be over faster."

He smiled at her example, wanting to ask why she'd needed stitching. Had she been thrown from the beast horse she rode? Had she fallen from a tree? No doubt it was something as adventurous as she was. "I hope the pain isn't so bad as stitches," he said, letting his kilt drop to the floor. He heard her quick gasp and expected her to look away with a maidenly blush, but not Brenna. She stared, gaping at his cock.

"I'm not so sure…" She pointed uncertainly at him and swallowed. "I know people have been doing this all the time, but… Do you think that will fit?"

He pressed his lips together so as not to laugh at her question. "We're about to find out."

She climbed awkwardly on the bed and scooted up to lie stiffly in the center. With a sigh, he slid into bed next to her. He kissed her again, softer this time, and allowed his hands to roam over her subtle curves. Her fingers clenched in his hair, pulling him closer as he invaded her mouth with his tongue, and she eagerly responded in kind. Whatever she lacked in experience and seduction, she made up in courage and pure exuberance.

He moved between her thighs and began to have his doubts as to whether he'd fit. There was barely room for his hips between hers. He reached down to the thatch of hair and touched her gently to determine her readiness. She was wet for him and made a soft noise of pleasure as he ran his thumb over her heat a few more times.

He considered taking the time to taste her and kiss her skin in places other than her mouth, but she was new to these things, and he didn't want to frighten her further. He paused to gather his courage when he was lined up where he should be. He'd never been the one to push someone into womanhood before. He paused at her warm entrance, loathe to cause her pain.

She smiled up at him. "I'm ready," she said in a soft, more convincing voice than when she'd shouted her willingness earlier. Her encouragement made him smile.

Here he was, a man of experience, and this slip of a lass had to encourage him to continue. With a sharp nod, he moved his hips forward and pushed inside her the entire way. He felt the breach of her maidenly defenses and shuddered.

"Are you well?" he asked when he was fully seated. He couldn't bear it if she wept. It would kill him. Fortunately, she smiled up at him.

"Aye. It wasn't so bad as the stitches."

He returned her smile and kissed her lips and her neck as he began to move inside her. To his surprise, she moved beneath him, writhing upward against him to meet each stroke. The sounds coming from her made his blood heat. He'd felt women take their pleasure before, but they'd not been so uninhibited about it as his new bride. He found he liked it very much.

In that moment, he could see how a man might give up his will to a woman. He might wish to do all that was necessary to make her happy. Was this how it began? The first deceit? The way a woman twisted a man to do her bidding?

He wouldn't have thought someone like Brenna was capable of such grand planning. She was no seductress. But her innocence was part of the ploy. He found it appealing enough that he wished to bring her pleasure and earn her smiles.

He didn't know what she was up to, having married him when she knew the truth. She didn't seem one to care for jewels. But perhaps that would have been easier. She'd be disappointed if she'd married him with some hope of earning his heart.

For she would hate him come morning.

Chapter Four

The pain had quickly subsided, and Brenna was encouraged by the pleasant feeling that replaced it. Every time Ronan thrust into her, she couldn't help but push up from the bed to meet his force.

It was as if her body knew exactly what to do, even though her sister hadn't prepared her for this enjoyment. Brenna seemed to be floating higher and higher toward…something… She didn't know what. Could it be heaven? Was she dying? Did she even care if she was?

Ronan shifted above her ever so slightly. It was such a tiny adjustment, but this slight movement had him touching something deeper within her. Something—

"Stop. Please, stop." She closed her eyes tightly, trying to keep the frightening thing away.

"What is it? Are you in pain?" he asked, his brows pulled into a frown.

"No. No pain, but I fear something is wrong.

Something is tightening, like it might burst inside me." She was out of breath, and the words were hard to speak.

He smiled, and she fought the urge to hit him for his reaction. Did the man not have any feelings at all? She'd thought he had a tender heart under the gruff exterior. She'd seen a hint of it from how he'd taken care of her earlier. His kisses were sweet at first and only slowly moved to scalding.

"Has no one told you what happens after the pain, lass?" he asked, his head tilted to the side.

She blinked at the unexpected question and shook her head. "My sister told me some women enjoy it greatly, but I didn't think I would because I don't enjoy many things other women enjoy."

He gently shifted a stray wave of her hair away from her cheek. "I think maybe you were wrong about that. I believe you're going to like it a great deal. You're very responsive."

"That's good?" She winced. Generally, her responses were all wrong.

"Yes. I like that you are not shy."

She smiled, happy to earn his admiration. But she still worried something was wrong with her body. He wasn't a woman. How could he be sure she wasn't about to burst into pieces?

"The tightening is a good thing," he said, making her think she might have spoken her worry out loud. "If I do my part well, you may indeed burst, but I promise all your pieces will remain intact, and no harm shall be done, only pleasure. Just relax and enjoy it. All will be well, I promise."

She swallowed nervously, then nodded. She would trust him. They had agreed to be honest, and she had to believe in him.

"Ready?"

When she gave a more determined nod, he slid deep inside her again. This time, slowly. She'd no idea this marital duty would be so...pleasurable. She'd thought it would be something she would have to endure, but she hoped she'd be made to endure it every day.

She did as he'd instructed—relaxed and allowed the feeling to rise again. Her insides tightened more and more with each stroke. She did her best to remain quiet. He bent to her ear and nibbled the soft skin there.

"You don't have to hold back. Make noise if ye wish. I like that, too."

Again, he liked something that came naturally to her. Hope soared. The moan that left her throat enhanced the experience, especially when he joined in with his groans.

He continued his pace, somehow getting deeper inside her with each stroke...until she did burst into tiny pulses of pleasure so great it stole her breath and made her shout at the same time. Her muscles tightened and then melted. The tremors slowed as he continued to move inside her, but now she felt everything within her so much stronger than before. She felt his heat and the moisture between them.

His thrusts sped up, and then suddenly, he pushed into her as far as he could, and she felt his pulses and a pleasing fire shoot deep inside her. She gasped as she realized what had happened. Her sister had been wrong about nearly every part of this experience. If Brenna could write, she'd send Hannah a letter telling her the truth so she'd know what to expect on her wedding night.

Her husband pulled from her slowly and laid his head near hers. His chest hammered against her ribs. She ran her fingertips through his soft hair, the color of sunshine on a wheat field. When she felt his heartbeat slow, she finally spoke. "I have no experience, but I think you are quite good at this."

"Thank you." His breath was still short, but she could hear a smile in his voice.

"Did your other lovers also burst into pieces?"

"I don't wish to speak about other women in our marriage bed."

This seemed like an excuse, but she allowed it because she didn't want to hear about other women in their marriage bed, either.

"Will you take other lovers now that we're wed?" She probably shouldn't have asked, for she knew other men had mistresses and lemans. His grandsire had suggested it, but she didn't like the idea. She didn't want to waste a single night with her husband.

"We'll discuss it later. Sleep now."

It was easy to concede to his command since her body was so heavy with pleasure and exhaustion. But she didn't stay asleep long. Not used to sharing a bed, she woke to feel his heat on her back. She reached behind her to touch the silk-covered hardness between his muscled thighs. As she stroked him, he woke and murmured something about her being lusty. He did not seem to mind. He pushed into her from behind.

There was no pain beyond a dull soreness. From this new, exciting angle, he was able to get deeper, and his hand held her hip as he drove into her harder than the first time. She liked the pace, and a blissful moan escaped her lips.

The sound ignited him, and his thrusts came faster and faster. When the tightening in her body began this time, she welcomed it, knowing what to expect. The wonderful currents of pleasure rippled through her, and she clutched his fingers between hers.

***

Ronan glanced over at his wife in the early hours before dawn. The low light from the embers in the hearth softened her features into beautiful lines. Maybe his initial frustrations and lack of options had made her seem less appealing than she was. True, she didn't have many womanly curves, but in sleep, she looked like a devilish angel sent to earth to torment him.

He was intrigued by how she'd responded to their joining. He'd expected someone of her age and inexperience to be timid and fearful of relations in a man's bed, but she'd embraced them with determination and, in the end, even pleasure. He should have known Brenna wouldn't be like other women. She'd done nothing but surprise him time and time again. She didn't seem to fear anything, his brave wife.

The familiar pang of guilt twisted his stomach for what secrets he kept from her. But one thing that would never come between them would be another woman. He'd always known when he married, he'd remain faithful to his wife for the rest of his life.

It was his right to take a mistress if he wished, and it seemed she almost expected it. His grandsire and uncle indeed did. But his stepfather would not find honor in that behavior. The idea of a mistress was considered a weakness to the MacPherson laird, who had never strayed from Ronan's mother, regardless of how manipulative the woman was. Ronan wouldn't be regarded as weak. Many couples started as strangers but had been happy ever since.

Could it be the same, one day, for him and Brenna? Or would she come to hate him for what he planned now? Something far worse than taking a mistress.

"Forgive me, lass," he whispered before slipping from their shared bed.

***

Brenna woke up late.

The heavy drapes over the windows were outlined in bright light that was only possible from a sun hung full in the sky. She was used to waking at dawn when the light was still weak. Jerking up in the unfamiliar bed, she worried she'd be scolded for being tardy to the morning meal, but her body reminded her of the reason for her fatigue. The sheet under her was marked with proof of a successful consummation.

A smile came with the memory. She was no longer a maiden—she was Ronan's true wife. And she was in Strathspey, the Grant seat—her new home. Ignoring the sore muscles and tenderness, she washed and dressed quickly to see her husband as soon as possible. She wanted to thank him for their time together the night before. He was a most skilled lover. She had enjoyed lying with him and looked forward to doing it again as often as he wished.

Well, as soon as she fed her grumbling belly.

She walked into the hall, her gaze instantly searching for Ronan at the high table at the front. But only the laird and Ewan were seated there. The laird waved a hand at her, and Brenna sat beside him on his left since Ewan sat to his right in Ronan's place.

"How do ye fair this morning?" the laird asked with a tender smile.

Brenna felt herself blush furiously. "Very well, thank you."

The older man's smile grew, and he patted Brenna on the shoulder. "Good. I'm glad for it."

One of the serving girls brought her food, and she dug in with a hearty appetite.

"Ronan must have put on a good showing to have you this starved in the morning," Ewan said with a mocking laugh.

She swallowed the food in her mouth, hoping she wouldn't be expected to respond as he leaned forward to glare at her. She couldn't help but notice the blue around his eye and the scab holding his split lip together. She wasn't sure if it had come from his tumble the night before or if someone had given the man a thrashing. She hoped for the latter.

She felt Ewan's gaze but had looked away again. "Where is Ronan? It's not usual for him to sleep through the morning meal," the man asked after her husband.

"He's not in our chamber," Brenna said.

She noticed the frown that had taken over the laird's wrinkled face. Had something happened to her husband? The food turned to ash in her mouth, and she choked it down with a hard swallow.

"I'm afraid he will not be here for some time," the man said while staring at her with something akin to pity in his eyes.

"What are you saying? Where has he gone?" Had he left her for another woman? Her chest felt like it might break apart and spill her heart upon the table.

"Ronan left before dawn for France. He will be away for a while."

Ewan slammed his fist on the table. "Tell me you did not allow him to go off with the MacPherson bastard to fight the French."

The laird held his hand up to stop him. "Aye. Ronan and I agreed, and I granted him leave."

"But we only just married."

Ewan stood. Brenna looked up to see his eyes narrowed on her.

"You have scared him away."

"Nay," the laird said. "That's not why he left. He'd wanted to go for some time, and I hadn't allowed it, not until he agreed to do his duty and marry."

Brenna's world splintered into a thousand painful shards. She fled from the hall and through the castle gate, not stopping until she was deep in the forest, eventually finding herself kneeling beside a wide river feeding into a loch. She needed to escape the truth, but no matter where she might run, she'd never be able to escape the terrible reality. The hurt overwhelmed her, and tears flooded her eyes. Her husband preferred to risk death in a foreign land rather than stay with her. She had asked for honesty, and he had betrayed their accord in the worst way.

She would never forgive him.

Chapter Five

Scottish Highlands
June 1695, five years later

Brenna braced herself as she sat next to Ewan at the head dais for the morning meal. As usual, he looked ill and appeared asleep at the table.

Already seated on her other side, Will, the war chief, nodded and wished her a good morning. She returned his greeting and offered a smile to her friend. Placing her hands in her lap, she awaited the laird's arrival.

"Go ahead and eat. He's not coming," Will told her.

She glanced up in surprise. "Why not?"

"He nicked his arm. It was a small cut, though he said it festers and bothers him. I sent Moira to his chamber to mend him. She'll give him some foul-tasting broth from her basket, and the stubborn old bastard will be good as new."

Will meant no dishonor when referring to the laird with such words. She knew their bond was deep and full of respect. If Will said anything else, she didn't hear it. She was instantly on her feet and hurrying through the hall to the stairs. Her guards, Gabe and Malcolm, followed close behind. She hated to cause them to abandon their meals, but it couldn't be helped. She knocked on Geordie's door and waited for permission to enter.

She found the laird sitting in bed, his face flushed but smiling when he saw her. "Why did you not call for me when you were injured?" she asked, hurrying around the side of the bed to see his wound.

Will had said it was only a nick, so she wasn't prepared to see the angry wound on the inside of the laird's forearm. A peculiar red line trailed from the gash and continued to his elbow.

The healer had noticed it, too. She frowned at Brenna from the other side of the bed. Brenna had seen this before…with dying men. "Will he be all right?" she asked the older woman.

Moira pressed her lips together but said nothing. Brenna didn't like the healer's silence. It did not bode well for the man she'd come to love as a father.

"I need to speak to you about the running of the clan," he said, his voice stronger than he seemed capable of.

She shook her head. She didn't want to speak of such dire things.

"You are the laird. You must get well and see to the running of the clan as you always have."

He smiled and patted her hand with his icy fingers. "I intend to do just that, but it is a foolish leader who does not plan for any possibility."

She nodded. He'd taught her many things in the five years since she'd come to live at Strathspey. He'd welcomed her thoughts and opinions in matters of the clan and explained his rulings so she might understand.

"What do you wish me to do?"

He shook his head. "It is already done. I've sent a message to Ronan asking him to return. It's time he come home and do his duty."

She tried to swallow, but her throat had gone dry at hearing her husband's name.

"If something were to happen before he returns, you will be in charge."

"Me? But I'm not a Grant by blood." She and Geordie shared a look, and despite the silence, she understood what he would never say aloud. If not her, the duty would fall to the next in line. Ewan. And he wasn't capable of such responsibility.

After taking a steadying breath and wiping away a tear that had escaped, she gave a firm nod. "As you wish, my laird. I will do my best to make you proud."

"You already have. I've signed a decree with my wishes, which was witnessed this morning by Will and Hugh. I know the clan is in safe hands."

She leaned forward to press a kiss to his soft cheek. "Aye. I might not be a Grant by blood, but I am a Grant in my heart." Before she'd finished speaking, Geordie had closed his eyes and drifted off to sleep. She went to sit by the window so she'd be close by if he woke and needed her. She looked across the fields to the southern border and wondered how long it would be until Ronan arrived.

It had been five years since they'd married. Much had changed in that time. She was no longer a silly girl, hoping her charming husband might love her someday. His extended absence and uninterrupted silence had told her everything she needed to know about Ronan's feelings and the kind of man he truly was.

***

Brenna woke the morning of the laird's funeral unable to breathe. After his last words to her to take charge of the clan, he'd drifted off to sleep and didn't wake again. That considerable responsibility placed on her shoulders was sure to cause a panic.

But the struggles with her new duty weren't what was causing her inability to take in air. It was Ewan's hands grasped tightly around her throat that caused her distress this morning. It was light enough for her to see him clearly as his weight pressed her to the mattress.

Years ago, Brenna took to barring her door before she slept to keep her husband's uncle from intruding. More recently, the laird ordered Malcolm and Gabe to protect her at all times, standing guard by her door as she slept. Which meant Ewan hadn't come to her room through the door. His clothing was wet, and his hair dripped upon her face.

The bastard had most likely climbed up from the loch outside to her window. She'd have not thought him capable of such a strenuous plot, but how he got there wasn't nearly as important. She needed help. Reaching out, she knocked the bell from the nightstand, causing it to clang to the floor.

"Lady Grant?" Gabe's low voice called right away. "Brenna?" he yelled louder when she didn't respond. Or instead couldn't.

"They won't be able to save you," Ewan said. For once, the sour smell of ale and whiskey didn't assail her senses. He was sober, not the malleable slug he usually was. It made him all the more dangerous.

Her hand searched the nightstand for the other item she always kept there—her dirk.

Ewan laughed. "It's not there." His whisper was barely heard over an axe splitting through her door.

Her vision began fading and fluttering around the edges, but she needed to hold until her guards could assist her. Just a few more seconds, and maybe a few more after that. With both hands holding her throat, her hands were free. She initially tried to remove his grip or fight him off, but he was too strong. But she had another plan.

She reached under her pillow where she kept her *sgian dubh*. She was rarely without a blade, even in the bath, all because of this man. She was tired of living in fear. She gathered all her remaining strength to end his terror once and for all.

But he noticed the weapon a moment before she would've stabbed him in the kidney with the small blade. It would have been a fatal wound, but instead, he released her throat to fend off her attack.

Her lungs sucked in the needed air as she fumbled with the blade, grasping desperately to find purchase. He hissed with pain and pulled back, allowing her to move for his throat. Another miss, but the blade caught the skin on his jaw and cheek. A moment later, his weight was off, and she could breathe more fully.

"The kitten has claws." He laughed again while wiping the blood from his face with his dirty sleeve. "You'll pay for that."

He moved toward her again but spared a look for the door, which was splintering to pieces. Malcolm reached through and tossed the bar off the brackets, and the mutilated door swung open as three guards rushed in to seize Ewan. Gabe came to her side with wide gray eyes.

"Are you injured, my lady?"

"Nay. I need to catch my breath," she answered, her voice rough. Gabe winced at the sight of her throat. No doubt it was bruised from Ewan's grip.

He spoke by her ear so the others wouldn't hear what he said. "He has gone too far this time, my lady. Ye would be justified in hanging the bugger."

"Aye," she agreed with a nod. At the moment, with her throat burning and her heart pounding, she wanted nothing more but to see Ewan Grant's lifeless body swinging at the end of a rope. But as her breath slowed and reason returned, she shook her head and changed her mind. "Nay."

"You are in charge of the clan and well within your right to seek punishment for his treachery."

"I know. But I was only given this power yesterday. How would it look to the clan if I exercised such a right the day after the laird passed?"

"It would look quite good," Gabe answered.

She might have laughed at his expression if things weren't so dire. She shook her head again.

"While I refuse to end his life, I want him exiled from Grant lands. No weapons. No food. No water. Perhaps if he spends time focusing on foraging for his meals, he'll have less time trying to overthrow me."

"How will I hunt without a weapon?" Ewan shouted at her.

"You might have thought of that before you attacked and nearly killed me. My ruling is more than you deserve, you spineless cur."

"Ye might as well run your wee blade across my throat, for I'll not survive in the wilderness."

"I will not stand before Ronan and tell him you died by my hand. But know this: if my men or I see you on Grant lands again, you'll not get another warning. You will be dealt with immediately. This is your final chance and more than you should have. Take him away. I never want to see him again."

"Aye, my lady. We'll see it done."

"And then join me at the kirk to say our goodbyes to a great man and a kind laird."

The rain did not let up as the priest performed the service, and the gathered crowd dispersed. She remained behind, allowing her tears to mingle with the raindrops that ran down her face and dripped off her chin.

She'd loved the man as a father or a grandsire. He'd treated her with more kindness than her own family ever had, and as he'd never had a daughter, he came to dote on her as if she was of his blood. She would miss him greatly. When a small sob escaped, Gabe and Malcolm stood closer. Always on guard to save her from any possible threat. Even sadness. A few of the remaining clan people looked over at her with confusion in their eyes.

No doubt they wondered why the laird had put her in charge of the clan. She was not a Grant by blood and had not been trained for such a duty beyond the times she spent sitting in the hall while the laird listened and ruled his people.

They probably didn't realize the true laird of the Grants had been summoned and was most likely already on his way. Her husband, Ronan, the man who had married her and then left her after their single night together, would be returning.

As usual, when she considered such a thing, she was overcome by conflicting emotions. Happiness, betrayal, hope, and disgust all warred in her mind and heart. Ronan would be here soon, and she had yet to determine how she felt.

Chapter Six

Ronan wanted to be angry at his brother for the slow pace he kept.

As soon as they'd crossed over into Scotland, Ronan had wished to nudge Brimstone into a trot, all the faster to get home. But he couldn't. His injured leg was troubling him something wretched, and a faster pace would be excruciating. And yet Shane meandered, making it seem their speed was at his request rather than Ronan couldn't keep up.

While Ronan's leg was a constant reminder of their time at war, he'd not complain, for Shane's pain was not physical. He'd lost a wife in France and had not been the same since.

Shane was a good brother. He'd kept Ronan alive the last five years they'd fought in France. And now they were both going home or instead to their respective clans. Ronan had called the MacPherson clan home for the ten years before he left, but now he'd return to take over as laird for the Grants.

He'd gotten word from his grandsire in July it was time to come home. The missive had arrived only days before Shane and Ronan planned to leave France anyway. Geordie would have only written such a message if the situation had been dire. Ronan hoped to arrive in time to say his goodbyes, but their slow pace had made that unlikely.

And now, somehow, Ronan would be expected to rule his clan, which he hadn't called his own in many years. It wasn't only the duty to his people that awaited him at Strathspey, but his duty as husband to Brenna. His wife. The thin lass he'd left only hours after consummating their marriage.

As he had many nights looking up at the stars, waiting for sleep to claim him, he tried to conjure an image of his wife's face. He recalled hazel eyes—green shot with amber and gold—but he couldn't recall the tilt of her brows or the curve of her lips. He remembered her being quick to laugh but couldn't summon the sound.

It had simply been too long. His grandfather had told him to bed her and forget her, and while the suggestion had seemed vile at the time, Ronan feared it had come to pass without his realizing it.

But once he was home, he would have plenty of time to relearn everything about her. Including the intimate knowledge they'd shared that one night. It had been a difficult five years, but he'd remained faithful to his vows while away.

"Are ye ready to be home?" Shane asked on their last day together.

"In some ways," Ronan answered as honestly as he could. He worried about the reunion with his wife. She would surely hate him for leaving without a word. "What of you?" he asked Shane rather than overthinking what awaited him at Strathspey.

Shane shook his head. "I am not ready to be laird. I just got done being captain. The last thing I want is people yipping their complaints at me all day. It may sound selfish, but I wish I could have time to myself."

"Ye are welcome to my cottage if ye wish a respite before returning to the castle and all the responsibilities that await you there. A rest would be well deserved."

"What things are you looking forward to on your return?" Shane asked.

The first thing that came to mind at the question was sharing a bed with his wife, but he didn't answer as such, mainly because his brother didn't know Ronan was wed. It seemed silly now, but when they'd left, Ronan worried Shane might not take him along if he'd known Ronan had just married the day before their departure. So he'd not mentioned it.

Later, when it would have been too late for Shane to return him to the Grants's, their discussions had turned to other things. Eventually, Ronan felt too much time had gone by to bring it up, and what did it matter anyway?

When Shane married, Ronan saw the man change from a gruff soldier to a doting husband. Much like Shane's father had with Ronan's mother. Ronan would not fall prey to such a demise. He might respect his wife as he should, but he'd never lose his heart or head in such a way.

If Ronan had met an untimely end, Shane would have sent word to Strathspey, and Geordie could have told the clan what happened. Not long ago, Ronan worried such a letter would be dispatched. After he'd injured his leg, he'd lain in fever for several days. Shane later told him he was sure he'd be returning from France alone. Fortunately, Ronan had lived. In his fevered state, he'd dreamed of many unsettling things, but it was the fact he would die without having read the words his wife had written to him in the few letters he'd received. Letters that remained unopened in his pack even now.

Eventually, he and Shane reached the place on their journey where they would part ways.

"Do you wish me to see you home to Strathspey?"

They'd watched over each other, fighting back-to-back, for the last five years. Their subsequent battles, whatever they be, would be faced alone. "Nay, brother. We both have duties waiting for us. I'll not keep you from yours."

Shane cleared his throat. "Speaking of that, I may take you up on the offer of your cottage for a few days before stepping into the duty that awaits me. I feel I could use…some time…to prepare."

Ronan nodded. "That sounds like a suitable plan. You're welcome to my home for as long as you need." After all, Ronan's home was with the Grants now. He nodded toward the east where the Grant lands lay. "I will no longer need it."

"Mayhap when you come to visit," Shane suggested.

With a clasping of bracers and a hearty pat on the back, they left each other to head off to their fates.

"Godspeed, brother."

"May we both have the strength to find our

happiness," Ronan answered and stood watching until his brother was out of sight before turning Brimstone toward home and everyone who waited for him there.

After making camp for the night, Ronan continued for home the following day. A cool rain made Ronan's leg ache, causing him to pull Brimstone into a slower walk and extend his travels even longer. He'd wanted to spend the night on Grant lands, but as evening fell, he knew he'd not make it that day. Surely, the following day, he'd be able to breathe in the mountain air of his home. Knowing he was only a day from seeing the towers of Strathspey on the horizon brought a smile to his face despite the grim day.

He was about to stop to make camp when he saw a man walking along the path toward him. As he drew closer, the man looked up, and Ronan was hit with recognition, though his tired mind couldn't quite make the connection—not until the man smiled. Despite the raw wound on his jaw, Ronan realized it was his dear uncle.

"Ewan!" he shouted as the man laughed. It was good to see a familiar face, even if it was significantly changed. The man had not aged well. His muscles had gone to waste. His eyes, once filled with mirth, were red-rimmed and bloodshot. Ronan knew this as the telltale trait of a man who spent too many hours in his cups.

Ronan recalled his wedding day and the way Ewan had been drunk. It seemed the man had spent much of the last five years in the same state.

"Nephew! I'd expected you'd be coming home this way. I'd hoped she'd sent word your dear grandsire has passed."

"The laird wrote to me when he'd fallen ill. He told me it was dire that I come home but not much else."

"Ah. Well, you've missed him. The funeral was long past, not that I was permitted to attend."

Ronan moved slowly to dismount so he could look at his uncle and oldest friend. Before Ronan had spent all his days with Shane, he'd lived at Strathspey with Ewan, and the two of them were as close as brothers. They hugged, and then Ronan considered what Ewan had said.

"What do you mean you weren't permitted to attend the funeral? Who would keep a man from mourning his father?"

"Your wife, or dare I say Queen of the Grants?"

Ronan didn't understand. Surely, the slender lass he'd left wasn't in charge of the clan.

"Much has changed here, Ro. Your woman is as slippery as your mother. She has honed the skill of manipulating men, and while she is not as beautiful as Deirdre, she knows how to get what she desires by casting favors on the men."

Ronan nearly choked at the thought. His mother was a wily woman, but she'd only manipulated one man. The laird of the MacPhersons was obsessed with Ronan's mother from the day they'd met and offered marriage the same day. Ever since, he'd done everything he could to make her happy.

Ronan had vowed never to allow a woman to claim him in the same way. Hearing his wife had learned such a skill made a chill crawl down his back.

"She did this." Ewan pointed at the angry cut

across his face. "Ones on my arm, wrist, and chest, too. I barely escaped her attack with my life. Like a venomous spider, she came to my chamber to rid herself of the only competition to her rule while I slept. Then had her men cast me out. Threatened a rope if I stepped back on Grant lands ever again. Left me with nothing. Not even a knife to hunt with or put myself out of my misery."

"The slip of a lass I left here has done all this?" Ronan couldn't believe it. Ewan might have been rowdy, but he'd never been one to lie. This story seemed beyond anything one could conjure up. So absurd, it must be true.

"You know well how women get when they are desperate. And how they come into their powers of seduction as they grow into womanhood."

"Seduction? Brenna? You jest."

But Ewan shook his head. "You left a knotted-haired mess of a girl when you escaped to France. You return to a bonny temptress."

"And she's seduced men while I was at war?" he asked, his blood churning as his anger grew. He'd spent years aching with need and held tight to his vows while she'd warmed her bed with his clansmen?

"Aye. I'm ashamed to say I almost fell for her charms but stopped myself because of my fealty to you, nephew."

"And the rest of the Grants? Who do they pledge fealty to?"

Ewan rubbed his jaw and shook his head. "Her claws are sharp. Many are afraid to speak against her."

"We make camp tonight, but tomorrow we arrive together to take down the witch who has claimed our clan."

"You won't want to show up with me. She'll be furious. She and her loyal guard have banished me."

"*You* are my blood. She has no right to throw you out of Strathspey. You will return with me to your home."

"Then I shall go with you and serve as advisor so we might win back what is ours, or rather *yours*."

"Aye." And Ronan would make sure his wife understood who was in charge of the Grants.

Chapter Seven

The poor weather of the last few days gave way to a warm, sunny sky as if somehow knowing how important the day was.

Ronan was returning home. The border scouts had sent word he'd be arriving within the hour.

Brenna jumped into action to prepare the kitchens for a hearty feast, one worthy of the return of their new chief. Gabe and Malcolm stayed with her while Will and Hugh ordered the rest of the guard into formation in the bailey to greet the man who would take over as laird.

She was more than happy to give up the duty. She'd never heard such a bunch of griping and complaining as during her few weeks as acting laird. She hoped she'd honored the old laird by making the decisions he would have made had he been there. The clans people had obeyed her rulings, and peace was maintained.

The larders were stocked, and the venison was

on the spit, ready for the feast. Kegs of ale and a cask of the keep's finest whisky sat at the ready, prepared for her husband's return. Now, a gaggle of maids were helping her into her best dress and taming her wild hair into submission. She wanted to look her best when her husband arrived, though why, she couldn't explain, even to herself.

She toyed with silly fantasies of his captivation with her upon his arrival. She was still no great beauty, but she'd grown into a woman while he was away, and she hoped he'd take notice. She'd been lonely the past years. His showing her what happened between a man and a woman had been a disservice, for she'd known what she was missing. She ached for his touch and warmth. She struggled with wishing she'd never known what it was like to share a bed with Ronan Grant and wanting to do so again every night he'd been gone.

Would it be different tonight? She'd heard the warnings of the women in the kitchens when they'd told her not to expect he'd been faithful while he was in France. They told her men craved such things more than women, and Brenna was sure she'd die from wanting him, so she couldn't imagine what he'd dealt with. They would be together now. He wouldn't need to spend his nights with strange women. She wanted him to spend them with her. If only she could let go of her anger, they might have a happy life.

She had just stepped into the bailey when the gate guard called out that there were riders. The following minutes ticked by excruciatingly slowly.

"Calm yourself, lass," Gabe teased. "You look like you plan to grab him down from his horse and steal him to your room for the next week."

"I'd guess a month," Malcolm said with a devilish grin.

"I hate you both," she quipped, earning a chuckle from the men behind her.

"If I had a coin for every time ye've said as much…" Gabe said as the gate began moving.

She was in danger of twisting her fingers clean off, and then, as he came into sight, her breath and blood seemed to leave her body.

"Bloody hell," Malcolm cursed. "What is *he* doing here? He's been banished."

Ewan's icy gray eyes found her easily, and he tipped his bare head and offered a sneer.

"Ronan is the laird now. He may overturn my ruling. It's his right."

"And do you think for one minute he did so because that demon told him the truth of why he'd been banished?"

"If Ronan believes him, we'll not change his mind. We must hold our tongues so as not to seem defensive. It's up to Ronan to decide what he wishes to believe. If he chooses Ewan, no one will convince him otherwise, and you'd be punished for raising your sword against the laird's uncle. Stand down for now. We'll bide our time to speak to Ronan when he's ready to hear us."

"You have the patience of a saint, lass." Malcolm shook his head, and she chuckled at the irony of that statement.

"We vowed to keep ye safe and will do so no matter what Ewan or the new laird has to say of it," Gabe stated.

She wanted to cry. She was grateful to these young men who'd only recently joined the guard.

They'd initially thought it a disgrace to be tasked with such a job as protecting the laird's granddaughter by marriage, but a more dangerous job she hadn't known.

The men dismounted, and Brenna noted the way her husband favored his left leg. Had he been injured? She wanted to go to him to see how she might tend to his injury, but with Ewan so close, she remained where she was on the steps to the keep. She was high enough there on her perch to watch as her husband searched the faces in the bailey, passing over her. Finally, he called out to one of the soldiers.

"Where is my wife?"

The guards behind her hissed in a breath, and she feared her heart might drop right out of the gaping hole in her chest.

Her husband had been told years ago to forget her, and it seemed he'd taken that instruction to heart, but as he stood there looking at her, he clearly didn't know who she was.

"He has forgotten me," she whispered as what was left of her heart shattered.

***

Ronan's gaze drifted over the happy crowd once more, pausing on the beautiful woman waiting on the steps of the keep. He'd known Brenna was rather plain with curly brown hair that acted more as tentacles, capturing his fingers as he'd toyed with tendrils after they'd made love. But this woman, whose hair was confined in an elaborate twist, was too fetching to be his wife. Then he recalled what Ewan had said, that she'd become a seductress in his absence.

"She is but there, my laird," Will, his old

friend, said while pointing to the woman he'd noticed. He didn't want to make a scene in front of everyone who had come to greet him, but he wouldn't tolerate his uncle being tossed from the clan a minute longer.

He let his gaze set on her, allowing no recognition to show on his face. She was beautiful. His scattered memories hadn't done her justice. Her low-cut gown did more than hint at the soft curves lurking under her bodice. Her hair had shots of fire he didn't remember; her bottom lip was trapped anxiously by her teeth. She was as bonny as any lass he'd ever seen. He felt as if he was under a spell as he took a stiff step toward her.

Pain flared in his leg, reminding him of his uncle's dire warning not to fall into her trap. He had nearly done just that. She came to stand in front of him, offering a low curtsy and a nervous look. She was right to be worried. The smile he'd attempted to remember all these years did not appear on her lips.

"Welcome home, husband," she said. The tilt of her head spoke of defiance. She wasn't happy to see him. Or perhaps it was Ewan who had her uneasy.

"You welcome me home, yet ye banished my uncle?"

She stood her ground though he towered over her. Her green-gold eyes flashed. "I had no choice."

"This is the home of the Grants. *You* are not a Grant by blood. Ye have no right to order anyone from our lands. Do you understand?"

The only sign she was shaken was a quick swallow and a slight nod. "That is true. Now that you've returned." He didn't miss the slight rise of her chin as she twisted her words of defiance to sound agreeable. Ewan was right. Brenna was a crafty one.

The crowd that had been cheering a few moments before fell silent except for a few murmurs Ronan couldn't make out.

"Did ye do this?" Ronan reached for Ewan, pointing to the cut on his face.

"Aye," she said, her gaze not moving from his.

"Did ye put him out of the castle without a weapon, with no way to feed himself?"

"Aye." Her chin notched up.

She stood there, claiming every accusation as truth. She didn't even attempt to hide it, which only infuriated him more.

"Did ye keep him from attending the funeral of his father?"

Another swallow, but she didn't falter. He expected her to break into tears, maybe even lie to save herself. His wife's strength intrigued him as she continued to stand before him and said with that same defiance he'd noticed earlier, "Aye."

"Ronan, if I can say something," Will said as he stepped up behind her with two young warriors at her flanks. Will hadn't changed, but his usual smile was now replaced by worry.

Brenna put her hand up and shook her head to silence him. "Don't, Will."

To Ronan's surprise, he obeyed her. Had all his men fallen into her web? It was better that Will remained quiet. Ronan couldn't stand to hear his betrayal.

"There's no defense for putting a member of my family out of the castle without so much as a way to hunt." Despite his words, he paused, hoping she might offer a plausible excuse. His journey home had been spent thinking of her, wanting her. Now that he was here, he was ashamed to say he still wanted her, even though it appeared she was a conniving witch. When she said nothing, he moved on to his other needs. "I'm hungry. I assume the hall has refreshment for its new laird?"

"Aye. I've planned a feast for your arrival," Brenna said quietly. "This way."

He grit his teeth and followed her inside, careful not to show his pain. He managed to display only the slightest limp. Since she walked in front of him, she wouldn't have noticed. The sway of her hips enticed him, but his anger forced him to look away before he fell victim to her wiles.

He was reminded of the way his stepfather chased after Deirdre to the detriment of his duties to his people. He would not fall into the same trap.

At the head table, she stood by the chair next to the laird's and waited.

"You are dismissed to eat elsewhere."

If he'd expected her to argue, he would have been wrong. He noticed a tremor in her bottom lip as she nodded and stepped down from the dais. She didn't deserve to sit at the family table when she'd treated his family so hideously.

The two young warriors followed after her, but the sour looks Will and Hugh gave him surprised him. They had all been friends once, but it seemed they, too, had fallen victim to his wife's charms.

"Your grandsire put her in charge of the clan over his own son. Mayhap you should consider why he did so," Will said while glaring at Ewan.

Ewan shook his head. "I told Ronan how she'd manipulated the old man to do her bidding."

"And did you tell Ronan why she gave you that mark across your face?" Hugh asked.

"Careful, friend. Your loyalties seem to be skewed," Ewan said.

"I'll not foul my meal by eating next to a snake," Will said with a glare in Ewan's direction.

"You may sit wherever you choose." Ronan wasn't expecting so many of his men to take him up on the suggestion. This was not a small matter. All of his men were loyal to his wife. Soon, he was sitting at the high table alone with Ewan, and his entire guard sat with Brenna.

Ewan had said she was out for power, and it seemed his men had given it to her. Will and Hugh were Grants; they would never bow to a woman who was only a Grant in name—unless there were something else afoot.

"Why did she cut you?" Ronan asked his uncle, who was digging into his meal like a starving dog. Ewan had once been Ronan's best friend. They had been like brothers. He trusted the man as he would believe his mind.

Even after the debacle that caused Ronan to marry Brenna, Ewan had told the truth of what happened despite the consequences. He and the other man had been drunk and gaming. The other man had pulled a knife on Ewan when he'd not liked the way his luck had turned. Ewan had defended himself, even admitting that he'd taken the matter too far by killing the other man.

Ewan sniffed before setting down his eating knife. "I see they've planted a seed of doubt, just as she wished them to."

"You haven't answered my question."

"Very well. It happened the night my father died. He was very sick, and Brenna told him the time had come for him to name his successor until you returned. She suggested herself, and she did this when I disputed her claim. I only wished to preserve the seat for you, and this is what I got."

Ewan was already on his second mug of ale as he turned back to his meal. If it weren't for the fact Ronan had known Ewan all his life and had never heard him lie in all that time, he might question the man. But Ewan had once saved Ronan's life while Brenna was unknown to him. Except for that night they'd shared, he didn't know her.

He'd seen how her sister manipulated everyone to get what she desired. At the time, he'd thought Brenna was the victim. But perhaps she was merely a pupil waiting for an opportunity to unleash her skills on her new clan.

Still, Ronan couldn't shake the feeling something was wrong. If his wife was the power-hungry tyrant Ewan made her out to be, why would his grandfather and his men follow her unthinkingly? One thing was sure—he'd find out the truth soon enough.

Chapter Eight

Brenna glanced up at the high table to see Ronan glaring in her direction. At his displeasure, she worried about the men who'd graciously sat with her.

"Ye should not have come to sit with me. Your loyalty should be with your laird."

"My duty is to protect ye," Malcolm said. "I gave the late laird my word and plan to honor it."

"Aye. As did I," Gabe added.

"And you don't know how much I appreciate that. But Will and Hugh made no such promise, and neither did the rest of the men. You should have stayed with Ronan."

"Even if he is talking nonsense and listening to that rat?" Hugh said. "I'd rather eat with the pigs. They don't smell as bad as that rotter."

"Aye. I don't know why we don't all march over there and toss the man out again. Ronan wouldn't be able to stop us," Ephraim, one of the older men, said, getting a few ayes with his plan to rebel against their leader.

She needed to stop this before it went too far.

"Please, wait. We must be cautious. I don't know what Ewan plans. He will show his scales soon enough. Until he does, I would feel better knowing you were close enough to protect Ronan. We all know Ewan was willing to kill me to become laird of the Grants, and at the moment, Ronan is what stands in his way. I can't help but feel Ronan is in danger."

Will shook his head. "Nay. The two of them are like brothers. Ewan may be a snake with ye, but I don't think he has the strength to do ill to his blood."

"And if you're wrong?" Brenna asked. "We'd all pay for such a mistake. Ronan, worst of all. I don't wish to see him harmed." Despite her anger with the man, she couldn't let the clan fall to Ewan.

"Even after he disrespected you in front of the clan?" Malcolm retorted on her behalf.

She wouldn't lie. That had stung a great deal. But she didn't expect better from the likes of Ronan Grant. She'd been a foolish girl when he'd left, with dreams of earning his affection. Those dreams faded into the mist the next morning when he'd left her without so much as a word.

The years had fed the fire of her anger until she feared she might catch flame in his presence. It had taken all her strength to remain calm when he'd called her out in front of everyone.

"Surely, you can agree that disrespecting one's wife isn't a crime punishable by death. Please, I ask ye to watch over the laird. Hold your tongue against Ewan for now. Ronan will see the truth soon enough."

At least, she hoped he would. She knew only

how easily Ewan twisted the truth until it favored him, leaving her with no defense.

"I'll not lie for him," Hugh said stubbornly, with Will and the other men nodding.

"Nay. I'm not asking you to lie. I'm asking you to wait to tell Ronan the truth about his uncle until he is ready to hear it." She reached across the table and placed her hand over Hugh's. "I told him the truth today, and it only proved Ewan correct."

"Because he twists the truth."

"And Ronan is no fool. He will untwist things soon enough. Until then, I want you to stay close to the laird and offer protection until you are asked to provide counsel."

"I'm not sure how smart Ronan is," Gabe said. The truth was both Gabe and Malcolm were young and would not have known Ronan. It wouldn't be easy to persuade them until Ronan gave them a reason to earn their respect. As to her husband's intelligence, she couldn't be certain herself.

"Don't worry about me. His words don't matter." Brenna no longer cared what Ronan thought of her. He'd forfeited the right to her consideration five years ago and had done nothing to earn it back. She thought things might have been different when he returned but seeing him in the bailey today only solidified her anger toward him for what he'd done when he'd left her without a word. Still, her anger wasn't enough to let Ewan win.

"The hell it doesn't matter," Will said. "You're planning to sit there and not tell Ronan the truth while Ewan fills his head with more bitter stories? We'll stand by you, my lady. Ephraim is right. Ronan will have to listen to all of us."

She shook her head. "Not today. Be patient." The last words were more for herself than William. She might be thrown out of the castle if she confronted her husband right then. She almost wanted to leave on her own, but that would leave Ronan with Ewan, and she wasn't quite sure if that was safe. So far, Ewan had only made threats against her. But was he dangerous to Ronan, as well? She needed to stay close enough to keep an eye on him, which meant not getting banished.

"As Hugh said, I'll not hide the truth to cover for that wee snake," Will huffed.

Brenna shook her head. "No. We will not lie. If Ronan asks us a question, we will answer truthfully. But we will remain silent for now until Ronan is in a place to hear us."

"We should have hanged Ewan when we had the chance," Gabe muttered.

Brenna couldn't argue. She regretted her decision to delay justice even though she felt she'd done the right thing.

"It's too late for that now. We'll have to wait him out."

"Aye," Will said in his commanding voice. "You're the level-headed lass the old laird saw ye to be. We shall watch over Ronan as you have requested." The other men followed along with their war chief and nodded in agreement, some even holding a fist over their hearts, pledging their oath on the matter.

She relaxed, knowing her husband would be protected. Ronan might not be the leader she'd hoped for, but he was all that stood between them and Ewan running the clan.

"For as quickly as Ewan is tossing back that ale, he'll not be a problem tonight," Gabe noted.

Brenna looked up at the table where Ewan was guzzling down the ale as soon as his tankard was filled. He noticed her and offered a slimy smile and a wink. "The man is even more dangerous when he's in his cups. It is, after all, why Ronan was forced to marry me."

She'd asked the laird about the conversation she'd overheard before their wedding. Ewan had run into one of her clansmen at a tavern and lost all his coin in a game. When he was tossed into the street, having lost everything, including his boots, he attacked the unsuspecting Innes.

Geordie said Ewan had told them a different tale then, but he'd sought out the truth, getting the facts from witnesses at the tavern.

It could have been seen as an act of war between the clans, being the laird's brother had murdered one of her father's warriors. But the marriage created the necessary alignment to keep the peace when the truth was discovered. Brenna could only be grateful she was married to Ronan instead of the vile man who'd done the crime. Her life had not been easy after Ronan left, but at least she'd not been Ewan's wife. The reason they'd wed was no longer critical. They were married; somehow, she'd need to work out her anger with her husband.

"Did you notice his limp?" As much as she wanted not to care, she did.

"Aye." Malcolm nodded. "I take it that is a new injury?"

"Will, can ye check on him and make sure he doesn't have a fever? And if he's in pain, have Moira bring him a draught."

"The man is fine." Hugh grimaced. "He deserves a bit of pain for treating you like he did. I might kick him in his other leg."

Hugh earned an "aye" from the other men.

"I thank ye for your loyalty, but I am no longer acting laird of the clan. It would be best if you protected Ronan. Starting now."

Begrudgingly, Will and Hugh stood and returned to the high table to speak to the laird.

"Are you sure you're well, my lady?" Malcolm asked.

She didn't know how to answer his question. Her heart was raw and hurting from today as well as the old wounds had been pulled open.

"We will have to wait and see." She had put her blood, sweat, and tears into this clan and earned a place of respect here after years of being the jester of her own family. She would not allow Ronan to take what she'd built.

***

The feast continued into the evening, and after the meal was cleared away, Ronan saw his wife directing people as the proper mistress of the keep. A lute player came in and began the night's entertainment.

He watched Brenna to see if she paid attention to any of the warriors, but other than the two that hovered close, looking serious and deadly, she stood alone. One by one, the people in the hall began to leave—first, the families with little ones who had fallen asleep, then the men who would be called to drills early in the morning.

Brenna kissed the bairns' heads and accepted

her thanks as a gracious hostess would. If not for the things Ewan had said about her, he wouldn't know she was anything but the efficient lady of the castle. And if she was so horrid, why did his people seek her out to thank her and wish her well?

He thought of his mother and how she stayed clear of the kitchens and anything resembling work. While the MacPherson laird waited on Deirdre's every word, the rest of the clan had not been as enamored of their mistress. From spending five years in battle, Ronan knew well enough the difference between a person who earned respect and those who grasped hold of their power with fear. These people—his people—respected Lady Brenna. He needed to find out more, though it wouldn't be from his uncle, who was hunched over the table, sleeping in a puddle of drool.

When she left to go toward the kitchens, he followed at a distance. Of course, her two pups followed as well. Ronan had watched them for any indication they lusted over his wife, but while they gazed upon her with affection, it was that of friendship and loyalty.

Leaning against the wall outside the kitchen, Ronan silently cursed his leg. He'd used it too hard today, and now it trembled, threatening to give out. He wouldn't be able to stand there long.

But perhaps it was long enough.

"The meal was wonderful, ladies. Everything was perfect. Thank you for all your hard work," his wife praised the kitchen maids. "Jane, did you have one of the maids get the laird's chamber ready?"

"Aye. 'Tis ready for his high and mighty," she said grumpily. "We heard what he did, casting you from your rightful place at his side for that worm. We should have put a rat in his bed since the new laird likes to keep company with them."

"I hope you didn't," his wife said, a bit of scolding in her tone. Of anyone, he would have thought she would be willing to set beasties on him, but it was clear she didn't stand for this.

"Of course not. The other girls talked me out of it."

"Good. I'll not have the housekeeper put in the dungeon when I need you."

After a moment of silence, one of the other ladies spoke. "Well, lads, there are some tarts here to keep you fit for the night. Watch over the mistress."

"Aye," one of the younger warriors said. "We will."

Ronan didn't understand why his wife needed such formidable protection. He backed away and returned to the hall to fall heavily into a seat near the fire. His wife and her entourage left the kitchen. Brenna paused briefly and nodded toward him before slipping up the stairs. Would one of the soldiers who followed her enter her room for the night? Anger surged once more at the thought of a man—or men—touching his wife while he'd been nothing but honorable all those years.

He stood, slower this time, and followed.

At the door to the room, he'd always called his own, the room he'd shared with her the night of their marriage, he heard his wife wish the warriors a good night. The men murmured to one another and flipped a coin. Ronan figured they were deciding who would take the first watch when one of them walked off, leaving the other guard who settled in, sitting in front of the door.

Why had his wife not moved to the more elaborate laird's chamber? And why did she need to sleep with a guard posted outside her door? He considered going to the laird's chamber, but curiosity kept him there as he heard the bar being settled on the door.

Was she afraid of him?

One thing was for certain—he would never learn the answers to his questions by sleeping in another room. And he wouldn't have his people thinking his wife had set him out of her chamber on his first night back. As he made his way down the corridor, the warrior jumped to his feet and waited with his hand on the hilt of his dirk.

"Do ye plan to stick your laird on his first night home, lad?"

The young man removed his hand from the dirk and uneasily held his arms at his side.

"Nay, my laird. 'Tis a habit when I'm guarding the mistress."

"What is your name?"

"Gabe, my laird."

"And what danger requires a guard posted by her door?"

The man pressed his lips together and cast a glance over his shoulder.

"Will you not answer?"

He nodded once after a brief hesitation. "Aye. She said if ye were to ask, we would tell the truth." He leaned a little closer and whispered, "She said we were to wait until you were ready to hear the truth. Are ye ready?"

Ronan was taken aback by the question but

nodded. "Aye. I'm sure I am."

"Ewan has been deviling the mistress for a time. I'm sorry to say he managed to get in her window. Malcolm and I had to take an axe to the door." He nodded to the new wood that made up the door to his old room. "She managed to cut him." He motioned toward his face in the same area as the cut on Ewan's face. The injury she'd owned to giving him. "He choked her. She was defending herself, my laird."

"And that is why she banished him?"

"Aye. We all said she had every right to hang the bugger for it. The auld laird had put her in charge. His orders were signed and witnessed. But she refused to kill your uncle for fear you might…"

"I might what?"

The lad had the cods to narrow his gaze on Ronan with anger. "She worried ye would hate her for it." He raised a brow, clearly calling Ronan out for his behavior.

Ronan saw nothing in the man's eyes to think he was lying. But if he weren't, that would mean Ewan had lied to him. Such a thing had never happened in all the years they'd known each other. "I'd like to see my wife."

The man's eyes went wide. "Now?"

"Yes. It is common for men to sleep with their wives."

Gabe swallowed loudly and looked toward the door before returning to Ronan with his shoulders back.

"I'm sorry, but I swore to the auld laird that I would protect the lady with my life, and I canna go back on it. It was his last order to me and my brother."

"And you think I plan to harm her?" He didn't know whether to be impressed by this warrior's loyalty or toss him in the dungeon for questioning Ronan's integrity.

"Ye made it clear you were unhappy to be in her company at the meal."

The man fidgeted nervously but stood his ground. Meanwhile, Ronan worried his leg might soon give out while arguing with the boy. But the lad was right. He had not hidden his dislike for Brenna, though now he had many questions for his wife.

"I don't make a habit of hurting women. You have my oath that I will not harm your mistress. Let us see if she will admit me." Ronan cocked a brow though he was unsure if Brenna would allow him to enter her chamber. He didn't know what he would do if she refused. He'd never force himself on a woman. He only wanted to speak to her alone.

Gabe nodded and then knocked at the door. "My lady?" he called loudly. "Ye have a visitor."

"Is someone ill?" Brenna called out.

"Nay," the guard answered, though Ronan thought the man looked a bit pale.

"Then who is it?"

"Your husband," Ronan said loudly and waited to be let into his wife's chamber.

Chapter Nine

Brenna stepped back from the door as if Satan waited on the other side.

She looked down at herself, dressed only in her shift. While the nights were cooler, it was still July, and the castle had remained warm after the sunny day. She was pulling on her robe when he knocked again. "One moment."

Running her hand over her hair, she cursed at the curls. They'd been bound tightly for the day, but she'd let them loose from their pins as soon as she'd entered her chamber for the night. She went to the door and slid the bar free, letting out a huff of anger and determination. What reason did she have to make herself more presentable for the man who'd left her years ago and hadn't had the decency to spare so much as a few words on a page in all that time? Even though she'd written to him numerous times. She did her best to put her anger aside. It wouldn't do to lose her temper with her husband during their first private conversation.

Perhaps he planned to apologize for his behavior earlier. Maybe he wanted to explain why he hadn't cared enough to tell her he planned to leave her behind without so much as a clue as to when he might return, if ever. She shook her head again. So much for putting her anger aside.

Nothing he could say would make her forgive him for forgetting about her for all these years.

Ronan entered the room and looked around, expecting to see someone else in her chamber. She could have laughed at the irony. The only man who'd been in her chamber since he'd left was his snake of an uncle. The man Shane had befriended and believed over her. And he surely hadn't been invited. But after Ronan was satisfied with the emptiness of the chamber, he turned his gaze onto her and was quite thorough about it. She told herself she wouldn't cower from his inspection. If he was unhappy, he could leave and find comfort elsewhere, just as she assumed he'd done every night he'd been away.

Perhaps he didn't have a woman in his bed *every* night. He *was* at war. She'd seen well enough the way battle wore on even the fiercest warrior. He would have needed sleep. And did he even have a bed, or had he slept under the stars each night?

She had so many questions. She wanted to know so many things about him despite not wanting to care at all. And was he always so handsome? She'd known he was attractive, but surely he couldn't have been *this* alluring five years ago when he'd made love to her.

He seemed larger, if that was possible. He'd been a man of eight and ten when he'd left, but now he seemed to carry more muscle. The room had somehow grown hotter since he'd entered. She stood straighter and looked him in the eye. Except he was not looking at her face. It seemed his gaze was hovering on her bosom. No. Perhaps a bit higher. Her chin? Nay. Her throat, where the bruises were all but gone.

She cleared her throat to shift his attention. "Is there something you wanted?"

"Aye. I would like…" He paused momentarily before answering with something she didn't think he'd originally planned to say. "It's late, and I'm tired from travel. I wish to sleep." He took a seat next to the empty hearth. She'd not wanted to give him an inch, but she couldn't help the surprise that had to have shown on her face.

"You wish to sleep here? But you are the laird. Surely, you would be more comfortable in the laird's chambers."

"This was my room, and my wife is still in it. I don't need the clan to think I was cast out of my wife's bed the first night of my return."

She swallowed and looked at the large bed. It felt enormous and lonely most nights, but now it seemed too small to hold them both. When last they'd slept there, they had been curled up together.

Why did her body want to feel the warmth of his skin so badly? Even knowing how much pain he'd caused her? She'd been upset earlier that he'd forgotten her, but it seemed her heart was already forgetting what he was capable of. Or at least her body's need was making it difficult to remember. Would he expect her to welcome him after he did not want to dine with her? Without realizing it, she had reached up to tug at the curls at her nape—a nervous habit.

She let go of the strands but didn't know what else to do. It seemed her hands had no place they belonged. He had utterly befuddled her.

"Calm yerself, lass. I can sleep on the floor. I'll not make myself a nuisance to ye. I don't wish to sleep in a bed where you've lain with most of the men of the keep anyway."

She sucked in a breath as if he'd punched her in the stomach. Had he just accused her of taking up with not one man but *most* of the men in the clan? "I assume you got that information from Ewan?"

"Do you deny it?" He crossed his arms over his broad chest. She was sure now he had not been so muscled before.

"Would you believe me if I denied it?" She mimicked his pose. She was not the besotted girl he'd left in the night while she slept. She was a woman hardened by anger.

"I'm not sure." Again, his gaze drifted down to her throat. The marks were hardly visible any longer. Had someone told him what had happened?

She knew the men wouldn't have said anything unless Ronan had asked. She only needed him to doubt Ewan, and perhaps there would be a chance to share the truth and warn him of the danger Ewan posed when he was back within the castle walls.

He stood and stepped closer. She noticed his limp was more pronounced than it had been since he'd arrived. Either it pained him more, or he was not trying as hard to hide it. Either way, lying on the chilly floor wouldn't hurt his injury.

"Your leg is hurting you. It would be best if you slept in the bed. I promise you, it is safe. You might not believe me, but you were the last man to sleep in here with me."

He made a sound between a sniff and a snort. "I'm sorry to say I'm good for nothing tonight. If you had any designs on reuniting, I'll have to put you off to another night," he said as if this information caused him more discomfort than the pain in his leg.

She shook her head quickly, putting him at ease. "I assure you, that suits me fine. I have no interest in...*that*," she managed to say without making it sound like the lie it was.

"That?" he repeated with a chuckle.

She turned away to the bed as her face burned like fire. Rather than remove her robe, she got in bed with it still tied around her waist. It only took a minute to realize she'd never be able to sleep, so she shifted under the blankets to free herself from the garment without exposing herself to the man unbuckling his weapons belt.

She turned away so as not to be tempted to watch him. But while she couldn't see him, she could still hear. The clink of his weapons as he hung them on the peg by the door. He took heavy steps as he approached the bed and set something on the nightstand where she kept her dirk. Should she have moved it?

Nay, he'd not use it on her. At least, she didn't think so.

The heavy thud of a boot made her jump, but she was prepared for the one that followed. Then the quiet hiss of fabric slipped over his body as he removed his kilt.

She hadn't breathed as she listened for the quieter sound of his shirt being pulled over his head. Instead, she felt his weight on the bed and the shifting of the blankets as he got settled on the other side.

A soft moan left his lips, and she couldn't help but ask at least one of her many questions. "Are you in pain?" she whispered.

"Nay. The opposite. It's the first time in a long time I've slept on a mattress. I've forgotten how wonderful it feels not to have the hard earth as a bed."

"It seems you've forgotten many things," she said, unable to hold her tongue.

If she thought to prod him into a conversation, she would have failed for no longer had she made her biting remark than his breathing evened out in sleep. She was even more irritated that he could find peace so easily while she lay there, unable to settle. It didn't help when his calm breathing picked up and turned to frantic cries for help. His body tossed and jerked as he fought off the demons that haunted his sleep. Unable to let him suffer, she reached out and placed her hand on his arm and rubbed his sweaty skin. "Shh," she said. "You're safe now, Ronan." She repeated the words several times until he stilled and relaxed with a soft whimper.

She wasn't sure what had happened to her husband in the five years he'd been gone, but it was clear he had been injured, and the damage was not just in his leg.

***

Ronan woke late in the morning. He hadn't slept so soundly since he'd been fevered from the wound to his leg. Shane had worried he wouldn't wake up, so close Ronan was to death during those days. Eventually, he came through it, feeling like the devil himself and wishing maybe he hadn't. This morning, he wasn't weakened or in great pain. Just the average amount of pain he'd become accustomed to.

His wife was gone; he wasn't surprised. Not only did she not seem the type to laze about in bed, but he imagined she had been counting down every minute until the sun rose so she could flee the room they'd shared.

He didn't know what he'd expected when coming to their room the night before, but it wasn't the shy woman who removed her robe under the covers. She appeared to be the same untried lass he'd bedded five years ago, in actions rather than looks.

His wife had grown beautiful—not in the way a man noticed right away, but in the way that made her more lovely every time he looked at her. He wondered briefly if it would continue to be like that as they grew older. Maybe his uncle was right, and she was a witch who'd cast a spell on Ronan.

Thinking such a thing made him question Ewan's other claims that his wife had bedded half the warriors. He hadn't missed how she'd worded her answer the night before. That no man had slept in the room since him. Ronan knew well enough that one didn't need to spend the night sleeping to take part in bed sport. After all, he'd never slept with a woman the night through until his wedding night. Not that it had been the whole night.

He'd dozed for some time with her in his arms, and then, as the sky was just being touched by the first light of the new day, he'd slunk from the bed, grabbed his knapsack, and headed downstairs.

His grandsire had been waiting for him, and Ronan recalled how he'd worried the man planned to return his offer to allow Ronan to go to France. But while he'd asked if Ronan was sure he wished to leave his young bride's bed for a life as a soldier, he'd merely nodded and asked Ronan to be careful and come back when he wrote for him.

Ronan had done precisely that. But now he wondered what his wife had been up to all that time. The men had followed her and stood by her door, but the way they watched their lady was not with the admiration of a lover but that of a protector. Ronan had seen how fiercely they respected her.

He didn't know the younger men but remembered Will and Hugh. They wouldn't follow a leader who hadn't earned the right to rule the clan.

So which was it? Was she a power-hungry witch, or did his grandsire trust her over his son to care for the clan until Ronan returned to claim his birthright? He'd looked for bruises on her throat the night before but saw no sign of the injury her guard had spoken of. Had Ewan threatened her life as the man had said?

Someone was lying. But if it had been Ewan, why hadn't Brenna told him the truth? The answer whispered in his ears. *She knew I wouldn't believe her.* The guard had asked if Ronan was ready to hear the truth.

"Yes," he said as he dressed. "Yes, I bloody well am."

Chapter Ten

In the hall, Ronan looked around for his wife and didn't see her among the people finishing their morning meal. He grabbed a few bannocks and made his way out to the bailey.

His leg always pained him in the mornings until he got it moving easily again. He worked to hide his limp despite the stiffness. Outside in the bright morning sun, the young lads worked through drills, with Will leading the warriors and Hugh instructing them in holding a proper stance. But his wife was not with them.

He halted a maid who was rushing toward the kitchens. "Do ye know where the mistress is this morning?"

The befuddled girl gasped and offered a quick curtsey, having realized who he was. "Aye, my laird. That is I suspect she is where she is most mornings. Either in the kirkyard on the hill or in the neighboring forest."

At Ronan's frown, she squeaked and hurried away. Ronan should have done better to ease the lass, but it was too late. He knew the kirk she'd mentioned well. His father was buried there, and he imagined his grandsire had also been buried there. It was not that far to walk, but Ronan wasn't up for it this morning with the pain in his leg.

Besides, it promised to be a bright July day, and he wished to ride on his lands and take in the views he'd barely remembered. At the stable, he had one of the lads saddle Brimstone, and Ronan held in a gasp of pain as he mounted the beast and rode through the gates. It didn't take long for him to settle into his seat, and he tilted his face to the sun's warmth. The mountains to the north seemed to have grown taller in the time he was away. Everything was washed in the green of summer, and the heather bloomed purple, splashing the rocky hills with bright color.

He headed toward the kirk, wondering what he might find his wife doing. He slowed Brimstone at the bottom of the hill and made his way to the kirkyard on foot. Until he was up the rise, his leg had eased somewhat.

No one was there, but a bundle of freshly picked heather rested on the stone that bore his grandsire's name. His father's mother—whom Ronan had never met—was buried on one side of the laird, just as he had wanted. His second wife, Ewan's mother, was buried further down the line.

Ronan would have expected his grandsire would have been buried next to Ronan's father, but another stone had been placed between the two men. The stone was blank except for a border of thistle around the edge, and a smaller bundle of heather was placed below it. So far, this morning only bore more questions and no answers.

Looking to the east, he saw a familiar horse tied to a tree at the edge of the woods. Merlin grazed peacefully and raised his head as if in greeting as Ronan came near. What was his wife doing in the woods? Had Brenna come to rendezvous with a lover? He stepped into the coolness of the forest and listened for voices or…noises.

He heard nothing but the birds high in the trees and the small scurrying of little animals escaping to their burrows and holes. He breathed in the rich smell of dark earth and leaves. As he stepped deeper into the woods, it took a moment for his eyes to adjust to the dimness in the shade of the trees. He spotted movement off to his left and froze as Brenna lifted a bow and nocked an arrow. She drew the weapon back in perfect form.

With a soft *thump*, the arrow hit its mark. She hurried across the small clearing and picked up a rabbit. After tying it to a line with two others, she checked her arrow and moved deeper into the forest. He followed behind silently. Occasionally, a stick would snap, but she was too busy concentrating on her hunt to notice. She was obviously accustomed to hunting here. She barely made a sound as she followed a thin path. He lost track of her after she'd collected the sixth rabbit. He followed again, causing a larger stick to crack.

"Ewan?" she called out. He froze, cursing his leg for catching on the branch. He remained quiet, waiting to see what she would say next, wondering why she expected Ewan to follow her.

"I know you're there," she said louder. "Do you not remember my promise to ye?" she asked, irritation lining her voice. Or was it fear? "I told you I'd give you no more scars. If you come near me again, I'd bury my dagger in your heart without a second thought."

Good God. Ronan knew his wife didn't care for his uncle, enough to banish him, but to threaten death? Despite her threat, he heard the underlying fear in her voice. What would cause a woman to promise such a thing unless she had been frightened? Rather than confront her about it, he decided to start with Ewan for answers. And this time, he would watch the man closely and look for a possible lie.

He slipped out of the woods without another word, glad he wouldn't meet up with his wife and her deadly dagger.

***

At the sound of retreating horse's hooves, Brenna hurried out of the woods with her dagger drawn, but Ewan had already fled. She took a few deep breaths to calm her pounding heart. How had he risen so early?

He was not one to be up and about before noon after a night of drinking. She almost wished he would have confronted her. She'd have been glad to have it done with. One way or the other. However, Ronan would never trust her if she killed his beloved uncle. With a sigh, she gathered her things and returned to the castle. Jane would be happy with Brenna's catch. And Brenna hoped the woman would be willing to give her some needed advice in exchange for a meatier stew.

When she returned, the men were still

working in the bailey. Upon seeing her, Malcolm nodded to his brother and approached closer. "You didn't tell us you were leaving the castle," he said with only the slightest hint of accusation.

"I'm sure you were still abed when I left this morning. Besides, you know Ewan is no threat so early in the day." She refrained from mentioning the run-in she'd had with him in the forest. Nothing had come of it. She'd managed to scare him, so it was nothing for them to worry over.

"I thought you were still in your bed chamber with…the laird."

She glanced over to see him looking her over. She'd seen such an inspection before when he'd been worried Ewan had caused her harm.

"He didn't hurt me."

"Did he…" He shook his head as if he was unable to finish his question.

"He didn't force himself upon me, either."

She held his gaze for a moment until he nodded and went on. "I'm sure it is none of my business. That's why we left your door unguarded for the night. Surely, Ewan wouldn't try another attack while the laird was close. Besides, Will told us Ewan was passed out in the hall. I think it would be wise not to go out unprotected."

"I'm glad you and your brother could get a good night's rest for once, but I will take your suggestion under advisement."

"That's a fair number of rabbits," he said, quickly changing the subject. "Do ye wish me to clean them for you?"

"That would be appreciated. Bring them to the kitchens to be added to tonight's meal."

As Malcolm left to take care of the rabbits, Brenna continued to the kitchens. She wanted to ask the women how she should handle her returned husband. Sleeping next to him had muddled her thoughts. She'd been angry at him for so long. It was an easy thing to hold onto because the pain was so intense. But seeing him deal with his pain had undermined her plans to keep him at a distance.

And having him in bed next to her had also caused her to remember the night she'd thought she'd long barred from her memories—their wedding night when the man who'd not wanted to marry her had been sweet and kind.

He'd made her feel things she'd never thought to feel, and then he'd held her afterward. She recalled the swiftness of his heartbeat and the way he trailed his fingertips over her heated skin until she'd been lulled to sleep. And then, when she slumbered into the deep sleep of the sated, he'd left her.

She was finding it difficult to hold on to the anger that had filled her heart since that morning.

She hadn't been paying attention as she walked past the stables and was completely surprised when someone yanked her behind the building. She pulled in a breath to scream, but a dirty hand had clasped tight over her mouth.

"If you scream, I'll slice your throat," Ewan said. "I want to talk, nothing more."

Brenna didn't think he would kill her any more than she would have killed him. And for the same reason. How would either of them explain their actions to Ronan? But she didn't trust Ewan. She would scream as soon as he gave her the chance. He must have known as much, for he didn't release her.

"Listen." He gave her a harsh shake. "I wish to call a truce. Ronan has returned to run the clan, which is his place. I want to put everything that happened behind us and move forward as family."

Was the man still in his cups, or had he finally gone completely mad? He'd never treated her as family, even though the laird had. Ewan had refused to accept the laird's rule for her to run the clan until Ronan returned. And she knew he wanted to be laird himself. She didn't trust him any more than she could tolerate his stench.

"Who do you think Ronan will believe if you tell him tales? He and I are blood, and *you* are an obligation he was forced into. He hates you and wishes you'd died while he was away. He told me as much, and I was ashamed I hadn't managed to do the deed and rid him of you. I'll never forgive myself for what he sacrificed for me by taking on the likes of you."

Ewan rarely spoke a true word, but she wondered if Ronan had wished she'd died so he could come home and marry whomever he chose. Did he realize how close she'd come after he'd left?

Her eyes watered as much from the pain of that memory as from the foul odor of the man's breath.

"Just keep your fool mouth shut, and things will be fine for all of us." He pushed her clear of him. When she turned, he was already gone. She wiped at her face, wanting to rid her skin of his touch.

No. She didn't believe he wanted her to be part of the family, but he had given something away. He was worried Ronan might not believe him and he'd lose his footing as Ronan's right hand. She needed to be patient and wait for Ronan to see his kin for what he truly was. Perhaps there was hope after all.

She hurried to the kitchens and breathed a sigh of relief when she was safe inside the warm room filled with the smells of roasted meat and simmering vegetables. This was one of her favorite places in the keep. The women had all treated her as a friend, and if Ewan dared show his face there, the room had plenty of knives and hot pokers available.

"You look like the devil himself was chasing ye," Jane said, causing the other women to look her way.

"You are not far off," Brenna responded, brushing a loose curl away from her eyes.

"Ewan? Doesn't he grow weary of pestering you day after day? Where is your guard?"

"I asked Malcolm to clean up some rabbits I took this morning. I was only walking to the kitchen. It is ridiculous that I cannot go anywhere without Ewan lurking about."

"You should have hung him when you had the chance," Corinne said as if they hung people every day at Strathspey, which was far from the truth. It was a rare necessity.

"You are not the first person to point that out, and I regret I didn't see it done more and more each hour. But it's too late now, and Ronan seems to believe Ewan's lies. He doesn't know me well enough to decide if I am to be trusted, so it makes sense that he listened to Ewan over me, even if his uncle is an unholy fiend."

All the women crossed themselves at those words. It didn't hurt to be careful.

"Ronan is a wise lad. He'll see the truth soon enough," Ada assured them.

"I believe Ewan is afraid of that as well. He told me he wanted to put everything that happened between us aside and start off as family."

The women laughed.

"Lord, you need to warn a person so I don't choke on my sampling," Corinne said with her hand over her chest.

"Don't you let your guard down for a minute. It's sure to be a trick."

"Aye. I wish I knew what game he was playing. I'll be watchful," Brenna said, hating that she always needed to watch out for danger and have guards with her everywhere she went. The horrid weasel had even found a way to ruin the small peace she'd found in the early mornings.

They went on with their work after Malcolm brought in the rabbits and left again.

"The whole clan is a-chatter about what happened at the meal last eve," Ada whispered loud enough for everyone to hear.

Brenna's cheeks went hot in embarrassment.

"Don't fash, lass. Everyone is wondering what was wrong with the laird to treat ye as such. There's no shame for you to bear. You've been a fine wife, better than he deserves if he plans to treat you the way he did last night." Corinne was known to speak her mind as much as the truth. "We all remember how things were when he left."

Brenna remembered as well. After that first morning when she came down to find out he'd left, she felt lost in a new clan with no one to help her find her way. She'd wanted to start over with a new clan, but she hadn't realized she would be so alone to do so.

She'd spent days in her room, hiding from the unknown. She couldn't even miss Ronan properly because she didn't know him well enough to have missed him. Still, it hurt that she'd been eager to start a life with him, and he'd...gone off and forgotten her.

But, eventually, she'd made friends with many of the people here, including the laird. For the next several months, she thought she would be fine. But then she was forced to face something so horrible she was sure she would die. And in those darkest moments, she found herself wishing he'd been there, hating him because he wasn't.

That hatred had rooted deep.

The other women frowned at Corrine's mention of those lost months she'd spent in agony.

"Ronan just needs some time to know ye as we do. All will be well. You'll see," Jane announced, motioning everyone back to work. Brenna shook off the memory of that pain and busied herself to help her friends until one of the maids came in with wide eyes.

"Ye must come quick."

***

Sweat trickled down Ronan's spine as he shifted in his seat. A laird had many duties, and ruling over his people was one that Ronan most dreaded. Having heard this second disagreement between feuding crofters, he had no answer.

"I will consider the matter and give you my ruling tomorrow," Ronan said again. It was the same decision he'd given the first time.

The hall broke into murmuring and pointed stares in his direction.

"Ye must give your judgment," Ewan whispered in his ear. The scent of sour ale twisted the unease in Ronan's already unsettled stomach. "Ye are the laird."

"I know that," Ronan said as he clenched his fingers. "And I wish to think further before making a rash decision." He knew well enough what came from making the wrong choice.

"It is a bit of grain that surely belongs to the older man."

"I wish to think on it. Next!" Ronan called, though he wished he could say he was done for the day.

When a small boy was pushed before him, Ronan rubbed his temple. The rounded man with the pinched face spoke his displeasure.

"This lad stole my bread."

Ronan stared at the trembling boy, wondering if his thin arms could hold a loaf of bread or if his scrawny legs could carry him and a loaf away.

"Is this true?" Ronan asked, giving the boy the chance to explain. But he only looked up at the table with wide brown eyes. Tears streaked down his dirty face as he bobbed his head in a nod.

"Ye must take his hand," Ewan whispered next to him. Ronan wondered if the hiss of his voice was similar to what Eve experienced from the serpent in the Garden. Then his words sunk into Ronan's thoughts.

"His hand?"

"Thieves have their hands cut off. Do you need a blade?" The man seemed almost eager to see a child's hand severed from his body.

"Nay. That is much too extreme," Ronan said

louder than he'd meant to.

"He needs to be punished severely. Otherwise, everyone will know the Grants accept stealing, and all law will be abandoned."

A few "ayes" caused Ronan to swallow and gaze across the people waiting for him to act.

"I should think on it and—"

"My laird, with all respect, letting him go now will allow him to run away without justice being served," the man, likely the baker, said with his beady eyes narrowed on the boy.

Ronan wanted to ask the man if he, with his ample belly, couldn't spare a single loaf of bread for a hungry child, but he also heard Ewan's words. Where would the line be drawn if such things were allowed? Didn't the baker deserve to be compensated? Making bread was his livelihood, after all. But he'd not take a boy's hand for trying to feed himself. There was no good answer. He needed more time to think.

"Fifty lashes, then." Ewan offered another equally distasteful alternative. This child would not manage fifty lashes. The baker nodded his approval of this option.

Ronan's mind began to buzz from one option to the next. A night in the dungeon might satisfy the salivating wolves while ensuring the boy had a fit meal. But how could he condemn a poor boy to a night in the dark? And what other prisoners were down there? No. That won't do, but it was undoubtedly better than a beating or losing a hand and perhaps having the boy work off the debt. But looking at the man who had forced him here, it didn't seem likely he would be kind to the child.

Ronan remained silent despite all the noise

going on in his head. He must say something. He must act. It was his duty.

"I—I—" But as he opened his mouth to try to do more than stutter, his wife rushed up to the dais.

"This clan does not whip hungry children. The auld laird would not stand for such a thing, nor will I." Brenna fairly sparked with her fury as she glared at him, or perhaps she was glaring at Ewan next to him.

"You are the laird. Ye must not let a lass overthrow your ruling."

Ronan didn't know what to say, for he agreed with his wife. He couldn't imagine his grandsire allowing a wee lad to be thrashed, let alone doing the thrashing himself.

"Where are your parents, lad?" she asked, her voice softening as she placed a hand on the boy's slim shoulders.

The boy shook his head. This child was alone. He was fending for himself to fill his belly. Ronan remembered the children who moved with the armies, looking for scraps. He was left behind by men who had died and women who'd left them to find better prospects alone. How was it fair that Ronan had two families when this child had none?

"Go to the kitchen and tell them Lady Grant has sent you. They will give you a meal."

"This is unacceptable, nephew. Stop this before you lose all control."

The people in the hall seemed to stare at Ronan, waiting for him to do something. But he felt the same paralyzing fear on the battlefield after making the wrong choice. He didn't know what to do. Every option seemed wrong. Ronan's words stuck in his throat along with the lump of anxiety he couldn't swallow down as Brenna dug about in the pouch tied at her waist.

She held out a few coins. "This is payment enough for the loaf, is it not?" she asked.

"It is, Lady Grant, but—"

"Then our business is done. You may go."

The baker looked up at Ronan briefly before dipping his head to Brenna and retreating. She was handling things; he could only be grateful for her decisiveness and compassion.

"Erek?" Brenna called, and a tall man came closer.

"Aye, my lady?"

"It has been three years since your wee angel was taken from you and Mary."

"Yes, and I know what you are thinking, but I beg ye—"

"No other child will fill the hole in your hearts she left. But this child needs a home and people who can take care of him and raise him to be an honorable man. I ask you only to take him for the night so that I might find another arrangement."

"Aye, my lady. For the night only."

She nodded, and even in Ronan's state, he could tell, as his wife did, that this Erek would not turn the boy out.

"She has made a mockery of ye, nephew," Ewan said.

"Why? Because she found a way to solve the issue without bloodshed? Isn't that what a leader should do? Spare his people any pain when possible?"

"A leader provides justice."

"And what justice is there for a child who did

nothing to deserve such a fate as being orphaned? His options are to turn to crime rather than starve to death. What of that justice, uncle?"

Ewan laughed with a sneer. "I would not have thought war could weaken a man, but I was wrong."

He shoved back his chair before standing and heading for the door.

The war had weakened Ronan. Some days, he wasn't sure his leg would be strong enough to support him. But it wasn't just the physical that had been damaged. His mind and heart had also been broken. Yes, Ronan had been weakened a great deal by the war.

Ronan watched Brenna as she ordered the other women in the hall to serve the noon meal. She then went to the other men waiting to have their issues heard and saw them nod before dispersing. She was putting them off to another day. While he was thankful for the reprieve, it was not her place to do such things.

He was the laird. As useless as he seemed, he needed to ensure she knew she was not in control. Had the MacPherson laird taken a firmer stance with Ronan's mother, perhaps she wouldn't have had so much power over the laird.

He stepped up as she was speaking encouraging things to a worried Erek.

"It is a good thing you are doing," Ronan added. "I appreciate you and your wife taking in the boy."

"Of course, my laird." Erek nodded to them before leaving them alone for Ronan to deal with his wife.

Brenna was beyond angry with the man she'd

married years ago. She tried to remember when she'd thought him kind but failed to recall why, for this man was as much a monster as his uncle if he'd thought to cut off a boy's hand for trying to feed himself. "I wish to end this marriage and return home," she said as anger forced words through her lips she'd not yet considered.

He blinked and then narrowed his eyes on her. "It is far too late for such a thing, not that I'd allow it anyway."

"I care not for what you allow and don't. You are no one I want to share a name with, let alone a bed."

"If you would let me explain, you might change—"

"My opinion of you was solidified the morning I woke up alone and remained utterly alone all this time. And seeing you agree to allow a small child to be punished so fiercely."

"I did not agree."

"You didn't *not* agree, either." She pressed her lips together as she ran the words back to see if they made any sense and found they were good enough for Ronan Grant. She couldn't remember being so angry and disappointed with another person all her life.

Even Ewan, the monster he might be, had never disappointed her so thoroughly. For expecting him to be ruthless was just that…expected. At the same time, she'd hoped for more from Ronan. She'd seen glimpses of what she'd thought might be goodness. But now…

"I was considering the dungeon," he said almost proudly, as if this were to sway her opinion of him.

"The dungeon? You wished to throw a child in a damp cell with hardened criminals?"

"Well, yes, I tossed that aside for the same reason. But I was never, not for a second, considering lashes or…" He swallowed before gesturing at nothing. "The other thing."

He couldn't speak of it. She stared at him as he struggled.

"The…" He pointed to his hand and shivered. "I would never. He was only hungry. A child left alone. I saw many like him in France. What would any of us do in the same situation but steal to fill our bellies? Even the baker would become desperate and do whatever was necessary to feed himself. It is instinct. And I would even say a plump man would not take long to be pushed to the brink of human nature."

She couldn't help but chuckle. She'd been wrong. He hadn't been silent because he approved; he'd been trying to find his way. And she'd…and then… Oh.

"It pains me to know you think so very little of me that I would go along with such a thing," he snapped, and she felt maybe she even deserved his displeasure this time.

"I don't know you, but I can see now that you are not without honor. I should not have stepped in. I should have allowed you to sort it out yourself."

"In truth, I'm grateful you stepped in. While I never would have allowed the boy to be harmed, I'd not yet figured out a way to solve the problem."

"I'm sure you would have if I'd given you time to do so. I am sometimes…" Words of her childhood flitted around in her mind. She'd been rash, impatient, unladylike, stubborn. Any number of words would suit, but she never considered the one he offered.

"Brave."

She started and looked him in the eye. If he was toying with her, she was not above ending their marriage. How many times had she considered it in those darkest of times? Why had she stayed? The auld laird had asked her to stay, but if she were truthful with herself, she knew Geordie was not why she'd remained at Strathspey. Or remained Ronan's wife.

"Brave?" she whispered, wondering how he might think such a thing of a person who had wanted to run away more times than she could count.

"You walked into the hall a fierce lioness ready to battle for anyone who might plan to hurt him as if he was your child."

Her breath caught as her chest blazed with painful burning. Her eyes stung, and her throat threatened to close. She took a step back.

"He is not mine," she rasped and backed away to return to the kitchens.

Brenna stayed hidden away, working with the women during the nooning, but her maid had helped her change in time for the late meal. She wasn't sure where she would be sitting. Would Ronan send her away from the high table again? Should she even try to sit with him? After her outburst, he may now be considering putting her in the dungeon. But he'd called her brave, and whether it was courage or obstinance that had her put one foot in front of the other as she went to the hall, she did not know.

She supposed it was his right as laird to invite

anyone he chose to dine with him, but she wouldn't recoil from rejection. Instead, she held her head high and entered the hall where she was pleasantly greeted by the families she called her own. Sparing a glance at the high table, she found her husband getting to his feet and holding out the chair that was hers. Ewan was nowhere to be seen.

This allowed her to speak to her husband without Ewan's glares and lies. She held his gaze as she walked toward the dais. It wouldn't do to shy away from his direct inspection. She had nothing to hide. At the table, she offered a curtsey and nodded before sitting. Jane had said Ronan only needed to know Brenna as the rest of the clan knew her, and he would see the truth.

This was her chance.

Chapter Eleven

Once again, Ronan was surprised by his wife. Not just for her beauty—yes, she was more lovely than the last time he'd seen her—but for her courage. After he'd treated her so poorly the night before, he expected her to be absent from the meal tonight.

He was glad he'd been wrong, for he'd found himself looking for glimpses of her throughout the day.

His uncle had also been absent, so Ronan could not question him about what had happened in the forest that morning. But he would have his answers soon enough. He sat next to Brenna, and she offered him a strained smile. She acted like he might roar at her any moment, and he couldn't blame her. He needed to atone for his earlier behavior.

"You look lovely this evening," he said, surprising her with a pretty blush. He noticed her hands on her lap, fingers clenched. Was she nervous or frightened?

"Thank you, my laird," she whispered.

She said nothing else as the maids served the meal and poured their wine.

"The boy is settled," she said, and at the same time, he said, "How is the boy?"

She smiled more easily this time, and her smile forced his grin. "Please, you first," he insisted.

"He—Matthew is fine."

He nodded. "Good. And how did you spend the rest of your day?"

She seemed frozen as she set her glass down. Did she think the question was a trap of some sort?

"I am only curious," he said, unsure why he needed to assure her.

She gave a nod before speaking. "I spent the early morning hunting, and then the afternoon and the rest of the day, I helped the ladies in the kitchen when I wasn't seeing to wee Matthew. Geordie always teased me for working in the kitchen like a maid, but I like to be useful, and I enjoy their company. They were the only friends I had here after…"

She looked away, but he thought he knew what she'd meant to say.

She'd been alone in a new home with a new clan. An outsider. Could he not have spared a few days to settle her before leaving her there? What a selfish arse he'd been to run off on their wedding night as he had.

He'd been so eager to get to France and the glory of war. But there had been no glory. He'd not become a hero in France, and he's undoubtedly not been Brenna's hero in recent years.

He smiled and tried to think of something to say when the silence continued. She hadn't said so much to him since he'd returned. He cursed himself again, for it was his fault she'd been wary to speak.

"You call my grandsire by his given name?" he asked because it wasn't typical for the auld laird to allow such a thing.

"He allowed me to," she answered quickly. His question had made her defensive. He wouldn't forge a connection with his wife in this way.

"He must have held you in high regard. He allowed only a few such liberties."

She pressed her lips together, and he wanted to hear the laugh she fought to hold in.

"What did I say?" he pressed.

"He didn't permit me exactly. He was being cantankerous, and I just used it as a scold. You should have seen his face. He was so shocked. And then he burst out laughing. After that, we were thick as thieves, having faced each other down like wild cats." Her smile faded.

"You miss him," Ronan said, though it was apparent.

"Aye. I didn't have a living grandfather, and my father was often vexed with me, but Geordie and I were very close. I often sat with him as he saw to business. He even asked my opinion on a few occasions."

"My grandfather asked for your advice?" Ronan could hardly believe such a thing. The auld laird was so set in his ways that Ronan could scarcely believe he had room to hear anyone else's thoughts but his own.

She nodded. "'Tis true. You can ask anyone if you don't..." She didn't finish the sentence; instead, she focused on her meal, but he knew what she didn't say—*If you don't believe me.*

Would this be how all their conversation would go? She started to say something but stopped so as not to rouse him to anger. He knew it was his doing but didn't like it. He didn't know what to believe. If this was a tale, it served no purpose to get anything from him. But he knew well enough a reason wasn't strictly necessary for a lie. Some people held no hold on the truth. He'd spent his life with a mother who plotted and schemed to get what she wanted through manipulation and deceit. He'd come to expect it from all women, but he'd known there must be some who were not out for their gain.

He thought of Maria, Shane's wife. She'd been faithful and steadfast. And Tory, his stepsister. She'd been a friend and always offered an ear when he needed to talk over a problem. In some ways, she probably knew him even better than Shane or had before they'd left for France.

Ronan decided to turn the topic to something else Brenna had said. "You hunt?" He'd seen her do so that morning. He didn't realize it was a common thing. He did wonder why she would leave the keep without her guards when, even now, they watched her from their place in the back of the hall.

"Aye. I used to go with Geordie. He enjoyed it greatly, even if I always caught more than he." Her fond smile had returned when she spoke of the old man. Ronan realized she probably knew the man better than Ronan had. With moving to the MacPhersons as a lad and then going off to war, he hadn't been around his grandsire much as a grown man. And he'd missed his chance.

"I caught the rabbits in this stew," she added

proudly.

"And then you helped cook it? You don't mind helping?" Ronan couldn't imagine his mother stepping foot in the kitchen unless she was looking for someone to scold for something she disliked.

"I enjoy it. The women who work there are good friends."

"The rest of the clan seems to like ye."

She shrugged and glanced at the empty seat beside him. The seat Ewan had occupied the night before. Ronan wasn't sure where his uncle was. He would worry about it another time, for now he was getting to know the woman he was married to. Just as things were being cleared away, his wife looked toward the side door of the hall and let out an excited squeal.

"Tonight's entertainment is my favorite. One of the mothers in the village teaches the children to sing. They are quite adorable."

Another thing he had learned about his wife. She liked children. He'd seen how she'd bent down to speak to them as she'd entered the hall with a bright smile. And yet he'd left her childless all this time. He had been selfish, not caring who he'd hurt to do what he wished. In many ways, he was no better than his mother. Deirdre never cared about those who were inconvenienced by her requests. Shame flared on Ronan's cheeks as the lute player strummed his instrument, and two women herded the children into somewhat of a line.

They began the first ditty about a boat. The group was sorely out of time and off-key, but Ronan understood why Brenna enjoyed it. For what the little ones lacked in talent they made up for in sheer exuberance.

His wife giggled, a slight sound of joy. When he looked over, she was squeezing her hands together at her chest as if overcome with happiness. Until she saw him watching her. She quickly straightened her posture and cleared her throat.

"They are quite excited," he said.

"Yes. They have no care in how they sound. They are each being their own selves. How wonderful not to have such worries," she said wistfully, and he remembered the girl galloping into the bailey on her monster horse with sticks in her hair and mud on her trews.

"I would clap if you sang with them," he said.

She laughed and shook her head. "Nay. No one could clap with their hands covering their ears."

She was witty, another thing he had forgotten about his wife.

Ronan found he was excited to learn everything about her, to know her as a husband should know his wife, and perhaps maybe even as a lover. She was a bonny woman; once again, he found her even more beautiful than the last time he'd seen her. His body stirred for her. It was not the usual ache he suffered when needing release; he wanted only her touch, her kiss. Her body against his. He'd stubbornly held on to his vows because it was right. But now he realized it was more than that.

He looked at her and wondered if what he saw was real or a facade crafted by a woman who traded in manipulations and lies. And a pretty smile and a twinkling eye could bring a man to his knees if he wasn't careful.

***

Brenna couldn't fathom the change in the man to her side.

Her husband had been horrid the night before until he'd joined her in their chamber. Tonight, he was the doting husband, asking her questions as if he wanted to know her better and how she thought of things. When he wasn't asking questions outright, he was watching her, perhaps learning more of her in that way than she realized. And all the while, she watched him as well. When his attention was pulled in a different direction, she stole glances, taking in his straight white teeth and how his smile hinted at a bit of mischief.

But she wasn't the only one watching the new laird. The warriors watched him with a narrowed gaze. And the serving maids cast alluring looks as they filled his cup more than necessary.

Brenna fought off the instinct to growl at them when they came near. She felt like a wild animal protecting its mate from intruders. How silly. She had no claim on him. Yes, they were married, but that meant little to him as he'd fled as soon as he'd had the chance.

Pushing away the bitter memories, she clapped loudly when the children finished and scattered to sit with their families, each accepting a hug and kiss from a proud parent.

"Thank you for your company this evening," she said, wanting Ronan to know how much she preferred this treatment than that of the night before. "I believe I shall retire to bed."

"I will join you. I fear despite sleeping late this morning, I'm still recovering from my journey."

She nodded, silently communicating she

welcomed him to join her. "Will you tell me about it?" she asked as she walked beside him to their chamber. Her guards hopped up from their seats as soon as she'd stood, but Ronan held up a hand to stay them.

Even at that order, they glanced at her for her approval.

She gave what she hoped was a subtle nod, letting them know she was okay. It wouldn't do for the laird to see his men obey his wife over his orders. Silent or not.

As they entered the room, he was chatting about how flat the land was beyond the highlands. She couldn't imagine such a sight, having spent all her days surrounded by mountains and hills. Having realized they were in the room alone, they both fell into a heavy silence. Her earlier courage deserted her, and she could not look him in the eye.

How was she to change with him in the room? She could manage her gown but used the excuse of needing to call a maid, hoping he would give her that moment alone. Instead, he offered his aid. She couldn't catch her breath as she shook her head. She couldn't allow him to help her out of her clothes.

She remembered their only night together when he'd done just that. Her cheeks went aflame as other memories came unbidden to her mind then. His kisses. The way he'd nipped the flesh on her neck. His rapid breaths near her ear and the other sounds he'd made. The words he'd said that made her feel cherished. But it hadn't been true.

As if icy loch water had been tossed on her, she remembered the chill of waking the next day alone and finding he'd left. The stares and cruel jokes. *"She must have been a fright in his bed. She scared the laird's heir clean to France."*

Standing tall with her indignation wrapped around her, she shook her head. "I do not require assistance from you." Her words sounded crisp and shrewish. Good. Let him know she had no interest in him in that way. She might be unable to keep him from taking his husbandly rights, whether he'd earned them or not, but she would make it clear she did not welcome his attentions.

The pain this man had caused her would never be forgotten nor forgiven. A few smiles and a bit of kindness could not erase the hurt.

Chapter Twelve

Ronan didn't understand the change in his wife as she turned her back to him and promptly moved to the far corner of the room. In the shadows where the light didn't touch her, he heard the soft swish of fabric over skin as she disrobed.

Somehow, hearing her nakedness rather than seeing it still enticed him. He was growing mad from his increasing need. He'd enjoyed the evening with her. Making her smile and laugh. Her witty sparring. He'd hoped to continue their easy banter until they drifted asleep. But she'd turned cold. Did she think he planned to push himself upon her?

He'd be lying if he said he hadn't thought of how much he'd enjoy making love to her. His body ached for release after years of loneliness but for his own hand. And that was only done on the rare occasions when he found himself alone. Tonight, her smile alone had made him swell with interest.

She was his wife. She was his. But as she

slipped under the blankets, keeping her back to him, he knew she didn't welcome his touch. He'd never force her, nor would he beg. He'd waited five long years; he could wait a bit longer. Tonight hadn't been about sex, though his thoughts had gone there. He'd only wanted to get to know her to better determine the truth.

What he knew so far was that his people and his warriors respected her. She didn't sit around all day casting orders for people to see to her whims. She was nothing like his mother. Or if she was, she'd found a more effective way to get the power she wanted. It hadn't gone unnoticed how the men in the hall hadn't stood down until she'd given a nod—her silent order to stay.

Ronan's order had not been enough.

He removed his belts and kilt and slid under the covers beside the woman feigning sleep. Her breathing was much too quick to be at rest. He stroked two fingers down her arm and watched as gooseflesh sprang to her creamy skin. She was interested in him, yet she denied him and herself the pleasure of a proper reunion.

That could only mean one thing. His wife was angry at him.

He didn't need to think long on why. He'd left without so much as a note. He'd been overwhelmed with excitement and anticipation the first few days after he'd left, but before he'd even made it to France, he'd started to think of Brenna each night before falling asleep.

He'd wondered what she was doing. At first, he thought she wouldn't have minded he'd gone and had even convinced himself she was likely glad since a stranger was her husband. And she had been a stranger to him. This was why he felt he didn't owe her anything more than his fidelity. But when her first letter arrived, he felt the first stirrings of guilt.

He'd wondered what words waited for him inside. Would it be a scold or angry threats? Or would it be worse than that? Would she wish him well and pray for his safekeeping? He didn't think he could bear to read her words of comfort or understanding. He surely hadn't deserved them back then. And he didn't deserve her kindness or patience now.

He wanted to apologize. To speak the words that would ease the way toward whatever life they might have together. But that was yet another thing he didn't deserve—her forgiveness.

What must she have thought that morning when she woke to find he was gone? Had she come down that first morning looking for him? Who had told her he had gone to France? It could have only been Geordie as he was the only one who'd known. How long had it taken for her to settle in here?

All these questions… She was right to hold on to her anger. He was surprised she hadn't run him through with the dirk she kept on the nightstand.

He didn't like to think she felt so unsafe in their home that she needed to sleep with a blade at hand. But the threat she'd made that morning in the forest seemed to prove that Ewan had hurt his wife.

He put out the light and settled just a little closer to her, feeling the heat of her body. He needed to know the truth. He wouldn't stop until he found out who was lying to him.

***

It took Brenna too long to fall asleep after she

and her husband settled in bed. She'd allowed her anger to grip her and ruin the pleasant evening. She'd let her guard down as they shared a meal and the children's entertainment. It was so easy to let go when he was smiling with those warm brown eyes open to her.

She wrestled with the strange feelings long into the night until she eventually fell asleep, only to be roused again what felt like minutes later in the worst of ways. She woke to pain, unable to pull in a breath. She scratched at the hand crushing her throat, but it didn't move. The weight above her pushed what little breath she had left out of her chest in a gust. Her only thought was that she'd been a fool to fall asleep without barring the door. Ewan would undoubtedly kill her this time.

But as she reached for the dirk on the bedside table, her hand found nothing but an empty bed. Warm from where Ronan had slept. Where was he? Had Ewan killed Ronan? Giving up on the dirk or trying to dislodge the hands at her throat, she moved her fingers up the arm and found a face. Pressing viciously on his eye, she heard a roar of rage. The weight lifted, and the man rolled over. Enough moonlight came through the window to see the man gasping beside her; it was not Ewan but Ronan.

Good Lord. Her husband was trying to kill her. Did he genuinely hate her that much?

She coughed and wheezed while he thrashed next to her, his eyes closed as he shouted out for help. As her breathing became easier, she realized he hadn't intended to hurt her at all. He was obviously in the throes of a nightmare.

She took some comfort in knowing he hadn't

intentionally tried to murder her in her sleep.

"Ronan—" She tried to speak, but it came out as a hoarse croaking sound. She nudged his arm and ducked when his hand came flying out as if holding a sword to slay an enemy. Twisting to the side, she used her legs and pushed him off the bed. He fell to the floor with a loud thump. A groan of pain had her out of the bed on the other side and around to light the lantern so to assess the damage.

He'd fallen on his side but had been spared more injury by the pile of clothes he must have discarded there before joining her in the bed. Again, she tried to speak but could not utter more than a whisper. She went to the pitcher and poured a glass of water to quench the burning in her throat, but she could barely swallow.

"Brenna?" her husband said, sitting up and watching her. "Why am I on the floor?"

"You— You were hav—" She tried swallowing again and forced out, "A bad dream."

He was up off the floor and standing before her in a flash. "Did I hurt ye, lass? What did I do?"

She pointed to her throat, and he moved her so he could see her better. Or perhaps worse was the more accurate term for his face crumbled. "Bloody hell. I could have strangled you to death."

"You're bleeding." She pointed to his temple, where a small cut oozed down his cheek.

"I don't care. Are *you* harmed? I could have crushed your throat and killed ye," he repeated, though she was well aware of how close it had come to being the case.

He paced away only to return to her immediately. He was having trouble reckoning what had nearly happened.

"I'm so sorry, Brenna. I didn't mean to—" He reached for her, but she pulled back on instinct, not because of what he had nearly done minutes ago, but because he was a man and thanks to Ewan, any such movements caused such a reaction.

And in truth, the memory of his attack was too fresh in her mind. She was rattled and didn't want to be touched. Not while her throat still burned.

"I'll get Moira. She'll know what to do." He stood and headed for the door in only his shirt.

"Nay." Brenna managed to stay him with a hand after taking in the enticing curve of his buttocks through the thin linen. She shook her head. "Sleeping."

"I don't care if she's sleeping. You need a healer right now. She'll come if I call."

Brenna rolled her eyes as he rushed out of the room. He came right back, snatched up his kilt, and hastily pulled on his boots before leaving again. She knew Moira wouldn't be able to do much. Some willow bark tea for the pain or honeyed mead to coat her burning throat was about all that could be done.

She heard Ronan's cursing before he entered their room again. "The woman is out helping with a birth in the village. I'll take ye to her." He moved to scoop her up from where she sat on the edge of their bed.

Brenna shook her head again and said, "Kitchen." She stood alone and went toward the door, picking up her robe. While he didn't move to try to lift her again, he quickly supported her when she wobbled. The stones were cool under her feet.

Despite the warmth of the July days, the castle

still turned cold at night. Together, they made their way down to the kitchens, where she made her drink, adding extra honey to sweeten the bitterness of the willow bark. The first sip burned a little, but she could swallow without discomfort after a few more.

Either the honey was working, or the mead was dulling the pain. Whichever, she didn't much care. "Do ye have nightmares often?" she asked, her voice a bit stronger.

"Aye."

"What are they about?" It must have been the mead. She wouldn't have asked him something so personal without the extra courage. Her defenses were low while her curiosity was in full force.

She'd seen how much he worried that he'd hurt her. The regret. That kindness she remembered from that night long ago. How he'd not wanted to hurt her as he took her in their marriage bed. Despite what lies Ewan had told him, Ronan was a kind man at his core. She felt her anger slip further and gathered it tighter around her.

He lifted a shoulder in a shrug, and she guessed he didn't want to tell her. She was no one he would like to share secrets with. Just the unwanted wife who had been forced on him. The wife he didn't want. Her throat burned again, but this time from holding back tears of resentment.

He surprised her when he finally spoke, his tone somber. "When I first went to fight, the number of deaths I witnessed was shocking. I'd been on several raids before that, so I wasn't new to battle, but war is much different than a skirmish with a neighboring clan. Somehow, it didn't feel real, so it was easy to sleep afterward. Keeping that part sealed off from my own life worked for nearly a year. But at some point, you're faced with the truth of things. He ceases to exist when you thrust your sword through a man's heart. There's no hiding from that reality for long."

Wanting to comfort him, she took his hand in hers. Without the bitterness, she had nothing to protect her. The unease of being vulnerable prickled as she stroked his palm with her thumb. For this moment, at least, she was safe from the anger he brought out in her.

She kept silent as he found the words to continue.

"When your mind fails to protect you from the truth, you start to think of those you've killed and who they were. They were your enemy, yes, but they were also men with kin and lives of their own. Were they even fighting for their homeland? Or were they hired from somewhere else, as was I? And then, as if that weren't enough, there is the matter of my men, the ones that died because of me."

"What do you mean?"

"Before I was injured, I was made captain. I thought it a great honor. Shane had been my captain and had recommended me for the job. A fool sees only a title and not the duty required to hold up such a thing. When I was called upon to make a crucial decision, I made a grave mistake, and lives were lost. I carry the burden of their deaths on my shoulders. Their faces still haunt me at night when I try to sleep."

She remembered his inability to decide what to do about the lad who had taken the bread and imagined that was why he couldn't act. Did he see every decision as life or death? His hesitation was born from this pain.

"I'm sorry," she whispered, wishing he'd not had to live through such horror even if he'd chosen that life over one with her.

"You've no reason to be sorry. Ye didn't tell me to go. You probably would have told me to stay and be your husband if I asked your opinion. But I dinna give you a say in the matter, did I?" He shook his head. "And now I pay dearly for that. As I should."

He bore these nightmares as a punishment. She could see that. Guilt washed over her. He must have seen her resentment earlier. She'd done nothing to hide it. He'd left her. He'd found a way to get out of being shackled to a woman he didn't want. But she'd been wrong to think he'd enjoyed his time away. He'd lived through hell. He'd been wounded inside and out.

Mayhap he deserved a small measure of compassion. He raised her hand to his lips and gently kissed her knuckles. "I'm sorry I hurt ye." His breath whispered across her skin, sending a shiver as heat washed her clean of bitterness.

This apology was short on words, but she thought she heard all he didn't say. He was sorry he'd hurt her throat, but he was also sorry for the other, more profound hurt he'd caused her. They were just words, much like the vows they'd shared. They only meant something if a person took them to heart. She didn't know if he regretted leaving her, but that didn't mean she enjoyed seeing his pain. Like Ewan, one would have to be a monster and not want to offer comfort.

"I'm sorry you are tormented as you sleep."

He offered a sad smile. "The truth is, even before France, I didn't sleep all that well. When I was a lad of eight, I followed Ewan into the loch to swim. Being a taller boy of twelve, I was quickly beyond my depth and couldn't touch the bottom. I struggled and would have drowned if Ewan hadn't pulled me out. He saved me. I owe him my life."

Brenna wanted to argue that he didn't owe that vicious cur a damned thing, but she understood how he had made Ewan into a hero in his mind, and words would never change his thoughts on the matter. She disliked the idea of being the one to force him to look at Ewan as the monster he was now and slay the person Ronan thought his uncle to be. Wouldn't he come to resent such a thing?

Wasn't there too much resentment between them already?

"Come. My throat is better. Let's try to get some sleep. Hopefully, the demons will leave us be if we face them together."

She held out her hand in invitation, and he didn't hesitate even a second before putting his larger, warmer hand around hers and offering a comforting squeeze.

"I vow to protect ye, if you'll have my back."

She smiled and nodded, but she wasn't sure who Ronan might choose to protect, Ewan or her.

Chapter Thirteen

Ronan hadn't meant to share so much with Brenna, but after he'd half-strangled her, he felt responsible for seeing her cared for and explained that his actions hadn't been about her.

But that hadn't been the only reason. When she'd touched him, he'd felt grounded in a way he hadn't in so long. After she set down her empty glass of mead, he helped her up to their chamber and tucked her back into bed. He fought the urge to join her when she snuggled under the covers and fell asleep. He was exhausted but couldn't risk putting her in danger. Instead, he frowned at the woman and turned to go.

The sun was hinting at the horizon, so he went out for a ride to clear his head. He didn't trust himself to give in to sleep again. He'd done enough damage already. His wife seemed pleasant enough, and he'd not seen any evidence that she'd betrayed him in any way other than banishing his uncle. Even the soft smiles and kind words didn't seem engineered to manipulate him. But he would stay his distance until he was sure she wasn't up to something. He'd not risk his heart with a feckless woman. And he'd not be led about by his cock in the way his stepfather was.

Brenna may have grown into a lovely woman, but she was still a stranger. He was guilty of leaving her, hurting her. But he'd learned over the years that everyone was guilty of something. What was his wife guilty of?

According to Ewan, the list was long. He needed to know for sure.

When he returned to the castle after his ride, he went to the hall to break his fast. Ewan wasn't there, but his men were filling their plates while casting glances in his direction. It was time to set things right with them. He was their leader, and it was time for him to start leading.

"Is this all ye do, stuff your gobs?" Ronan asked with a smile as he sat with them at one of the low tables. A serving girl brought him his meal, and he dug in.

"We have already done two sets of drills this morning while you were off taking in the sights," Will said, baiting him.

"Fair enough. I'll let you put me through my paces when we finish eating."

Hugh smiled with a touch of mischief. "I look forward to it."

As Ronan laughed at the implied threat, Malcolm gasped. Will's smile was replaced by anger, his hands fisting on the table. Gabe also looked up and sat back in shock, his mouth gaping open. Ronan turned to see Brenna approaching. She wasn't wearing anything that warranted this ill response. Then he saw what his men had responded to. The dark bruises on her neck were in the shape of his hand, and each finger was distinctly outlined.

Malcolm turned to him, his face tight with accusation. "Did ye not protect her from Ewan?"

To the others, the young warrior defended his lack of protection for their mistress. "I thought she'd be safe with him."

Ronan shook his head, feeling the familiar wash of shame heat his blood. "'Twas not Ewan who caused that damage."

Hugh slammed his fist on the table. "What the bloody hell did you do to her?"

Gabe stood and hurried over to Brenna as Ronan explained to the three men, glaring at him and snapping angrily.

"I had a nightmare, and the lass was unfortunate to be too close," Ronan quickly explained, though as laird he wasn't obliged to justify his actions. He did so because he didn't want anyone to think he was capable of abusing his woman. Or any woman, for that matter.

"How did she end up too close?" Will pushed. "She's stayed clear of ye because you treated her worse than a beggar when ye arrived. Is this how you plan to rule, laird? Strangling innocent women because they don't suit ye? Your grandfather would turn over in his grave to see you've touched the lass harshly."

"The facts are true as I've told them to you. She is my wife. It's not uncommon to share a bed with one's wife."

Hugh's anger seethed into disgust. "She's not

good enough to be treated kindly, but you'll rut upon her to get a bloody heir." He shook his head with a sneer.

Gabe returned and sat down. "Lady Brenna says the laird choked her while he was having a bad dream. She insists it's not his fault."

"Just as I said." Ronan glared at his men.

Will let out a breath and relaxed slightly. "Fine. If the lass says that's what happened, I believe ye."

"But only because *the lass* said it was so?" He didn't like being challenged by his men or for his word to be doubted.

"Aye." Hugh met his gaze unflinchingly. "You've been gone a long time, laird. I don't know your heart. And hearts have a way of turning dark with some people. I've seen it happen. Know this. I swear my fealty to you as my laird, but if you hurt the lass, I will defend her with my life."

"Aye, and I, as well," Will chimed in.

Malcolm and Gabe nodded in agreement from the other side of the table. Ronan didn't think his men would ever side with a power-hungry tyrant. Unless Ewan was right and Brenna had bewitched his men to do her bidding. Still, no woman deserved to be mistreated, no matter how devious she may be.

A memory stole over him. A crisp spring day. He was a lad, no more than eight summers, living here at Strathspey with his father. But he'd gone to the village with his mother. She'd said she needed to visit with a friend and told him to sit outside and wait for her. But he hadn't, not when he'd heard sounds and thought his mother was in distress.

He'd looked in the window and saw what he'd

thought at that young age was a man struggling with his mother. He'd run as fast as his scrawny legs could carry him to fetch his father so he might help her.

But when he'd arrived back at the house with his da, his mother did not look distressed. She was kissing the man he'd seen her wrestling with. And his father had gone into a rage.

He'd grabbed her and practically dragged her off to the castle. Once there, they'd gone to their room. Once again, Ronan had been left outside the door. He'd heard the yelling, the slap of leather, and his mother's wail.

His father left the room first, and Ronan went inside to see his mother. She'd been crying, and her lip had a bit of blood. He'd hurried to get a cloth to help her, but instead of accepting his offer, she'd snapped at him.

"This is your fault."

For the few years before his father died, he heard the same sounds coming from their room, and in his youth, he'd thought it was his fault that his father hurt his mother because of him.

But later, when he knew to shed light on what had truly happened, he'd realized his mother had betrayed her vows. And instead of accepting the blame for her misdeeds, she'd held Ronan at fault.

Later, when he was thirteen and living at Cluny Castle with his new family, he'd seen his mother sneak off to another man's home. Ronan had stayed far enough away to see but not close enough to hear the sounds coming from inside.

His mother smiled like a cat when she left the cottage to return to the castle. Ronan watched as his mother sat beside his stepfather with an adoring smile. She kissed him as if he were the only man holding her heart, and he foolishly believed all the sweet words.

It was a lesson he'd never forgotten. Women were deceitful. Women lied. Women blamed others for their wrongdoings. Only a fool believed he alone could win their heart.

But no matter their crimes, they should not be beaten.

"I would never deliberately hurt my wife. Ye have my word on it."

The only answers from the table were a snort, a sniff, and a rolling of eyes. He'd already betrayed that vow to them and guessed it was true. He hadn't tried to strangle her on purpose, but he had deliberately left her behind for five years.

The anger he'd seen in her eyes the night before was born of the pain he'd caused when he'd left. She'd likely thought the worst of his reasons. He needed to explain that his desertion had nothing to do with her. It was merely a temporary escape from the duty that had suffocated him.

He didn't get to explain it during the morning meal, for she left the hall. She hadn't even broken her fast. Curiosity had him on his feet to follow her. It didn't take long for him to spot her when he stepped outside. She didn't appear to be in any hurry as she secured a basket under her arm and headed for the village. She walked past the first two cottages along the path and knocked at the third.

A man opened the door. From how the morning sun shone in Ronan's eyes, he could not tell if the man was young or old, but he could tell by his height it was a man.

Just moments ago, he remembered watching his mother sneak off to another man's cottage, and now he was watching his own wife do the same thing. It seemed Ewan had been right that she'd taken a lover or many.

There was only one way to find out.

***

The mornings were Brenna's favorite time of the day. Not only was she usually free of worrying about Ewan, but the mornings offered a fresh start—the chance to find happiness.

She greeted Mr. Campbell as the children gathered around her. By now, they knew her basket contained treats, and they waited with big eyes for her to dispense the tarts she'd managed to get from the kitchen while the women were busy with other things.

She didn't want to have to explain what had happened to her throat. She'd seen the way her guards had reacted. Somehow, she expected the women of the kitchens to be even more fiercely protective than four strong warriors.

Brenna was handing out the first tart when she jumped at the sound of someone beating on the Campbells' door. Her first worry was that Ewan had found her and would hurt this family because he knew Brenna cared for them. Had he sought her out to threaten her again? Or maybe worse.

"Open up!" a man bellowed, and the pounding continued.

Like yesterday in the forest, she'd thought she'd been safe alone. It was too early in the day for Ewan to be awake. Perhaps Ronan's return kept the man from sleeping the day away in the beds of different women.

Brenna braced herself as Mr. Campbell opened the door. But it was Ronan, not Ewan, who stormed inside, taking up much of the small space in the cottage. His brows nearly touched in the middle as he took in the four small children gathered around Brenna and the baby in her arms.

"What's this?" he demanded.

"This is wee Rabbie. His mother is not feeling herself quite yet from birthing him, but she's doing a bit better today." She turned to hand the small bundle to the family's oldest daughter.

Mr. Campbell gave a quick bow. "I don't have much to offer you, my laird. But I can get ye a pint of ale if you wish."

"Aye. Thank you, sir." He grasped the man's shoulder. "Ye have a fine home and family. My apologies for barging in and frightening ye."

Brenna sniffed, knowing exactly why he'd barged in. He still thought her unfaithful. He could follow her around and make accusations until he ran out of breath, but he'd never find her guilty of such a thing.

"You are always welcome," Mr. Campbell offered. The man was nearing sixty. His five children and his first wife were grown and had families. Now, he was raising these five with a younger wife who suffered from spells of melancholy.

"Have you eaten today, Sarah?" Brenna asked the woman, huddled in a bed tucked in the corner of the tiny home.

Sarah shook her head.

"I think you will feel better if you eat a bit," Brenna said, stopping by the fire to ladle some stew into a bowl. As she handed it to the woman, the baby began to cry. Mr. Campbell had already gone out to get Ronan's drink, so Brenna took the baby from the girl and plopped him in Ronan's arms.

He looked stricken. "What am I to do with him?"

"Walk around and give him a little pat on his arse until he stops crying."

To her surprise, Ronan followed her directions perfectly as she helped Sarah sit up and take some nourishment. "He's soon going to need to feed. Will you try?" she encouraged the mother.

Sarah nodded and even tried to smile. Brenna had seen it before. Some women grew sad after giving birth, even to a healthy bairn. Brenna didn't understand why a woman wouldn't be thrilled beyond reason to have a child, but it didn't always work that way.

The baby stopped crying for a moment. When he started again, Brenna took the babe and held him out to Sarah, who fitted him to her breast like a woman who'd already had four bairns. Mr. Campbell came in and put a cup in Ronan's hands. The laird gave a nod of thanks and smiled at the other children, who were staring up at him.

"Who is this man? Why is he so big?" the older of the boys asked.

"This is the laird of clan Grant, Thomas. And he is big because he is a fierce warrior," Mr. Campbell said.

"Can I be a warrior someday?" the boy asked, not daunted by Ronan's solemn expression.

"Of course you can, lad," Ronan said, pulling the boy into his lap. "I would be happy to have a man as courageous as you to make sure the people of our clan are safe."

"I keep my mama and papa safe."

"I'm sure you do," Ronan said.

"Does your leg pain you?" the boy asked, and Brenna gasped, not wanting Ronan to be angry with the child for pointing out his weakness.

But the laird just smiled and nodded. "Aye. It hurts me today. I was walking on it faster than I'm used to."

Was she mistaken, or did he look over at her—almost in accusation—as he said that? She walked quickly; perhaps her husband had not easily kept up with her as he'd followed her this morning. She hid a smile.

"You should let Lady Grant look at it for you. Last summer, I fell from a tree and broke my leg. She fixed it up so it dinna hurt anymore. I could still do my chores."

"Are ye a healer, then?" Ronan asked, keeping his eyes on her.

"I just help out. Moira is getting older and can't keep up with all these fine bairns." Brenna smiled and picked up wee Joey, who was only three.

After she'd passed out the bannocks she'd brought and rechecked on Sarah and the babe, she picked up her basket and said her farewells.

The children came to the door to wave, and Mr. Campbell gave her a little bow. "I don't know what I would do if not for you," the man said. "She was much improved today. Thank ye, mistress."

"I'm glad she's in better spirits. Take care. I'll check in on you again soon." She headed back toward the castle with Ronan close behind. "Did ye follow me here?" she asked when they were alone. She knew the answer but wanted to see if he would admit it.

"Aye."

"I've told you already, I have no lover." She gave him an even look and glanced down at his leg when he winced, taking a step. "I'll make ye some ointment."

"Nay. Don't bother. It smells bad." His nose scrunched up, making her chuckle.

She knew the smell wasn't the real reason, or at least the only one. He'd been at war, and from the tales she'd heard, war didn't smell like a rose garden.

"It's my experience that not many things in healing smell good."

"True enough."

"Let's get you back to the castle, and I'll help you. You need to rest and give your leg time to heal properly."

He stopped then, and she thought the pain had made it impossible for him to walk. She turned to come back to him.

"I'm sorry for barging in like I did. I feel rather foolish."

"You're sorry for barging in but not for doubting me," she said, her arms crossed over her chest.

"Aye." He looked up at the sky as if it held all the answers. "Where I was, I saw many lonely people take comfort with those other than their husbands or wives. Ye didn't know me well when I left you, so I can't expect loyalty from such a brief association. You probably hated me for leaving, and that anger might have chased ye into another's arms." He opened his mouth as if he would share something else but stopped himself.

She kept silent at that. In truth, she had considered taking a lover on the nights when she was so lonely or times when she hated him for the pain he'd caused, but she never acted on it, and not just because she hadn't found a partner for such a tryst.

He rubbed his chin, looking uncomfortable. "I'm saying, I wouldn't be surprised to find you sought comfort in another man's arms."

"If I tell you I didn't lie with another man, will ye believe me?" She met his gaze, testing him.

He peered back at her, considering. They must have stood there a full minute while he took her measure before finally, he nodded. "Time will tell. You and I have plenty of that."

"Listen, husband, I have only shared my body with you."

He swallowed and nodded, though he didn't look convinced. She wanted to point out that if he'd been worried about her fidelity, he might have stayed to see she didn't stray himself, but the past was done. There was no changing it now. He didn't trust her, and she was so angry that she didn't think she cared.

She let out a breath and continued on their way. She moved to put an arm under his to help support him as they made their way to the castle.

"I don't need help walking."

"Fine," she answered, but her arm didn't budge, even when he made a noise of irritation.

"You're too small. I'll crush ye with my weight."

He was too big for her to offer much assistance, but she'd manage if it took some pain out of his eyes. She hated to see anyone struggling.

"I'm much stronger than I look."

He mumbled something that sounded like, "I don't doubt it."

He remained quiet except for a few curses as they slowly entered the hall and up the stairs to their chamber. He practically fell upon the bed while she went to light a fire despite the warm day. She would take care of her husband whether he wished it or not. She wouldn't see him suffer when she could do something to relieve the pain. Smelly or not.

Healing his leg could also be a step toward healing them. He'd been right when he'd said they had plenty of time before them. She would spend the rest of her days with this man who thought her disloyal.

Heaven help her.

Chapter Fourteen

Ronan had pushed himself too hard today, but he'd needed to follow his wife to catch her in the act of…helping someone. He frowned at the ceiling as she set a flame to life in the hearth and built up the fire.

He'd thought to find her in the throes of passion in that small cottage, just as his mother had done. But instead, she was easing someone's misery. Much as she was doing now, heating water and gathering linens to help him.

Shame brought heat to his cheeks in the already warm room.

She carefully wrung out the hot water from one of the cloths and lifted his kilt slightly to place it on his thigh, just above the knee where the scar marked his injury. He hissed from the contact, then shook his head at his weakness. His wife had just touched the same hot linen with her bare hands and hadn't so much as murmured a complaint.

"What happened here?" she asked when she changed out the cloth, taking in the scars on his leg.

"The enemy thought I didn't need this leg anymore. I decided I did, despite what the surgeon preferred."

She nodded. "How long ago? The wound doesn't look that old."

"I woke from the fever in time to get the message that my grandfather needed me to come home."

"I'm glad you recovered from the fever."

He felt her sincerity in the way she clasped his wrist. "You would have been fair in wishing me worse after what I did."

She shrugged. "There may have been a few times I stooped that low, but they were brief."

His lip pulled up at her admission. He rather liked her spirit. He couldn't be sure she spoke the truth about everything, but that he knew was true.

"You've overused your leg on your long journey home. It can't heal properly if you continue to use it."

"There was no time to wait. I needed to get back. I left as soon as I was able."

"As soon as you could ride well enough that you didn't fall from your horse, you mean."

"Aye." He nodded in agreement. "Shane would have caught me, I'm sure of it. Or at least seen me properly buried."

She winced as if she truly feared such a thing. She cared about him as she did the Campbells. What he didn't know was how much she cared *for* him. He had a lot of ground to cover if he had any hope of repairing this marriage. "I was not so bad. Though it's not the worst thing to have someone see to me." It was far from the worst thing and more than he deserved from her.

"You need to let your leg heal. I understand you wanted to get home, but you're home now. You should rest so you don't cause more damage."

He smiled at her nagging. He must be daft to enjoy such a thing, but her scolds amused him. She cared, even though she didn't want to.

"My leg is fine. Just a little sore."

"I disagree, but expecting you to stay in bed until it's healed would be too much."

She crossed her arms in that haughty way he was coming to enjoy because it called his attention to her breasts. He'd also noticed them when she bent to hand him the baby. He was a man, and his wife was appealing to the eye.

"Aye," he answered. "It would be too much to ask."

At his answer, her lips twitched with the beginnings of a smile. He remembered that smile. It had once been open and ready to break into laughter at any moment.

She'd been a happy lass the day they'd married, though he wasn't sure why she'd agreed to marry him in the first place. She'd overheard Ronan and his grandsire speaking of the situation.

Had she mentioned it to her father, she would have been spared the marriage and the Grants would have been at war with the Innes clan. It was something he'd wondered about all these years. "Why did you agree to our marriage?"

Her brows went up in obvious surprise, but other than tilting her head to the side, she didn't respond.

"You heard my grandsire. You could have told your father, but you didn't. You went through with the match. But why?"

She let out a breath and glanced briefly at him before answering. "It wasn't like a long line of suitors were waiting to ask for my hand. Perhaps it would have been the more merciful thing to do so you'd not have to wed someone you disliked, but I guess I was selfish. I wanted you to be my husband. I often thought your leaving was my punishment for greedily trapping you in the marriage."

Unable to bear her words, he took her hand, waiting until she looked up to meet his eyes before speaking so she would know the truth of his words. "You did nothing wrong, Brenna. Nothing. Ewan is responsible for the events that forced the match. I'm sure your father gave you little choice in the matter. I didn't leave because I didn't want you, Brenna. I didn't want a wife at all. I only wanted to go off on an adventure to France with my brother. It had already been decided long before I met you, but I used the duty to gain my grandsire's permission to go."

"So it wasn't that I was so unskilled in your bed that you preferred death rather than lie with me again?"

It was good he was already seated, for her words might have knocked him over. "No. Why would you think that?"

"I didn't, not until I heard others saying it."

He wanted the names of all the people who had said such things so they could be appropriately punished. Unfortunately, his name must be at the top of the list. Hadn't he caused the most pain? "It's not true. I'd been a foolish lad who could only think of the glory of war. I only wanted to avoid my responsibilities and put off the duty to my clan as long as possible. I'm the one who deserves to be punished. Never you, Brenna."

"Perhaps we can both give up this quest for punishment. Mayhap, it's time now for forgiveness."

"Ye are as wise as you are beautiful, wife."

She blushed prettily and turned back to the fire to change out of her clothes once more. He found he rather enjoyed causing her to blush. He didn't think a woman could feign such a reaction. He decided to watch for the clues her body gave for signs of the truth.

She changed the warm cloth on his leg, and instead of wincing, he let out a soft moan of comfort. It was nice to be home. And to be cared for by a bonny lass. When she leaned over him to add an extra pillow, he had a clear view down the front of her dress. He couldn't get enough of her breasts. They were bigger than they'd been when he'd bedded her so long ago; he was sure of it.

She left the room without a word and returned with a jar of something. He could only guess it was some foul-smelling concoction. But when she came closer, he didn't notice a harsh camphor scent. Instead, it smelled like her. A meadow warmed by the sun with a hint of roses. He wasn't fond of smelling like roses, but it was far better than the alternative.

She scooped some of the salve into her hand and worked it lightly between her palms. She turned to him and rubbed her palms up his thigh. He nearly came up out of the bed. Not that it hurt, but because it felt so good. Too good. He grew hard instantly and pulled a blanket across his lap to hide the evidence of his arousal.

"Did I press too hard?" she asked, glancing up at him.

He nearly groaned. "No. It's fine. Thank you."

With a quick nod, she touched him again, lighter this time but working back into the deeper motions that had him throbbing. She wasn't trying to seduce him. It was clear her intent was only to alleviate his pain. But her scent and her touch drove a dull ache straight to his cock.

"How does it feel?"

Like heaven and hell colliding, making me yearn for more. But he didn't say that aloud.

"It's loosening up the stiffness." He managed to answer. The truth was it was not the stiffness of his leg that bothered him now as much as a different place.

After half an hour, Ronan had grown used to Brenna's touch enough that he no longer embarrassed himself. She continued her pattern, up the outside of his leg, down the inside.

When she finished, she stood and placed another hot cloth on his leg. "Keep that there until I return."

"Aye," he agreed easily, not wanting to move.

She didn't say when she'd be back, and he started to get up when she didn't reappear after many minutes. It was then she came walking through the door carrying a tray of food.

"I told ye to stay there." Her bossy tone amused him.

"I thought you'd abandoned me." His words echoed in his head, and he wished he could pull them back into his mouth. If he'd felt deserted after a few minutes, what must his years of absence have felt like to her?

She shook her head as she helped him settle back in bed. She changed out the cloth again before setting the tray next to him. There were two meals on the tray, and he was happy she planned to sit with him, but when the silence dragged on, he hated the awkwardness that had settled between them.

He knew not every woman was like his mother. Shane's Maria had been faithful based on what Ronan had seen. But they'd not had the chance to be married long before she'd been killed. Ronan didn't know if Brenna was to be trusted, but how she cared for him was breaking through his doubts. He wanted to believe her. He wanted to trust her. But Ewan had never lied to him.

He'd seen the reactions of his men when they'd seen their throats. Every one of them seemed sure Ewan had hurt her. They wouldn't waste their time trailing after Brenna unless it was warranted.

He and Brenna both seemed overly interested in the room rather than the other. The chamber was slightly different from the one they shared years ago. Back then, it had been an open guest room assigned to him. Now, it looked like a room that belonged to someone. A small table in the corner held a few books and a pot of ink.

He wanted to ask when she'd learned to write and read, but that topic could easily turn to the letters she'd written to him. Letters he'd not read for worry they would make staying in France even more difficult.

"You should have seen your face today," she

said as if hearing his thoughts and knowing he couldn't take much more of the quiet.

"How do you mean?"

"When you practically pounded down the Campbells' door to catch me in some lewd act." The smile hinted again but didn't give in completely.

"I'm glad you found it amusing."

"I'm glad you have so much extra time to spy on me while also making a mess of your leg."

"It feels fine now." His pride spoke before his brain had any say.

"Well, of course it does. I just tended it." She shook her head, irritated.

"Thank you for taking care of me," he said. "And thank you for taking care of the Campbell family. You're a kindhearted woman."

"But you still don't trust me."

She frowned when he didn't answer right away. He hated to see her disappointed, but he didn't want to tell her he trusted her until he could be certain it was true.

He decided the best way to get honesty might be to give it.

"My mother was unfaithful to my father and my stepfather. I saw how easy it was for her to leave her lover and become a besotted wife. The way she turned them into besotted fools to get what she wanted. And when she was caught, the way she twisted things so she wasn't at fault. I know not all women are that way. I don't know how to know for certain."

"I don't know if it is something you can ever know for certain. Trusting someone is a matter of faith."

He nodded but said nothing in response. He didn't know what to say. And maybe it wasn't a matter of not trusting her but of not trusting himself to see if it was safe.

She busied herself with changing out the hot cloth again.

"'Tis helping greatly," he said, turning the conversation back to easier things, like his mangled leg.

"We'll continue treating it with heat tonight. In the mornings, before you go for a long stroll, give it another good rub and stretch the muscles a bit first to tease them into working better."

"Very well." Did that mean she wasn't planning to tend to him in the morning, to rub his leg for him? Worried she was about to leave, he groped for something to keep her in place. "How did you learn so much about healing, or did you already know such things before we met?"

She sat next to his bed again. "I enjoyed healing in Innes, though Hannah constantly fretted over it. But here, Geordie didn't seem to mind, so Moira taught me, and I would help by sitting with someone when they were ill. It meant fewer hours for each of us."

"So you've tended many of the villagers?"

"Aye. I've been there at the joy of a new birth, as well as the sadness of a passing. When I would return in tears, Geordie would tell me it was the circle of life. You hear of such things, but until you see it—a birth and a death within hours of one another—you don't truly understand it."

He nodded. "I was surrounded by only death. Not many births going on near a battlefield."

"Will you tell me about it?"

"You wish to hear of the hell of war?" He couldn't imagine why she would want such darkness in her life. Unless she thought to draw some of it upon herself to ease his burden as she'd done with Moira.

"Maybe not every detail," she admitted. "But I'd like to know what it was like, what you lived through. And I'd like to know how you were injured."

He hadn't given her the details when she'd asked before. He hadn't wanted to delve into such gruesome discussion for fear she might swoon. But his wife was strong and wanted to know him. He understood her curiosity better now.

He looked at her hand resting on his skin and nodded. He wasn't sure why it felt comfortable to tell her. Maybe it was simply because she asked when no one else ever had. Shane knew the same hell as he, so they never spoke of battle. Mostly, their conversations focused on what activities took place at home. They both received letters from his stepsister, Tory, and occasionally from Deirdre.

The four letters Ronan had received from Brenna remained unopened in his pack. He couldn't bear the weight of guilt her words would have brought, so he'd kept them unread. But he could lean on her now to know his truth. He didn't think she would offer pity or false words of understanding. She would listen and let him purge himself of the memories tinged in blood. She'd told him he needed to have faith in her.

He opened his mouth and allowed the words to come.

Chapter Fifteen

"As I said last night, I thought going to war would be a grand adventure—a way to see more of the world than just the Highlands. As far as that, I did see more of the world. Though it didn't turn out to be a very appealing journey." He cleared his throat and continued.

"When I arrived in Spain, I was clothed in a proper uniform, given a weapon, and shown how to fire it. I was fed like a prince, and the wine was supplied aplenty. But after we left for France, everything changed."

"How so?"

"I'd arrived with my horse—Brimstone served me well—so I was permitted to ride. But we couldn't get ahead of the men the whole way. While their feet ached, my arse and back hurt like the devil from being seated from predawn to well after dark. I found someone willing to trade off and let me walk awhile."

"I'm sure he was happy to give his feet a rest,

as well," she suggested.

"Aye." Ronan nodded. "We got to the camp at midday. There was hardly time to throw down our things in the tent before we were whisked away to battle."

He looked at her slim fingers and remembered that first day. "I rode out onto the battlefield and was immediately bombarded by men coming at me. I didn't have time to think about anything. I started fighting through them out of survival rather than wanting them dead."

She let out a breath. "Was it different? Killing a man who was not your true enemy?"

He understood her question. It had been different when he'd protected his lands during a raid. There had been purpose to it.

"Aye. I didn't know the man who threatened my life, and he didn't know me. Most likely, we didn't even speak the same language. I understood why he wouldn't want me on his land. It would have been enough to draw a sword across his throat without thought if he had been on Grant lands. But as it was his land, I thought about its wrongness."

"Did you win that first battle?"

"Aye. I fell onto my bedroll that first night with nothing but a few scratches to show for the day. My head, however, was filled with thoughts and regrets that turned into that numbness I spoke of earlier. The soldier who'd rode my horse earlier in the day hadn't lived. Shane and I found our feet quickly. Fighting back-to-back, we were invincible, or so we thought."

He nodded toward his leg. "I went to fight because Shane had told me of the adventure it would be. It didn't take us long to realize how wrong we'd been. There was none of the glory we were promised. I knew right then I'd made a mistake."

Her fingers tightened slightly.

"I held on to that mistake the whole time. Using it to spur me into fighting. Using that anger at myself to keep me going."

He went on for hours, telling her other stories while sparing her the worst gore. The day wore on. She brought him dinner when they grew hungry again. Her hand remained on him the whole time he spoke, tethering him to the room, the castle, and home. He told her of that last battle where he'd been caught in the leg by a boy who couldn't have been older than thirteen. He was telling her of his fevered dreams when her hand slipped from his arm. Had he finally disgusted her enough that she no longer wanted to touch him?

But when he looked to her, he saw she had slumped over in sleep. He smiled. She hadn't found him disgusting, simply boring. The sun had left them hours ago, and she'd been up early. Not to mention the lack of sleep the night before because he'd awakened her and nearly killed her.

After watching her sleep for a few moments, he slid from the bed and slipped off her shoes. He picked her up from the chair, expecting his leg to protest. But thanks to her care, he only suffered a minor ache.

He settled her in the bed, wishing he knew her well enough to remove her dress so she'd be more comfortable. But he didn't want her to think him improper for undressing her while she slept.

He was her husband and, by rights, would

have been allowed to disrobe her, but he wouldn't until she was awake and able to give her permission.

Once he was in bed beside her, he pulled the blanket over them, ensuring she was covered. She burrowed in, making a sweet sound of contentment. Aye, he'd definitely made a mistake when he left home to find adventure. Perhaps the adventure he'd been seeking had been right here all along.

With her.

***

Brenna dreamed about battle—the sounds and the chaos. If this was what war felt like, she would gladly follow the drum. She was so warm and comfortable. She was probably too close to the fire and would go up in flames at any moment. But she couldn't care enough to make herself move.

She opened her eyes to see a hard, naked chest in front of her face. Her hand rested over Ronan's heart, and she smiled at the steady thump, proving he was here, healthy and alive. If he'd succumbed to fever, she would never have had this moment with him.

Or this second chance.

Was that what she was hoping for? Where was the anger she'd been gripping onto to help save her from the pain he would inevitably cause? A tear came to her eye at the thought of losing him, but she pushed it away. It was silly to be sad about something that hadn't happened.

Knowing he was sound asleep, she pressed her lips to his warm skin—checking for a fever, she lied to herself.

Slowly, as not to wake him, she pulled her hand across his taut stomach. She paused momentarily to caress the sprinkling of hair she encountered, but eventually, she removed her hand and slipped out of bed without disturbing him.

Brenna wasn't sure how she'd ended up in bed the night before, but she was happy to have slipped out from his heavy arms without waking him. She had things to do, and morning was the only time of day it was safe to walk around without her guard. Not going would have been a missed opportunity.

She smiled up at the sunshine as she left the hall and went to the stables. After packing a few oat cakes and honey mead she eagerly rushed off to enjoy the August morning without worrying about Ewan being around.

Jamie, the stable hand, smiled and waved as she stepped into the stable and went to her horse's stall. Pulling the stall door closed behind her, she wiggled off her skirts so she was in her trews and shirt. It was easier to ride without a skirt, but she didn't go about the keep dressed like a man.

Leading Merlin out of his stall, she whistled a tune while saddling him. The groom smiled and left her to work, knowing she liked caring for her horse. The tall stallion reminded her of the day she'd married her husband when they'd gifted each other their horses.

When Merlin was ready, she hopped up and swung her leg over to mount. It wasn't the most graceful approach, but she'd learned to mount without a block so she could get on and off her horse wherever she wished.

She trotted him out of the gate and through the village. The horse had tensed in anticipation, and when she gave him the nudge, he flew into action across a field and over a short wall. The horse slowed on his own as they approached the kirk. It wasn't their first visit, and he knew the way well.

After dismounting and selecting a handful of flowers, she entered the graveyard and placed the bouquet on Geordie's grave. Resting her head on her knees, Brenna took a moment to enjoy the warmth of the morning sun on her back. Usually, it was earlier when she came, the sun too low to offer much heat.

She remembered the heat from Ronan's body when she woke that morning. "Ronan has returned," she told his grandfather quietly. "He's had a few injuries but is in otherwise good health. I worry more about the injuries one can't see. He has nightmares, and I wish there were something I could do to help him."

She touched her tender throat, recalling how those nightmares haunted him. And how dangerous one's mind could be. "I wish you were here. I miss you."

She stood and brushed the grass from her backside. She placed kisses on each of the headstones. "I love you." Letting out a sigh, she went to her horse to retrieve her bow.

Feeling like someone was watching her, she pulled her dirk from the scabbard at her hip. She would not allow Ewan to catch her unaware. In the forest, she stepped quietly behind a tree and waited.

A few minutes later, someone stepped into the woods on the same path she'd used. She'd thought she at least had the peace of the mornings, but now Ewan had also ruined that. She sprung out to attack as soon as he walked past the tree where she was hiding. Kicking the backs of his legs caused him to stumble down to his knees, and she took advantage by grasping his hair and jerking his head back to place her dirk at his throat.

"Good morning, wife," Ronan said calmly.

She released him immediately and then helped him rise to his feet. "My apologies. I thought…I thought you were someone else."

"I guess I should be grateful you didn't wish to kill me. Who were you expecting?"

She shook her head, not wanting to tell him she might have killed his uncle if the opportunity presented itself. "A woman must protect herself, even on her lands. It is a sad truth, but the truth nonetheless."

"Interesting you speak of truth while you avoid it."

Her eyes went wide as he called her out.

She'd told the warriors to be patient and wait until Ronan was ready to hear the truth. She'd told them to answer honestly if he asked a direct question. But here she was, not following her own orders.

"Very well. I thought you were Ewan come to trouble me. I normally have peace in the mornings for the drunkard sleeps until noon most days. But the other day he…" She paused and considered. "*You* followed me to the forest that morning as well?"

"Aye."

She couldn't help but roll her eyes. "Trying to catch me in a tryst with my imaginary lover? Is that why you came here today? I thought you would have given up this ridiculousness yesterday after you visited the Campbells' home."

"I have."

"Then why do you slink about following me

and nearly scaring the life out of me?"

"I believe it was I who was in danger." He glanced down where she still held tight to her blade.

"If I'd killed you by accident, I would have never forgiven myself," she said while guiding it into the scabbard at her hip.

He smiled then, the crooked pull of his lips that showed his dimple to distraction. "I'm sorry for scaring you."

"If you are not trying to catch me up at something, why are you following me?"

He shrugged. "As you guessed, I saw you as you came to the woods to hunt. I wondered if I might join you today." He nodded to the bow and quiver of arrows he'd dropped to the ground during her attack. He looked about and frowned. "I dare say we've probably scared any game away."

She nodded and pressed her lips together to hide her smile. They'd surely not see anything out of the stomping and shouting they'd done.

"Mayhap we could go for a walk instead?"

A walk with Ronan? "Very well."

They secured their weapons back with the horses and followed the path into the cool forest. She paused to look down at his leg. "Did you remember to stretch it out this morning?" she asked.

"Aye. I followed your orders, and it doesn't trouble me much today." She looked up to see if he was reluctant to admit she'd been right, but he merely smiled down at her.

"Still," she said. "We shouldn't walk far. I did say you should let it rest."

"Ye did. And then you kicked me in the very leg that was injured."

Her eyes went wide again as he chuckled. She opened her mouth to apologize again, but he raised his hand to stop her.

"I'm only jesting. You didn't hurt me."

"You're certain?" She felt horrible.

He smiled at her again and shrugged. "Maybe I should have feigned a bit of pain so you would tend to me again the way you did yesterday. I enjoyed it more than I should have."

He looked at her unashamedly, and she met his gaze. He'd liked her touch. She imagined the surgeon hadn't thought to rub the sore muscles. She paused and looked back at him, remembering the day before when he'd grasped the blankets and pulled them across himself.

Was he... Yes, he was flirting with her. But why? She was standing before him in men's clothing. He couldn't possibly have liked her touch in that way. She swallowed down the many questions that came to her lips and ignored him instead. "Should we sit over there on that downed log? I brought food if you're hungry. I generally break my fast out here rather than in the hall." Not wanting to miss a moment of the time she could be alone in the woods.

"I've already eaten," he answered. "But I would be happy to join you."

They settled on the damp wood, and she pulled the oatcakes from her pack. She offered one to him, and he took it. She pulled the cork from her flask and offered it to him.

She focused on her meal for the next few minutes and what she might say to the man next to her. She could feel his curiosity like a living thing sitting with them in the calm of the dense trees. She wanted to move the conversation back to how he'd felt when she'd touched his bare leg. She had not been unmoved by the action herself. It was strange for all the times she'd touched people she helped heal; she'd never felt the tingle of anticipation she had when she'd stroked the muscles in Ronan's leg.

She'd indeed kept at it much longer than necessary, but she would never admit to such.

"You say you cut Ewan's face," he stated rather than asked.

His words caused her to jump. They were so far from where her thoughts had traveled. So it was back to this. She squared her shoulders, ready to defend herself. "Aye. I did," she said with no little amount of defiance. Let him judge her for it.

"And ye banished him from the clan without food, water, or a weapon."

"Aye. I have already said as much." Again, the words nearly snapped with annoyance.

"What you haven't said is *why*."

"You haven't asked."

"I am asking now." He raised his brows, and she knew it was time to share her story.

Chapter Sixteen

Brenna's anger flared to life like stirring the embers of a fire. Ronan had left her there unprotected with a madman. While he'd spent the last five years living in fear of war, she'd lived in fear of Ewan.

His threats had started the day Ronan left. As an outsider, Brenna was reluctant to say anything to the laird. She didn't wish to cause trouble. She thought it was just a matter of winning the man over. But it went well beyond that. Ewan hated Brenna and how close she had become with Geordie.

For years, she'd silently feared the man until one day, the laird caught him harassing her and took up her defense. She was so grateful to Geordie for choosing to side with her over his own son.

She'd managed to stay clear of Ewan for the most part after that. But she would be reminded of her error anytime she let down her guard.

When Geordie fell ill, he knew Ewan wouldn't honor his ruling to have Brenna run the clan and swore his men to protect her. They had saved her life more than once. Geordie believed her because he had seen Ewan harassing her with his own eyes. Would Ronan need the same proof?

"And you would believe me?" she asked him, challenge clear in her voice.

"We once promised each other honesty," he said with that charming smile back in place. "Do you remember?"

She'd assumed he'd forgotten their promise, just as he'd forgotten her. Still, she nodded, ready to keep that promise now.

"I want to hear your side of the story, Brenna."

"Very well. My side of the story is that the bugger snuck into my room by climbing in the window and nearly strangled me to death. I cut him so he would leave me be until my men could enter the room with axes. Everyone said I was within my right to have him hanged for what he'd done."

"But you didn't."

"Nay. He is your kin. I thought you would hate me if I'd sought such justice." She let out a breath. "Not that it matters, as you hate me anyway."

His face showed his surprise. "I don't hate you." His brows pulled together as if he had considered his words. "I may have been angry when I arrived. But no. I don't hate you. I don't trust you, but I don't trust any woman." He paused for a moment before looking at her again. "Do you hate me?"

His question surprised her. She remembered all the years she had thought to hate him for how much pain he'd caused her. She didn't think her heart could hold all the animosity she felt. But now…?

"Nay. I don't hate you, Ronan." She shook her head. "I don't trust you, but then I don't trust any man." She turned his words for her use.

He grinned and gave a nod. "Fair enough. Mayhap we could start over?"

"Start over?"

"We were both young when we married. We hardly knew anything about each other, and I'd wager what we knew of one another before has changed greatly in the past years. Let's start anew in this marriage and see if we can find happiness. After all, we will be married for a long time, with God's blessing. Why not make the most of it?"

She wanted nothing more than to find happiness with this man. Perhaps it would have been wise to think the offer through, but she didn't. Instead, she grasped on with both hands.

"Aye, I would like that very much."

He held out his hand, and she placed her palm against his to shake. With his gaze locked on hers, he pulled her hand to his lips and warmly kissed her knuckles.

"As would I," he said in a voice so silky she thought she might fall over.

She wasn't sure what she'd just agreed to, but with excitement fluttering in her stomach, she couldn't care if it was a mistake. She would have to hope it wasn't.

***

After forging a truce with his wife, they returned to the castle shortly before noon. She'd said she wanted to get to the kitchens, but he wondered how much of her routine was out of fear of an encounter with Ewan. Ronan saw the distress in his wife's eyes when she thought his uncle had followed her into the woods.

Her story had matched up with what the young warrior had told him. And the fear he'd seen in her eyes that morning couldn't have been faked. Ronan believed her. He believed Ewan had tried to hurt her. What he didn't know was why. Ewan had been his best friend from the beginning of his life. Even after Ronan's mother had married the MacPherson laird, they had spent time together during visits with the Grants.

Shane had claimed the role of brother and best friend, but Ewan had still earned his loyalty. He couldn't help but think all of this between Ewan and his wife was a misunderstanding between both parties. It was the only thing that made sense.

He'd heard Brenna's side. Now, he needed to confront his uncle. After being directed to a cottage where a lively wench offered him favors in exchange for coin, Ronan escaped, with a suggestion he try the tavern. There, he came to learn Ewan had been tossed out. And to look for him in the fires of hell where he belonged. Eventually, he found his uncle in a heated argument with the blacksmith.

"You bloody bastard, do you not know who I am? I'm second in command of clan Grant."

"Aye, I know well who ye are, and if you ever become laird, that will be the day I pack up my things and my family and move to bloody England," the large smithy said.

"What's the matter here?" Ronan cut in.

Ewan stepped back in surprise. That made two of them. Ewan had always been an amiable man, a person to turn to for a laugh. This belligerence wasn't like him. Then again, neither was earning the ire of a woman like Brenna.

"Nothing for you to worry over, Ro." Ewan smiled widely, cutting a look toward the smithy.

"I'll decide what I should worry over. What's going on?" Ronan turned toward the smithy, awaiting a response.

"I'm sorry, m'laird, but your heir has commissioned a sword. I made it to his request, but he's trying to claim it with no coin."

The same charge as the tavern owner as for the reason he'd kicked Ewan from his establishment.

"Does his name not earn him credit?" Ewan had been correct about being second in command of the clan.

The man let out a breath and rubbed his forehead. "Aye. It's just that it's the fifth sword he's requested in the last two years, and I've not been paid for any of them. I have a family to feed, m'laird." He brought out the sword, reluctantly holding it out to Ewan.

But Ronan took it and turned it over, noticing the fine artistry in the blade. The inlaid hilt held a fair-sized gem. "What do ye need such a fancy sword for, uncle?" he asked.

Ewan laughed and slapped him on the shoulder. "You caught me out. It was to be a gift for you to commemorate your return."

"I thank ye for the thought, but if you do not pay for it, the sword is not a gift from you but from the blacksmith."

Ewan's charm faltered slightly as the smithy chuckled.

"It's the finest sword I've ever seen." Ronan

tested the balance as Ewan reluctantly pressed coins into the other man's hand.

"Thank you, m'laird. I'm glad you like it. I hadn't known it was a gift when I was asked to make it a few months back. It's good to have ye home."

Ronan wondered how many months ago it had been requested and if he had even planned to return at that time. He didn't like doubting Ewan, but something was going on with the man.

"Thank you. It's good to be home," Ronan said. "Now that your business is done here, I'd like to have a word with you, uncle."

"Of course." Ewan wasn't being his normally pleasant self. He was still frowning at the sword in Ronan's hand. Ronan was more convinced the sword had not been intended as a gift.

This was yet another thing that made him uneasy about Ewan. Something was wrong, and Ronan was determined to get to the bottom of it. He didn't like thinking badly of his uncle. But Ewan had changed.

"The cut on your face. Ye said it was Brenna's doing."

"Aye. Did she say differently?" His face changed at the mere mention of Brenna's name. Hatred practically dripped from him.

"Nay. She admitted to it. But I'd like to hear why she drew a blade on ye."

"Does there need to be a reason? I'm your blood."

"I'm the first to admit I don't know her well, but I've not heard from anyone else that she's injured anyone. I've seen the opposite with my own eyes."

Ewan laughed. "I see. She's using her wiles to

charm you into doubting me."

"I wouldn't say that. You do me a disservice by assuming I'm not wise enough to see the truth when it's in front of me."

"Have I ever played ye false?" It was a valid question and the reason Ronan believed Ewan without question initially. Ewan had never lied to him, which could only mean Brenna had.

"Nay. Never. But I want the whole story, and I'll get it from you or my wife." Ronan made a show of looking at Ewan's scarred cheek.

"'Tis nothing."

"Tell me how you got it. I'll decide if it's nothing."

Ewan's jaw tensed again, but he remained silent. Ronan continued his questions as they walked toward the castle.

"Why did she put ye out of the keep, Ewan? She's not quick to anger. Lord knows I should have seen her wrath if that were true—so what did you do to cause such a punishment?"

"You can't see her for what she is. She's turned ye against me."

Ronan was at a loss. Ewan was twisting things around without giving any real answers.

"I've told her I want to start over. I plan to have a life with her, Ewan. She's my wife. I don't know what has transpired between you, but until I get to the bottom of the matter, I want you to stay away from her."

"Me? Do you think I would betray you, nephew?" Ewan looked genuinely shocked…and yet his jaw twitched.

They had made their way up to the castle.

Ronan was ready to repeat his warning to avoid Brenna when Ewan glared at something over Ronan's shoulder. Ronan turned to see Brenna dumping some scraps for a few small dogs. Ewan's glare turned to surprise, and then he laughed. The sound alerted Brenna, who went pale before turning and rushing back to the safety of the kitchen.

Ewan's laughter faded, and he slapped Ronan on the back. "From the looks of the handprint on her neck, it seems you've found a way to deal with the wench."

Ronan batted away Ewan's hand, which had come to rest on Ronan's shoulder in a conspiratorial way. "That was an accident," he quickly explained as guilt washed over him. "I would never hurt her on purpose." He watched to see if Ewan would say the same, but he didn't.

Instead, he grasped Ronan's shoulder again and stared into his eyes.

"I'll never forgive myself for being the reason you were shackled to that scheming witch. Be careful, Ro. Every word she speaks is a beautiful lie to turn ye against me. You'll see the truth soon enough."

Before he could say anything else, Ewan had turned in the opposite direction and hurried away.

Ronan stood there in complete confusion. He still wasn't sure if it was Brenna or Ewan who was lying. Whoever it was, they were good at it.

Chapter Seventeen

Neither Ronan nor Ewan were seated at the high table for the late meal. After seeing the two of them together earlier in the day and the way they shared a laugh at her expense, Brenna assumed Ewan had turned Ronan against her yet again.

She'd been so hopeful after he'd asked if they could start over. She should have known better. Why did she still hope Ronan was the man she'd once thought him to be?

Having lost her appetite, she decided to go to the study to tend to the ledgers as she had done since Geordie had taught her how. She wasn't sure if Ronan planned to take them over, but she would ensure they were in order if he did.

She didn't make it to the study before being pulled into the solar at the end of the hall. She rarely spent time there in the spring and summer, preferring to be outside while the weather was warm. But Ewan had been lurking inside, apparently waiting for her to walk by.

He held her wrists high above her head, straining her shoulders and forcing his face close to hers.

"You fool, you still attempt to fill Ronan's head with lies."

"I'm not the one who has lied, Ewan." Antagonizing the man was probably not her best strategy, but she couldn't hold her tongue.

He laughed. "It doesn't matter. He doesn't believe you. He's playing at this starting over bit to earn your trust, and then he plans to get rid of you so he can take a wife of his choosing."

Brenna's face must have shown her shock. He chuckled darkly.

"What? Did you believe he'd want someone like you?" He laughed; the cruel sound made her sick. "A man just home from war hasn't tried to bed his wife. Have you not asked yourself why?"

He released her and backed away.

"Go on. I don't plan to harm you. I don't need to. Ronan will see to it himself. He lures you closer so no one will suspect anything if you succumb to an accident while hunting." He waved her out of the room, and she fled on shaking legs. "Do take care. A woman in the woods alone could befall many dangers."

She didn't believe Ewan. He lied simply for the joy of lying. But he hadn't made any of his usual threats to force her silence. He didn't seem worried at all about losing control. Could he be telling the truth? Ronan had said they would start anew in their relationship. Was it, as Ewan said, a ruse so no one would suspect him if she were to be injured, or worse?

No. Ronan, indeed, had no plans to harm her. Except...he hadn't touched her, hadn't even attempted to. But for a bit of flirting, he hadn't seemed interested in her at all. And he'd never wanted her to be his wife. Even the day they were to marry, he'd wanted Hannah, not Brenna.

Letting the ledgers rot, she went to her room and barred the door and the window. Once she was alone, she gave in to the doubts. The tears that gathered and ran down her cheeks angered her even more. Exhausted from the early day and the stress of what unknown displeasure was to come, she eventually drifted off.

If Ronan had ever come to the room and tried to get in, she'd not heard him. Perhaps he'd spent the night in the village in the company of the women who invited Ewan to their bed. What a fool Brenna had been to believe Ronan could care for her. She still didn't think he would resort to murder, but she would be careful.

She went about her routine, stopping by the kitchen to select a few warm bannocks and a bit of butter. She filled her skin with ale and placed everything in her pack. She retrieved her horse as always and rode out to the kirk. She visited her loved ones and crossed the forest to hunt like any other day. Her heart took to pounding when she heard someone ride up and dismount. A moment later, her husband entered the woods carrying a bow. She wanted to think it was nothing more than Ewan's words and her imagination, but what if Ronan had other plans?

"Brenna?"

Her breath seemed stuck in her chest as she

froze in place. Was he there to end his marriage to the woman he never wanted? She could shoot him from where she hid. She could tell everyone it was an accident. But who would believe her? And did it matter if they did if she would sooner die herself than hurt him? And what if she was wrong? She was sure she was. After all, Ewan had been the one to plan this seed of doubt.

"It isn't true," she whispered before speaking louder. "Here."

He smiled, though it seemed strained as he came closer. "Do you mind if I join you on your hunt today?" he asked. He blew out a breath. "You're wondering where I was last night," he guessed. "I went to sit by the loch to think, and years of sleeping outside made it easy to doze off until the sun woke me."

He rubbed at his leg. "I'm paying for my foolishness this morning. My leg didn't take to the cool ground."

They stood silently for a few minutes as she studied him, waiting to see what he planned. He interrupted the silence and pointed. "There, a rabbit," Ronan whispered next to her, his breath warm on her ear. He nodded when she didn't respond. "Go ahead. Take the shot."

She nodded and drew back her bow. Trying to calm her breathing, she waited and released the arrow, which missed by a few yards. Damn, her shaking hands.

He looked at her in surprise. "What happened? I've never seen you miss."

The day before, they'd not shot anything, but then she remembered he'd said he'd been in the woods with her that first morning when she'd thought it was Ewan. He'd seen her shoot then. With a shaky breath, she ran a damp palm over the thigh of her breeches. Was there any reason to drag this out? To pretend? To carry on as if she didn't know why he'd joined her out there?

"Your hands are shaking. Are ye well?"

Since he'd asked, she would be honest. She wouldn't attempt to talk him out of this. She wouldn't beg. But she'd be truthful.

"I don't want to believe it, but it's just if I'm wrong... Well, the dying part has made me nervous."

"Dying? Why do you think you're dying?"

She waved her hand to the forest. "I don't want to believe such a thing, but I can't eliminate the idea, for I know you can't remarry and breed an heir with someone else as long as I'm alive. So if you came out here to rid yourself of me, I ask that you get on with it. The wondering over it grows tiring."

"You think I came out here to murder my wife?" His eyes went wide with surprise.

"Nay, or rather, I'm not sure." She shrugged, trying to seem courageous while facing death. "Ewan told me of your plan. To win my trust with that proposal to start fresh and find happiness together only so you can get rid of me, freeing you to marry someone of your choosing. And it's a fact you never wanted me. So is it true?"

He looked down at the ground momentarily, cursing quietly to himself. He was a seasoned warrior who'd just returned from war. Surely, he could drop her quickly if he'd just done it already.

"He said you wish to make it look like an accident."

"An accident...?" He shook his head. "If one of us deserves death, it's me for what I've done to you. I've been a poor excuse for a husband and don't deserve ye." He rubbed his forehead and bent over, resting his hands on his knees.

She didn't know if it was some trick or what he was after. He held out his dagger with the handle toward her. Was he offering himself to her?

Stepping away from the knife, she shook her head. "No. Not just because the whole clan would come down on me, and I'd be hanged anyway, but because I don't want you dead." She winced and added, "Perhaps there was a small moment when you first arrived when I may have wished it before I took it back."

To her surprise, his mouth pulled up on one side. "You took it back?" he asked, walking closer. He sheathed his dirk.

"Aye," she admitted. "I want to hate you, but something keeps me from doing it very well. Even now."

"I am a lucky sot indeed." He stopped in front of her and reached for her hand. She jumped but relaxed when it was empty. Just his palm held out, waiting.

"What do you want?" she asked.

"In truth, I came out here because you are so happy. You seem so free. I want to be with you. I really want to get to know you how I should have when we were first wed."

He let out a breath. "I can't go back and change anything that has already happened. I would if it were possible. But I do want you."

He took another step and lowered his head to

place a soft kiss on the corner of her lips.

"I beg you not to toy with me," she whispered, her voice trembling. She so wanted to believe him.

"My uncle has lied to us both, Brenna. Let's not allow him to ruin what could be between us."

And like that, all her defenses fell and her anger fled. If Ronan were lying, she would be caught unaware, but she wouldn't miss the opportunity to kiss him. Reaching up, she grasped his long, blond locks and pulled him to her lips, where she kissed him with all the passion that had been stored up these past years.

"Dear God," he whispered as he lowered his mouth to the skin on her throat. "I'd only wanted a kiss, but when you do it like that, I can't help but want more."

His hands had lowered to her arse, where he grasped her close to him. She felt the ridge of his erection, and her head spun with his words.

He wanted her. This knowledge spurred her into action. She reached for the buckle of his belt, getting the leather tangled as she frantically tried to release him from his clothes. Stepping back just enough to reach for her trews, he fumbled with the fall.

A low growl left his lips. "I generally like seeing the curves of your arse in the tight leather, but I find myself wishing for the ease of a gown at the moment."

She realized then what would happen if they continued down this path, and she froze.

"What is it?" he asked, staying his hands when she stilled. Then he looked around them as if only then realizing where they were. "Christ. What am I doing? I'm sorry, Brenna, truly. I didn't mean to tup you like a randy lad in the woods. Forgive me, I got carried away."

"I'm not so fancy I'd care about being in the forest. In truth, I can see how it might be quite nice since I enjoy being in the forest, but it's just…" How did she share her fears? It's best to be outright with it. "I only wonder why you would wish to lie with me. Surely, I'll do the same things to displease you."

"Displease me?"

"It was made quite clear to me in the days and weeks that followed your leaving how you preferred to travel to fight another country's war and face death rather than be forced to lie with me again. I must have been truly dissatisfying. Everyone said so."

She recalled the whispers, the fear of being alone in a strange place with a new clan. But she'd thought she'd have her husband there to help. But what she'd gotten were rumors and scandal.

And then such pain she didn't think she'd survive it. But she had—alone.

Chapter Eighteen

Ronan's brows pulled together, and his fingers clenched into fists. He couldn't be sure who he was most angry with. His people for their cruel jokes at his wife's expense, his grandsire for not assuring she was protected from such vicious gossip, or himself for leaving her to face everything alone.

Had he stayed, people wouldn't have spoken of such things.

"Ye think I went to fight for France because you displeased me in bed?"

"That was my understanding." She pulled herself up to her full height and glanced away. "I have since spoken to a few women about such things that happen in the bedroom, and I suppose…I may have seemed stiff and unyielding. At the time, I didn't realize it was encouraged that I…do things for your pleasure. I thought I was supposed to stay still until you were done." She cleared her throat. Her cheeks had long since turned crimson. "Maybe if ye had said something, I could have done it better. I would have tried."

No seasoned seductress could fake a maiden's blush like that or be utterly oblivious to a man's interest in her. Whatever his wife had become, he was more confident it was not an adulteress.

"Brenna." He turned away, shame tinting his voice. "I'm sorry."

"I understand I shouldn't think badly of ye if you took comfort with women when you were away. Men need release, and whatever ye may have taken when you were away was physical. Geordie said I was not to be hurt by it. I—I am not." Her words did not match the hurt he saw in her eyes as she glanced down at her hands.

His grandfather had expected him to betray his vows. He took a step closer, wanting to ease her pain, but he stopped when Brenna flinched. He'd frightened her with his harsh words and his anger. Shame and guilt, his constant companions in the days after he left returned with a vengeance.

This was not her fault, none of it. He didn't deserve to take his pleasure until he was sure she understood and trusted him. Until it was something she wanted as much as he did. "I had planned to leave for France before I even met you, Brenna. You heard the promises exchanged between my grandsire and me. I was to wed you and consummate the marriage, and he would approve. You may not have understood everything from the other side of the door, but I promise you, I didn't leave because you displeased me."

She smiled shyly. "It was a nice kiss."

He returned her smile. "Aye. It was until I got

carried away and nearly took you here where anyone could happen upon us. That is not the way I want our reunion to be. You deserve better than that."

She looked like she might argue as they turned for the horses. He knew waiting for trust between them was right, but if she wavered, he didn't think he'd be strong enough to stay.

"I'll race you back to the keep," she said, surprising him.

She took off running, and he jumped into action. His horse was closer, and he took advantage of the opportunity to wield it around and head for the castle gates. She was fast, but he was quicker and had a head start. Even taking Brimstone around to the far side of the stables, he was dismounted and striding down the row of stalls as she rode in.

Her hair was coming free of her braid and her cheeks were full of color, this time from excitement rather than embarrassment if her wide smile told him anything. While he had handed Brimstone off to a groom, she brushed down her horse herself. He pulled the saddle from Merlin to help her finish the task quicker.

When she led the stallion into the stall, he followed behind her and closed the door, ready to steal another kiss. Or two. Although he wasn't sure if it was stealing when his wife so clearly approved.

He brushed a few loose strands of windswept hair back from her face. And before he could utter the request to kiss her, she stood on her toes and pressed her lips to his. This time he made sure to keep his urges to kissing. Even when his wife's hand trailed down his back to hover just over his arse, which had his control near to breaking.

He refused to take his wife in a horse stall any more than he would have made love to her in the forest. Both things seemed exciting and adventurous, something he wouldn't mind exploring, but not this first time they found their way back into each other's arms.

To do it justice, he needed a proper bed and the whole night without interruption. He had waited all this time. Once he got started, he might need the next day as well.

He was contemplating all the things he wanted to do to her when Merlin grew restless and stomped his foot. Ronan didn't know what was amiss.

Brenna whispered, "Oh, no." She wound a rope through the door and pulled Ronan behind it.

"What is—"

"Shh…" She gave him a frantic look. "You wanted the truth. You will hear it now if you only listen," she whispered a moment before Ronan heard his uncle's voice.

"Brenn-na," he said in a sing-song voice as if they were playing a game. "I know ye are in here. I saw you ride in."

The door was tested, and the horse reared up, his hooves catching the edge of the stall. Ewan chuckled. "Very well. I don't need to see you. You need to listen."

"I don't wish to listen to more of your lies. You said my husband wanted to kill me, and I nearly believed you, but then I remembered who I was dealing with."

Ronan watched as his wife held a trembling finger to her lips reminding him to be quiet. She had said this was his chance to hear the truth, and he understood what she meant now.

If he remained quiet, he would hear how Ewan treated Brenna when no one was watching him. Ronan wasn't pleased that his uncle had frightened her with such a lie. Ronan would never hurt Brenna.

"I saw the fresh bruises on your throat. Everyone in the clan knows he did it."

"A nightmare." She spat the defense.

"That's what he wants everyone to believe, so when he finally chokes the breath from you, he can say he did it in his sleep. You'd do well to find another bed to sleep in."

Brenna rolled her eyes at Ewan's suggestion, though it was possibly the only true thing Ewan had said so far. Ronan did fear hurting his wife while in the throes of a night terror. But not on purpose. Never.

"Do you keep that blade close by your bed to protect yourself? It might come in handy," Ewan taunted.

"What do you want, Ewan? My guards will come looking for me soon, so say your piece and go away. I know you care nothing for my neck as you tried to choke the life from me that night I marked ye."

Ronan was impressed by her bravery. Her hands shook, which spoke of her fear of Ewan, but she stood up to him as if she had the courage of a lion. How horrible it must have been for her all this time to live like this. He would reward the loyal men who'd protected her when he couldn't, or rather didn't.

Ewan chuckled. "He won't believe you."

Ronan shook his head, for he'd already

believed her even before this.

"Everyone knows you wanted me out of the way when the laird put me in charge. I'm not the only person telling him what happened."

"My father shouldn't have put *you* in charge of the clan. *I* should be laird."

Ewan's anger caused his voice to shake, and he must have slammed his hand against the stall door.

"You mean *Ronan* should be laird," she corrected him, though this time even she seemed surprised.

"For now. But it never should have been you. What a disgrace."

Ronan's hand tightened into a fist. His muscles readied to jump from their place behind the door where Ronan could punch his uncle for his rudeness. But Brenna placed her finger to her lips again, reminding him to remain quiet.

"Geordie made the decision, not me."

"He was weak and blinded by your manipulations. Ronan won't be as foolish. He'll see you for the menace you are and deal with you swiftly."

The door moved again as if the man kicked it, startling the horse before the heavy tread of footsteps faded. Brenna took a few deep breaths before looking at him.

"I don't wish to harm you more than I have already. I don't know why he would lie. He never…" Ronan shook his head. Ewan had always been a close friend and trusted ally. They might not have been as close as Ronan and Shane, but they were like brothers.

"He is terrified you will find out who he is."

"This raving lunatic is not the uncle I knew all my life. I don't understand what has hardened him so."

"I'm sorry, Ronan."

He was surprised by her apology. After everything she'd gone through because of him, he was the one who owed her an apology.

"Why are you apologizing to me? I left you here unprotected, and then I took his side without even allowing you the chance to explain. What kind of husband doesn't stand with his wife? It is me who is sorry."

"I'm sorry he isn't the man you once looked up to like a brother. To find out your friend and uncle is not who you thought him must surely be a disappointment, and I'm sorry for it."

He leaned closer and pressed a single kiss to her lips. This woman continued to surprise and captivate him each minute he spent in her presence.

"I thank ye, for your kindness. But know this: blood or no, I will do whatever I need to do to the bastard if he tries to harm ye. He will not come between us. Do you understand?"

Ronan blamed himself for everything that had happened to his wife in his absence, but he would see she was safe from this moment forward.

Chapter Nineteen

Brenna nearly collapsed in relief, so glad Ronan had believed her even before Ewan had shown his colors and outed himself. But something still bothered her about the exchange with Ewan in the stables.

He'd said *he* should be laird.

Until then he'd always said he should be laird over Brenna because he was blood and she was not. While it wasn't pleasant, Brenna at least understood why he might think that. She'd questioned the laird's choice because she was not a Grant by blood and had only lived with the clan for five years.

But now it sounded like Ewan thought he should be laird over Ronan. The laird's son as opposed to his grandson. However, that wasn't how these things worked. Ronan was the firstborn son of the firstborn son—the rightful heir of the clan. Geordie had once told her he always favored Edward, Ronan's father, because he'd been born of the laird's first wife, who also happened to be the love of his life, while Ewan had been born of his third wife.

Because of this, Ronan had been favored simply because he was all that was left of the bond between Geordie and his beloved wife. Had Ewan known and resented it? The auld laird was not shy about saying such things. Perhaps this had turned Ewan against Ronan as well as her.

"I would ask that you be careful, husband," Brenna said.

"Me? You need protection, and I'll see your guards are given a proper reward for keeping you safe."

"Thank you," she answered, grateful he understood. He now seemed set on whatever was required to keep her safe. Which meant she would be free to watch over him.

It was clear Ewan's interruption had doused their earlier kisses. Ronan offered to escort her to the kitchens' safety so he could speak to his men, though she'd have rather spent the day in their chamber. Instead, she would spend the afternoon with the ladies as usual. Even if so much about her felt different.

"No rabbits today?" Jane noticed right away.

"Oh, uh…" Brenna should have had a ready excuse, but she'd had much to consider.

"Why has her face gone to red like that?" Corinne asked.

"It appears there is a juicy reason why she has no rabbits today," Ada commented. "Perhaps the laird accompanied her on the hunt this morning."

As much as Brenna tried to think of something else, she could feel her face get even hotter, causing Corinne to squeal with glee.

"I don't think they spent their time hunting. Are your lips swollen from his kisses, lass?"

Brenna instinctively put her fingers to her lips to feel for herself, but it only proved Corinne's assumption correct. She'd fallen for the trick.

"Tell us everything. Did he make up for lost time?" Ada asked.

"Girls, don't trouble the mistress. She may be our friend, but she is the lady of the castle and deserves privacy," Jane came to Brenna's defense.

"Oh, poo, Jane. The laird's been away for five years. I would expect nothing less than for our lady of the castle to walk straight for a few days."

Their ribald humor was always amusing until it was focused on her. Fortunately, Jane changed the subject and moved their focus to the tarts they planned to make that day.

Other than a few comments, Brenna made it through the day unscathed.

At dinner time, the laird escorted her to their table. When Ewan came to take his seat next to Ronan, the laird shook his head.

"Please move down, Ewan. This seat should be for my war chief. Will should be along shortly."

If Brenna thought her face had been red under the scrutiny of the women, her cheeks couldn't have come close to the purple of Ewan's flesh when he was forced to move to the end of the table to make room for the guard.

The glare he sent in her direction spoke of his unfettered hatred for her.

"And uncle…" Ronan added once Ewan was seated. "If you don't stay away from my wife, you'll take your meals in the dungeon. Do ye understand?"

"What has the witch said about me? She lies to turn you against your blood."

"*She* told me nothing. Perhaps when you threaten people in the stables, you'd be wise to see they are alone first."

All the blood that had turned Ewan's face purple seemed to flush from his body as he went pale and wide-eyed. He jumped from his seat a moment later and rushed from the hall, moving faster than Brenna had seen him manage.

"All the better," Ronan said as he patted her hand and welcomed Will to take his rightful spot at the laird's right hand; the rest of the warriors filled in. Hugh was next to Will. Malcolm and Gabe were next to her.

"What has happened?" Gabe asked as Malcolm leaned across him to hear.

"I told Ronan the truth, and he believed me."

"It's about bloody time."

"Aye," Ronan said. "I will see you and Gabe rewarded for doing what I didn't see to do myself. I'll be forever in your debt for your protection of my wife."

"It was an honor, my laird," Malcolm said.

They continued with the meal, and Brenna relaxed, grateful to have the people she cared for at the table with her—even better because Ewan was gone.

The maids continued to bring food and drink to the table as the men quickly worked on the venison stew being served. But one of the maids Brenna didn't know well came to the table to fill their glasses and stopped as if frozen in place. At first, Brenna thought the girl was just nervous about serving those at the high table, but as the girl finally came closer and picked up Ronan's glass to refill it, her hands began to shake, and she broke into tears.

"Larrie?" Brenna said, thinking that was her name. She and her young sister Amie had come to them from the Gordon clan. Their aunt was a Grant, and Larrie and Amie had come to live with her after their parents died last winter. She was always shy, but not like this. "What is the matter?"

"I canna do it," the girl gasped.

"I can help you." Brenna found her husband intimidating, but not enough for this reaction. But when Brenna reached for the pitcher to help the lass fill the glass, Larrie held tight.

"Nay. It's poisoned." That last part was whispered.

Brenna pulled her hand back as if the earthenware pitcher contained a snake.

"Poisoned? Why would it be poisoned? Who poisoned it?" So many questions.

Tears ran down Larrie's rosy cheeks.

"A note said Amie would be harmed if I didn't poison the laird's glass. I love my sister and would do anything for her, but I can't kill the laird."

Having heard her outburst, Ronan took the pitcher from the girl and set it far from him. "Where is the letter?"

She pulled it from her apron and held it out with trembling fingers. Ronan took it. Brenna watched his eyes move as he read the letter while Larrie explained.

"I canna read. I had to have one of the other maids read it to me. But they told me it says harm will come to my wee sister if I don't pour the vial's contents into the laird's drink."

"Who would do such a thing?" Brenna said, looking into Ronan's startled face. Before she asked the question, she knew who had done it.

Ewan. He'd been outed for the traitor he was, and now he was retaliating in the worst way.

Ronan folded the missive and answered slowly. "According to the note, the order came from you, wife."

Brenna wished she was the type to swoon because now would have been the perfect time to melt away.

***

Ronan watched his wife's eyes go large in surprise. If he'd had any niggling doubt she had nothing to do with this attempt on his life, it would have vanished at seeing the shock across her face.

He'd learned recently that his wife was not a skilled liar. She preferred to blurt out the truth when asked whether he was prepared for it. With the threat coming only an hour after he'd sent his uncle away from the table, Ronan didn't have to guess who might want to poison him.

"Ronan, I swear I didn't do this to you." His wife's hand on his arm thrilled him despite the ill-timing.

It brought forth the memories from that morning of them kissing in the forest. How heated they'd become for each other. But that was ill-timed as well. As much as he would have enjoyed frolicking in the woods with his tree sprite, it wasn't the honorable way to reunite with one's wife.

"I know it wasn't you. I didn't think about it for a minute. And not only because you have sat next to me through the whole meal. When would you have had an opportunity to do such a thing? We'll deal with Ewan soon enough. Right now, we must find Amie and make sure she is safe. Would he injure a child?" Ronan would like to think his uncle above such hideousness, but something had changed in Ewan over the years. Ronan had been away, and now...

"I'm not sure."

Ronan turned to Will, who immediately organized the men to start the search for the girl. Larrie described her sister to aid in the task, and the men were off—except for Malcolm and Gabe, who stood by Brenna with matching expressions of obstinance Ronan had come to expect from the brothers.

In the past, he'd been irritated by their constant presence, but now he realized why his grandsire had sworn them to this duty, and he was ashamed he'd not seen the truth sooner.

"Brenna, will you take Larrie to the solar so these men can better protect you?"

She nodded, and he appreciated her easy agreement. He was sure she would have argued to come with them if not for the poor maid crying on his wife's shoulder.

Whatever the reason, he would be glad to know she was safe. She reached out her hand and squeezed his fingers. "Please be careful."

Her concern took him aback. It wasn't uncommon for a wife to worry over her husband. She sent him letters when he'd first arrived in Spain with the army. He'd never read them, unable to shoulder the guilt her words would bring, but he always liked to think she'd ended each message with those words of affection that showed she cared for his health and well-being.

And as he stowed the letter in his sporran unread, he sent out the same hope for her.

With a smile, he squeezed her fingers to reassure her. "I will. I promise."

With a nod to her guards, he followed Will and Hugh out of the hall to start the search.

"You know Ewan is behind this plot. Which means he's trying to gain control of the clan," Will said. "It would probably be best if you stayed with Brenna."

Did his men expect him to hide away in the lady's solar while his brother blustered and threw a childish fit?

"I'll see he is punished for this."

"That is just it. He is like a brother to ye. When the time comes, can you do what needs to be done?" Hugh asked.

"What needs to be done is that he be captured and locked in the dungeon until we can question him. Do ye understand?"

He gazed around the ranks of warriors to be sure they all heard him.

They nodded their agreement.

"Find the girl and bring Ewan to me. I want to look into his eyes when he explains why he has done this."

As they dispersed, he heard one of the men mumble to another, "He wants to be the bloody laird; *that's* why he's done this."

It seemed a plausible reason, except that Ewan had not seemed to care about being laird when they'd been childhood friends. Yes, they'd both been trained for the duty, as any heir and spare had been. But that day at the loch, when Ronan had nearly drowned and Ewan had saved him, didn't speak of a person wanting to remove his competition.

Something in his stomach twisted at the memory. He worried he would be faced with acknowledging Ewan's betrayal soon enough. He took a moment to mount his horse, rubbing at his aching leg, and rode out of the gates with Will at his side.

They would find Ewan. What happened after that would be up to Ronan. Will's earlier question still plagued him. Would Ronan be able to punish Ewan? Ronan thought that he could, and the reason surprised him. It wasn't that Ewan had tried to poison him, but it was for the fear he'd seen in Brenna's eyes earlier that day in the stable. The knowledge that she had lived in such fear all these years.

The man needed to be stopped. And Ronan planned to stop him.

Chapter Twenty

Hours later, Ronan entered the great hall. He paused to order his men to bring food, as some had missed their meal while others ate whenever food was available. Climbing the stairs, he greeted the men at the solar's door. He was relieved to see a welcoming smile rather than the familiar scowl, as Malcolm reported.

"All's quiet, my laird. How did you make out?"

"We found the lass wandering alone in the meadow on the southern border. The girl said the man who held her didn't show his face and that he'd ridden south. I think it is safe to say Ewan left clan lands after he realized we were chasing him."

The brothers exchanged a look.

"Until we're certain, Gabe and I would prefer to keep watch over m'lady when she's not with you."

"Aye. I agree. I do not wish to be careless with my wife." He paused. "I wish to thank ye both for protecting her when I wasn't here to do it."

They nodded in unison and then moved aside for Ronan to enter the solar.

Inside, he smiled seeing his wife sleeping on the chair by the window, as if she'd nodded off while watching for him to return. She would have seen the gate, well-lit with torches, from her perch.

The young maid, Larrie, slept on another chair. Ronan woke her and told her quietly that her sister had been returned to her aunt and was unharmed.

She hurried off after a hug that surprised him for its fierceness for such a slight girl.

Brenna stirred and sat up. "Did you find her?"

"Aye. She is fine."

"And Ewan?"

"He has gone. We think he's left Grant lands, but we'll continue to keep watch for now."

She nodded and glanced through the windows.

"I'll see that you are safe. And when I can't be with you, your guards will remain with you as they have done."

"It's not myself I'm worried about. He seems determined to be laird, which makes *you* his target."

It seemed odd, this danger hanging over him. In France, the threat was always head-on. He knew what front to protect. This was infuriating. He had only spent a few hours in this danger and was already restless about seeing an end to it. How had Brenna lived like this every day?

Ronan nodded. "Ewan planned to stay close until he had the opportunity and could make it look like an accident. Now that I know the truth, he no longer needs to pretend."

"I'm sorry, this must be difficult for you. To think him a friend and a brother only to be betrayed."

"He has made his choices. Power can make an otherwise rational person abandon their honor. I've seen it with my mother. I don't think there is much she wouldn't do to ensure her place of power and riches. I'm sorry if I expected that from you when I returned."

"Ewan played on your fears. It is what the best villains do."

It was true, but he'd hoped he wouldn't have fallen for the ruse so easily. He'd never even considered his wife was innocent.

"Besides," Brenna said, "now that you know the truth, we can move forward without these lies between us."

How forgiving she was. Not just for his lack of faith in her but for leaving her. For never writing back, for doing his best to forget she was waiting here for him. "I have many other things to be sorry for, wife. I've treated you horribly."

She shook her head. "The past is behind us."

"And our future is before us," he said with a smile. "I intend to make it a pleasant one indeed."

The soft blush on her cheeks proved she'd understood his underlying promise.

"Shall we retire for the night?" he suggested in a low voice that hinted at what he intended when he got her behind their closed door.

Her blush deepened, but she nodded. Taking her hand in his, he brushed a kiss across her knuckles.

"Let us go to bed, wife."

***

Brenna had thought herself tired only a

moment ago. After the day's early start and harrowing events, she had been exhausted. But at Ronan's invitation to go to bed—with him—her heart began galloping in excitement. Sleep forgotten, she had to rein in her steps to avoid running to their chamber, dragging him behind her.

She could imagine how he would laugh if she'd given in to her desire to do so. But seeing the gleam of excitement in his warm brown eyes, she thought maybe he wouldn't have minded. She'd heard his desire in the roughness of his voice when he'd spoken of taking her to their room. He'd told her he'd been true to her all this time. She knew his need must be even worse than her own.

Inside their room, where they wouldn't be disturbed, they stopped a few feet from one another and stared. They'd managed quite well earlier in the day, but now they both seemed at a loss as to how to start.

In the woods, she wasn't sure who had moved for whom. They'd just been standing there one moment and kissing in each other's arms the next. He opened his mouth, floundering for words that would get things underway. But before he could speak, she rushed forward, stood on her toes, and kissed him.

With that first step out of the way, they returned to where they were that morning, ready to move forward. His warm tongue invaded her mouth as his hands seemed to be touching her everywhere at once. She'd changed into a gown for dinner, and she half expected him to do as he'd wished before, and she tossed up her skirts to get to her. Instead, he tugged at the laces in the back of her gown as his kisses became hotter.

A few curses escaped when he struggled to get her dress open. She pulled away and spun so her back was to him so he could free her from the gown.

"I've half a mind to pull my dirk and cut the blasted things."

"'Tis my best dress."

"I'll buy you a new one."

Fortunately, it didn't come to that. The laces relented, and soon her husband was tugging the gown over her hips to drop to the floor. She removed her own boots and reached to untie the stockings, only to have her husband stop her with a hand over hers.

"Leave them."

She didn't know why he wouldn't want them removed, but seeing the heat in his eyes forced her quick agreement to move on to his clothes.

He'd kicked off his boots and stockings, and at the same time he reached behind his neck and drew his shirt over his head. She gasped as she took in the ripples of his stomach and the flat plains of his broad chest. She touched the light sprinkling of hair on his face and smiled as it tickled her palm. When she inadvertently stroked her hand across his nipple, he jolted and hissed in a breath.

Could it be that her husband's smaller nipples were as sensitive as her own? Perhaps men were not so different in some ways. Feeling bold, she leaned closer and slid her tongue across the tiny nub, earning another hiss. Before she could explore that area further, his kilt dropped with a thud at his feet, and Brenna's attention became fixed on a different body part.

She'd seen him before in this same state of arousal. She knew well what happened next. But even knowing that part of him fit splendidly inside of her, she felt the same wonder at how it all worked. And the fact that he felt this way with her.

"I must make my apologies to ye now," he said, his voice coming quick as the words came between kisses to her neck.

"Whatever for?"

"It's been so long. I'll not last long. Just seeing you look at me the way you are has me close to spending, and I've not even gotten inside of you. I promise to make it up to you the second time."

She nodded as she untied her shift and let the fabric slide over her body, leaving her naked except for the stockings he'd insisted remain.

He cursed again, a whisper before he spoke louder. "The third time. I shall make it up to you the third time."

She lay back on the bed and bent her knees the way he'd shown her all those years ago when she'd made room for his body against hers. But instead of lying atop her or even next to her, he bent down. It took a moment for her to realize his intention. She might have protested such a thing, but only until his tongue slid across her most intimate flesh.

The sensation left her unable to speak. She could only moan. The feeling was exquisite torture. So good she wanted more. She was so sensitive she didn't know how she would stand it. But Ronan wasn't even close to stopping. Instead, he'd settled closer to her as he stretched out on the bed and continued to lap at her center until that intense feeling she'd nearly forgotten began to rise.

With each touch of his tongue, the tension built and came closer until it was right there on the edge of oblivion.

"Please."

He didn't make her wait. He growled against her flesh as his fingers entered her, and everything seemed to stop for the smallest of moments before all sensation came crashing over her. Her mouth moved with words, but she didn't know what she was saying. Maybe his name. Maybe she thanked him. Perhaps she told him she'd never make it to the third time.

She wasn't sure, but he smiled at her when she could open her eyes. It was almost a surprise to find she was still lying on the bed in the same room. It seemed she'd flown a great distance.

She smiled at her husband as he came closer and kissed her. They shared a look as his body aligned with hers. She arched up to welcome him home.

Chapter Twenty-One

Watching his wife fall apart nearly undid him. He hadn't been lying when he'd said the first time would be over quickly. He'd barely seated himself inside her when she thrust up against him, and he erupted.

He might have felt shame for it, except he was hard again immediately and able to continue as he'd wanted to. He thrust into her as she arched up to meet him each time, her body moving in perfect time with his. Unfortunately, he soon became distracted by the pain in his leg, which threatened to give out on him from the exertion.

"Bloody hell," he said, and Brenna looked up at him, clearly confused. He reassured her quickly, not wanting her to think she displeased him in their bed. "'Tis my leg. It is not used to such effort."

Always a willing healer, she asked, "Do you want me to rub it?"

"Nay," he said as he rolled over, bringing her

above him without breaking their contact. Her eyes went wide as she looked down at him. "Ye don't need to rub my leg, but I would be much obliged if you could take over."

"I—I'm not sure..." She frowned but moaned in pleasure as he pressed up from the bed into her.

"Move as you like, however you like."

She did, and after a few moments, she found her stride. Her eyes closed, and her head fell back in pleasure, exposing herself to his gaze. He reached up and caressed her breasts, making her gasp and jerk by playing with her nipples.

He'd never seen anything so beautiful in all his days as his wife riding him toward their pleasure. There had been many times over the years he considered taking pleasure with one of the women who offered it. When his need became more than he thought he could endure. But now that he was here with his wife, he was glad he hadn't.

She'd been prepared and even expected such, but he knew now it would be different between them had he strayed. Their loyalty to one another made this reunion all the sweeter.

"Ye are mine," he said amongst his other ramblings of how lovely she was as she cried out his name. He hadn't thought much about it as it crossed his lips, but hearing the words in his strained voice sounded right.

His wife responded with a moan and a confident, "Yes. Only yours."

But he wouldn't allow it to be one-sided. She was his equal, and he wanted to make it clear. "I am yours, Brenna."

"Yes," she said. "Only mine."

As he reached his peak this time, she joined him, taking everything he had to give, body and soul. She collapsed atop him, her unruly curls covering his face, unleashing the honey scent as he caught his breath. Her heart raced against his chest as he smiled for the sake of smiling. Eventually, she shifted and managed to throw the covers over them. He wasn't nearly done making love to her, but he'd take advantage of a rest.

"Was it how you remembered?" he asked her.

He felt her shake her head, though her answer came a few breaths later.

"Nay. It was better."

"No pain?" he guessed, remembering the reluctance he'd felt to hurt her when he took her maidenhead.

"Well, yes, but that was not what I thought."

"How was it different?"

"We know each other a little better than we did then. There is a comfort in that."

"Aye. You're right. I'm glad we've not taken our pleasure with anyone else," he said. He was still holding her close, so it was easy enough to feel her body tense. The silence went on for some time.

Rolling her onto his back, he looked down at her.

"Have you taken your pleasure with another?" he asked. She'd told him she hadn't lain with another while he was away, but it had been a long time. If she had... She merely shrugged.

"Is it a difficult question, wife? Has another man touched ye and made you tremble as I have?" He tried his best to keep the anger from his voice, but the thought of another man touching her... He couldn't bear it, even knowing he would have to accept it.

He was the one who left. Brenna bit her bottom lip and winced but shook her head. "What is it?"

She looked away, but he nudged her chin back to meet his anxious gaze. "Please just say it."

She let out a breath and the words in one quick exhale. "I brought pleasure to myself."

He could feel the heat of her blush and see it even in the dim light of the room. He smiled and rolled back over, pulling her against him.

"Did you think of me when you touched yourself?" he asked, knowing she would be embarrassed to discuss it further but having many questions all the same.

"Of course. Who else would I think of?" she said into the protection of his chest. Again, he coaxed her face up to look at him. He wanted her to see how happy he was and how he accepted her.

"I thought of ye when I touched myself as well."

This surprised her. And then she blinked and glanced away, clearly not believing him. She'd been told she'd displeased him, scared him to France. He needed to convince her that she was everything he desired.

"It was rare for me to have enough privacy to take care of my needs. And when I did, it was only a few minutes, so I conjured up images to help me finish the job quickly."

She still avoided his gaze as he continued.

"Sometimes, I thought of the sounds you made, though those memories faded quickly no matter how desperate I was to hold onto them. I thought of the way ye responded when I touched ye. The way you cried out my name when you reached your pleasure. When it had been a long time since I'd had a release, it didn't take much at all, and I would think of the curves of your arse when you hopped down from your horse that first time we met."

"In my trews?" Her brows rose in disbelief.

"Aye. That buttery leather held you the way I wanted my hands on you."

"Now I know you jest. You couldn't find it attractive when I wear men's clothing."

"I may jest, but I assure you, my cock is not a humorous fellow."

She laughed, and the sound warmed his heart. To prove his words, he pushed against her. She gasped when she felt his arousal yet again.

"Are you thinking of me in my trews now?"

"Nay. I'm thinking of you touching yourself and want to see it for myself."

"I couldn't possibly—"

"You asked me to promise you honesty. Do you remember?"

"Aye."

"I will ask you for something as well."

She nodded.

"I want us each to feel safe with one another. It is safe to ask for anything or tell each other anything we need or want without fear of being shamed or judged. Our bed will be a safe place to share our desires."

"That sounds lovely." She bit her lip as she considered his request. "I imagine the honesty we promised would also play a big part in this."

"Aye, I believe so."

"Yes. I agree."

"Then will you show me how you touched yourself when you thought of me? And now it is what I desire." He moved aside to give her room and helped by kissing her knuckles and placing her hand where it would be easier for her to touch herself. As her fingers moved across her folds, he reached out as well, following her movements.

At first, her eyes remained open, focused on him, but as she stroked her warm flesh, her eyes fell closed, and her head tilted back.

Soon, soft cries of pleasure escaped her kiss-swollen lips, and he ached for release once more. He waited and watched his wife as she brought herself closer and closer to the edge.

Only when her breath caught did he shift and slide into her, feeling the tightening of her body around his as she shouted so loud that he expected everyone in the castle might have heard. He didn't care if they did.

***

They were awakened hours later by loud whispers outside their room. For a moment, Brenna was confused until she felt the large, warm body pressed against her back. And the reason she could feel him so easily was because she was naked.

Ronan. The memories of the night before flooded her mind, bringing a smile to her lips until the whispering started again.

"I'm a-tellin' ye, Mal, we should go get the axe and take down the door."

"And I'm tellin' ye, if you take an axe to this door, the laird will likely take an axe to you."

"He's not wrong," Ronan whispered before

kissing her temple.

She turned toward him with a smile. "We should at least knock and ask to see the mistress to be sure she's not tied up."

"Hmm... I might like to tie you up," Ronan said. "Do you have any ropes about?"

She was not overly familiar with bedsport, but she could see why tying each other up might be fun. To torment the other by restricting their ability to touch. But alas, she had no ropes in their chamber.

"I suppose I should go to the door and tell them all is well," Brenna said, though she didn't wish to move. Even to appease her guards.

She'd relied on their thoroughness for the last few years to ensure her safety. And not long ago, being trapped in her bed chamber would have alerted them to the danger within. But there was no danger this day, far from it.

"I'll take care of it." Ronan cleared his throat and shouted firmly. "You on the door!"

"Aye?"

"Your mistress is well." He squeezed her and whispered, "Well-loved."

"If it is the same to ye, laird, we'd like to hear the mistress say so herself."

"That's it. I'm getting the axe," Ronan grumbled but only snuggled closer to her under the covers.

"I am fine, Gabe. I don't need anything." Even conversing with them through the door when naked while Ronan nestled against her breast made her cheeks warm with a blush. One should not be forced to converse in such a state.

"Let's not be hasty," Ronan said and turned to

shout. "Men. Your mistress is rather famished. Send for a tray, will you?"

"What, are we maids now?" Gabe grumbled from beyond the door. They had no idea of how easily they were heard.

Brenna giggled as the men stomped off, but her laughter was cut off in a gasp when Ronan stroked his hand up her thigh and over her heat.

"Again?" She could hardly imagine he had any strength left, even after sleeping the few hours they'd managed. She didn't want to move.

"Can you still walk?"

"In truth, I'm not sure. I haven't attempted to in many hours."

"And I'll see to it you won't need to for many more hours."

She'd remembered their first night together and how he'd woken her through the night to make love to her again until she was so exhausted she'd slept like the dead.

So still, she'd not roused when he'd packed and left her. That thought brought a shiver through her body and not the delightful kind that Ronan's kisses inspired.

"What is it?" Ronan paused in his nibbling of her neck to look at her, concern evident on his face. She had no reason to worry he would leave her again. He'd said as much, and she decided she would believe him unless she had a reason not to.

Their bannocks and porridge were cold when they rose to retrieve them, but neither seemed to care as they dug in. Ronan had not been lying when he'd told her guards she was famished. She couldn't remember being so hungry.

She could barely wait for Ronan to drizzle a bit of honey over her bite of pastry. When he spilled some of the honey on her hand, he watched her intently as he glided his tongue, cleaning her skin of the sticky sweetness.

From there, the honey barely made it to the remaining bread. They made quite a mess as they found other places to dribble and delight. When they were not caught up in passion, they napped and talked quietly. She coaxed more stories from him about his time in France, and he asked her about a few of the clanspeople he'd met.

For all they talked, they avoided some topics as if they weren't yet ready to discuss them.

"Oh my," she said when his stomach growled. "Have we spent most of the day in our room? We must dress and go down for dinner."

"I'm against anything that requires you to be dressed. I like ye just how you are."

She slid from the bed and went to stand to wash. Eventually, with a loud sigh, Ronan relented and got himself ready.

"It is only because I am so hungry from my exertions that I agree to leave this room."

She leaned up on her toes to kiss him. "Duly noted, my laird."

When he was ready, she tucked her hand in at his elbow, and he escorted her into the hall. They made it a few steps toward the dais when someone hooped and started clapping. The rest of the clan shouted and clapped along as well.

Brenna felt her cheeks go red at the attention, but Ronan held his head high with a smile.

"Don't worry, lass. If you'd like, I'll tell them

how grateful I am to have you in my bed and that wild horses wouldn't drag me back to France."

"That won't be necessary," she said. "So long as I know you are here to stay, that is all that matters."

His grin slipped slightly.

"I never should have left ye the first time. I've learned my lesson, wife. I'll never leave you again."

She hoped that was true.

Chapter Twenty-Two

Ronan bore the cheers and clapping with good humor and was pleased that Brenna was not too upset by the attention they'd gotten coming to dinner late after hiding away in their room the whole day.

But they had a lot of time to make up for it. It was a lot of pleasure, yes, but many conversations as well. They had missed a lot of each other's lives, and he found for everything she shared, he wished he'd been there next to her, good and bad. It had been his place as her husband, and he'd not been there.

He sat next to Will, noticing how Malcolm and Gabe scurried to Brenna's side. He gave her a thorough inspection before relaxing into their meals. They were both young and didn't know Ronan at all. He couldn't blame them for their concerns and was grateful they were such watchful protectors.

"Ye seem unsteady on your feet, laird," Hugh teased.

"I'll remind you I arrived home that way, and

it's not any fault of my wife's attentions."

"What about the shadows under your eyes from lack of sleep?" Will asked with a slight grin.

"Now, *that* is my wife's fault," he whispered so as not to embarrass Brenna further. "I hope you have reason to miss some sleep someday as well."

"I'm glad the two of you have found happiness. I wasn't so sure when you arrived."

Ronan frowned. "I was an arse."

Will shrugged. "I'll not be accused of disagreeing with my laird."

Ronan looked over to Brenna, who requested a second helping of stew for both of them.

"Thank you, wife," he said as he dug in. "I might think ye have a reason to keep our strength up."

Her cheeks pinked, and it was all he could do not to scoop her up and carry her back to their room despite the laughter that would surely ensue. They remained below stairs for the meal and entertainment, though he couldn't say what songs the man might have played, for he was paying more attention to his wife and thinking of what he wanted to do when they returned to their room.

He glanced around at his clan and saw a number of smiling faces that had previously looked at him with suspicion and anger. It appeared his clan approved of him treating his wife as a husband aught.

When they finally turned for their bed, his wife paused at the top of the stairs.

"What is it?"

"I have a surprise for you, though now I'm unsure if you will like it."

He pulled her hand from the other, where she twisted her fingers nervously. "Why don't you tell me what it is so I can show you how thankful I am?"

She let out a breath and nodded. Instead of continuing down the corridor to their room, she stopped at the double doors with the Grant crest engraved in the wood.

"The laird's chamber?" he said.

"When you were speaking with your men, I had the maids prepare it for us. I thought…" Her cheeks flared with another blush, and he could hardly stand not knowing what she was thinking.

"You thought what?" he encouraged.

"It is only that the bed is much bigger in this room."

His grin grew into a full smile. "And ye thought we could use more space for our activities?"

She shrugged but looked up at him, a coy smile of her own tilting her lush lips. "I also thought to get some rope."

"Dear Christ Almighty, woman, you are going to be the death of me, and I won't even mind."

He picked her up, despite the soreness of his leg and carried her into their room like the proper groom carrying his virgin bride. But as soon as the door was shut behind them, they became the ravenous lovers they'd been the night before.

They slept until late in the morning, and Ronan was grateful not only for the larger bed but also for the heavy curtains surrounding it, which kept the sun out.

"I must go about my day," she murmured as he woke her with kisses. "We can't spend another day in our chamber. I'll not be fodder for the men's jests again this evening."

"I can put them out if they tease you if that be

your wish, my lady."

She laughed. "That is not my wish, laird. When they are not laughing at our expense, they are quite valuable as warriors to defend us against other clans. Besides, you know I will not be the kind of mistress who punishes their people simply because she is displeased."

"Can I be the kind of laird that punishes his warriors because his wife is displeased?"

"Nay." She laughed at his eagerness.

"Can I be the kind of laird that punishes his warriors for being the reason his wife chooses to venture out instead of spending another day with him abed?"

"Hmm… It seems it falls to me to save your men from their fates by giving into your whims and staying in your bed. What sacrifices I make for my people."

"You are a benevolent mistress. It shall be noted in the history books."

They fell in a laughing heap back to the bed. And soon, giggles turned to moans and gasps.

"We shall go out tomorrow, I promise," he said as he slid into her.

"We shall see," she whispered. "We do not need quite so many warriors. We could surely spare a few."

***

Brenna straightened her shoulders and took a deep breath to steady herself before opening the door and entering the kitchen.

Rather than walk with her husband into the hall directly from their chamber, she'd decided to help with the late meal and join Ronan at the high table before it was served. It was a poor ploy to draw attention away from the fact they'd spent most of the day closed up in their bedroom again that day.

"Look who it is, ladies. Our mistress is walking a bit bow-legged this evening," Corinne said loudly as the other women stifled chuckles.

"Go on. I knew I could not sneak in without a few jests," Brenna said.

In truth, it was much easier to face her friends than the warriors in the hall. Many days they'd spent in this very room talking about the things they shared with their husbands in the privacy of their bedrooms. Brenna had not had much of anything to bring to their bawdy discussions. Even now, she didn't plan to share the intimate details of what went on with her and her husband. But she understood better why they teased each other.

It was a way of letting the others know they were happy for each other.

"Does he treat you well?" Ada asked quietly.

"Yes. I worry I may never stop smiling for how happy I am. I never expected it to be this way between us," Brenna blurted out, her eyes filled with happy tears.

She didn't mean to be such a mess, but she couldn't help herself. Soon enough, the other women dropped what they were doing to hug her.

"You deserve nothing less for all the sadness you've endured all these years," Jane said. The other women nodded in fierce agreement.

"I am quite happy. Happier than I ever expected."

Each woman reached out in some way, either with a hug or by squeezing her hand, to show how much they cared.

"Now," Corinne said, clearing her throat. "How large is the laird?"

After avoiding Corinne's naughty inquisition as best as possible, Brenna helped them finish the meal and headed to the hall.

She glanced up at her husband seated at the high table with his men around him. She smiled at seeing him, like some silly girl with her first crush. Only this was so much more. At least, it was in her heart. She knew her husband cared for her and enjoyed lying with her, but did he love her as she had come to love him? She was aware these things were different for men.

Ada had told about how her husband hadn't realized he was in love with her until she'd had difficulty with the birth of their child, and then he'd become overwhelmed with fear of losing her.

Did Ronan love her? She thought perhaps he did. Just then, his gaze landed on her, and he stopped speaking to Will so that he could jump up and walk across the hall to meet her. In front of everyone, he bent to press a kiss to the back of her hand.

"I've missed ye, wife."

She might have mentioned she'd only been away from him for less than an hour, but she'd missed him as well.

She allowed him to lead her to the table and help her settle in her chair. Instead of entertainment, Ronan explained they'd be hearing complaints from a few clansmen and making rulings. This was common, and she'd spent many evenings after the late meal next to Geordie, as he did the same.

"Will you stay in case I need your

assistance?" Ronan asked, and it warmed her heart that he valued her opinion.

The first person to come forward was Samuel Grant with his daughter Isabelle, who was clearly with child despite her young age of ten and six. Brenna whispered their names to him as everyone quieted down.

"What challenge do ye present to me, Samuel?"

"My laird, I've come to see if you can make my daughter tell me who has defiled her so they can be made to care for her and the child. I haven't the room nor the coin to take on another mouth, and no one will want to marry the girl now." He gestured toward his daughter, who wiped at the tears on her cheeks but kept her gaze on the floor.

"Did someone force themselves upon ye, lass? I'll not hold with such things in my clan."

"Nay, my laird." She shook her head as her bottom lip trembled.

Ronan turned toward Brenna with a distraught look.

"I'd rather not drag something so personal out of her in front of everyone in the hall. Would you take her aside and look into the situation so I can better know what to do?"

"Aye." She placed her hand lightly on his hand before standing. "Isabelle, might you come with me?"

"I'll have the name," Samuel bellowed, and Ronan raised a hand.

"I'll see that there is some resolution. Let us be patient for a moment longer."

Brenna pulled her aside and whispered to the

girl.

"You're sure no one has forced you? We would see you protected if that were the case."

Isabelle's face crumbled as she shook her head again.

"Nay. It wasn't like that. I was willing. I thought…"

"What did ye think?"

"I thought he loved me. He said he did, but then…after…he didn't want anything to do with me. I feel like such a fool to have believed him. It was a mistake to believe him, but it would be an even bigger mistake to name him and have my father force him into marriage. I don't wish to spend another moment with him."

She lifted her chin and shook her head with determination and heartbreak in her eyes.

"Very well," Brenna said, hugging the girl before returning to explain to Ronan. She noticed Gabe and Malcolm talking in their usual whisper, which was louder than they realized, but she ignored them to relay the situation to her husband.

Ronan frowned. "The man should not be left without any responsibility for what he did."

"And Isabelle should not be punished further for believing the man's lies. To spend the rest of her life resented by such a man."

The brothers were still bickering, and Ronan looked past her to scowl at them.

"Do you think one of them is the father?"

"Nay. I can't think of two more responsible men."

Ronan nodded his agreement and turned back to the seething father.

Brenna didn't know what he might have said next since Gabe stepped out and spoke loud enough for all to hear.

"I'll marry the lass."

Ronan twitched his finger to bring Gabe closer. "Are ye responsible for this?" Ronan pointed to where Isabelle was standing with wide eyes.

"Nay. But I may have heard something of it when I was in the tavern, and there's no way she can marry the man. Even if he weren't on the run for attempting to poison ye, he wouldn't be fit, if you take my meaning."

It wasn't difficult at all to take his meaning. Ewan had done this. He'd preyed on this girl. He spun his lies and offered his charming smile to get what he wanted from her.

Brenna focused on her guard. "You would raise the child as your own despite who fathered the babe?"

"So long as it doesn't come out with horns and a forked tail, I'll do my best to raise the bairn to be a better person than his father. And Isabelle is lovely and witty from the little I've spoken to her. It would be no hardship to have her as my wife. As long as you keep me on as a warrior, I can provide for my family."

"Aye, lad. I'll see you're paid enough," Ronan said and clasped his hand on Gabe's shoulder. "It's an honorable thing you're doing. I'm proud to have you on my guard."

Gabe only nodded as if he had no use for praise.

Ronan spoke to Isabelle, "Will you take Gabe as your husband? I can speak to his nature. He's been watching over my wife, and he's a valuable soldier. He'd see you and the babe cared for."

Isabelle looked at Gabe for a moment and then nodded. "Aye. Thank you."

Ronan turned back to Samuel. "Does this outcome satisfy you?"

The man frowned but then nodded begrudgingly. Ronan turned to her as the next person came forward. "I thought this would be easier. Arguments over land or disputes regarding cattle. I don't know that I'm prepared to make such vital decisions."

Brenna looked up to see Angus Grant frowning toward the dais. She patted Ronan's arm.

"You did a fine job and are about to get your wish about the cattle."

"I'd much rather take you to our room and see to your pleasure."

"I'd prefer that as well. Let's tell Angus we shall buy him however many cows he wants so long as he's quick about it."

He laughed and kissed her in the mouth in front of everyone, and she didn't mind at all.

Chapter Twenty-Three

Three days later, Ronan was finally ready to leave their room and venture outside again. Brenna suggested they go hunting together, and they had awakened early enough to satisfy their desires and still make it to the stables in good time.

She gathered bannocks to break their fast, and he readied the horses and weapons.

He kissed her as she tucked the food into her pack and helped her mount the tall stallion. He had seen much of his wife's body over the past few days, but there was something about seeing the curves of her body wrapped in soft leather trews that made him want to carry her back to their bed despite the soreness in his leg that morning. Some things were worth the pain.

They rode silently for a bit, him watching her rather than where they were going. It wasn't until he looked up and saw the sun glinting off the surface of the water that he sucked in a breath. Brimstone, ever perceptive of Ronan's slightest distress, came to a stop.

"What is it?" Brenna asked as she came to a stop next to him. She glanced at the water and back at him. "Do you see someone? Is it Ewan?" She twisted in her saddle, looking about.

"Nay. 'Tis not Ewan. It's that I haven't been here in many years. Not since I was a boy. This is…" He swallowed and decided to force the information from his lips. "This is where I nearly died."

"When you almost drowned, and Ewan saved you?"

"Aye. We were swimming here."

Her brows pulled up in confusion. "This lake is not so deep. I didn't realize it was this pond. I'm sorry. I shouldn't have come this way if it distresses you."

He raised his hand to set her mind at ease and looked at it as she did. The body of water was more of a shallow pond than the dark depths he seemed to remember.

"Come, let us leave," she said.

He agreed, though he turned to look over his shoulder, still surprised to see such an innocent-looking place. Tranquil even. He nudged Brimstone into a trot and left this place's ghosts behind him again.

When they arrived at the forest's edge, where she preferred to hunt, he helped her down, lingering long enough for a kiss. His earlier alarm had gone. She smiled and he laughed with her. He didn't know he could be so happy. Not for the first time did he curse himself for being away all this time.

"Do you think we will ever have enough?"

"God, I hope not. In our defense, we have much time to make up for," he pointed out. So many years they'd spent longing for something they could have had each night if not for his selfishness.

"Especially since we both remained chaste all this time." She smiled, and he saw the pleasure his fidelity had brought her.

"It was worth it," he said easily now that he no longer needed to remain chaste. It was one of the most challenging things he'd ever done.

"Why did you?"

"Why did I honor my vows and be faithful to my wife?" he teased, though she was still waiting for an answer. He shrugged.

"It couldn't be for any respect for me personally. You hardly knew me, and I know it wasn't your choice to marry me."

He let out a breath and wondered if he'd ever forgive himself for his behavior when he'd first met his wife. Seeing how Gabe had stepped forward to marry Isabelle in her time of need shamed Ronan as he recalled his cowardice. He'd been nearly the same age Gabe was now. Yet the soldier didn't waver in doing what was right—even taking on a child that wasn't his by blood.

"I was a fool not to see how wonderful a wife you would be. I was an impatient arse."

"It is impossible to see the moon when the sun shines so brightly."

He didn't need to ask what she meant by that. Hannah. For all the ways his wife had grown into herself, it was clear this uncertainty remained. She'd heard him state his preference for her older sister, and it was yet another thing he regretted.

"I mostly prefer the nights when it is only me and the vibrant light of the moon," he said, hoping to convince her he was more than pleased with the sister whose hand he'd taken in marriage.

She smiled again but said, "You didn't answer my question."

He hadn't. She wanted to know why he'd remained celibate all those years.

"Two reasons, I guess. My father didn't think much of men who didn't honor their wives. My mother may have disillusioned my da, but he loved her deeply, as did my stepfather. I grew up seeing a man devoted to his wife in both homes. It may seem silly, but it was how I was raised and what I felt was right."

"And the second reason?"

He scrunched up his nose. "The poor women who follow the drum and offer their company for coin have hard lives. I'd not wanted to be part of that or succumb to one of the many unpleasantries they shared with the other men." He'd seen more than a few soldiers suffering from the effects of a few moments of pleasure that ended in painful diseases.

She smiled at him. "I thank ye for not bringing such horrors to our bed."

He realized then he should have voiced a more personal reason. But he knew she would have seen through such a thing. Years ago, when they'd wed, she'd asked him for honesty. He would do his best to honor that vow.

When her brow pulled together in a frown, he thought perhaps he'd been hasty, but he quickly saw she wasn't upset with him.

"What is it?"

"I seem to have lost one of my arrows. I'd thought I had five, but only four are in my quiver."

"You are welcome to one of mine."

She chuckled. "Yours are too long. Mine are made specifically for my size. That's why I tip the feathers with woad. No one likes to get one of my arrows by mistake."

He pointed to her four remaining arrows, white swan's feathers tipped blue.

"I've seen you hunt and know you'll show me up with the four arrows just fine."

She blushed under his praise and headed into the dim coolness of the forest. They stood side by side, waiting and listening. She tilted her head and lifted her bow. The flash of blue sailed through the air, silently hitting its mark.

"Good job. I'm afraid I am not one for stealth," he said as they walked together to retrieve her arrow and the rabbit she'd taken.

"War is very loud, I imagine."

"Yes. But amid the chaos and noise, I often found moments of quiet when all else was blocked out. In those brief moments, it was possible to hear a single breath from an enemy as he drew his sword, hoping to end my life before I ended his."

She placed her hand on his chest and looked at him. In her hazel depths, he didn't see pity or fear. Just understanding. He knew she couldn't know what war was like and was glad she never would.

He opened his mouth to say something, but she turned. Her eyes narrowed on something he couldn't see, and then, with a gasp, she quickly stepped closer to him and pushed him to the side. She jerked and then looked at him in surprise.

"What...?" he managed to say as blood bloomed across her white shirt.

"Run," she said as she slumped to the soft, dark earth. An arrow stuck up from her back. White swan feathers tipped blue. His wife's missing arrow had been stolen and had been meant for him.

He wanted to chase after Ewan and end this right then, but his wife was hurt. She could be dying, and there was no greater need than for her to live.

He dropped down behind some shrubs so he'd not be an easy mark. Tugging her shirt to the side, he saw the arrow had just come through her skin just below her collarbone. A lower shot would have been fatal. He hoped this higher shot had missed anything vital.

Years at war had him acting as he would have with any other soldier. It wasn't until he'd pushed the arrow through and broken off the tip to pull the shaft back through the entrance wound that he spared a moment to consider the frailty of his wife's smaller body. As much as he wished to see her eyes bright with laughter, he was glad for her unconscious state during that hideous task.

"Sorry, lass," he whispered frantically.

From his sporran, he pulled a bundle of clean cloth. Ripping them, he shoved a length into the front wound and then the rest into the wound on her back to staunch the bleeding until she could be properly tended.

The first thing he needed to do was get her to a healer and quickly. "Stay with me, Brenna. Don't you leave now that I've just gotten here. We have things to do, you and I." He spoke with the desperate need to keep her from fading off to the welcoming darkness many succumbed to.

He spared only a moment to worry if another arrow might come his way as he pulled his wife into his arms and headed for the horses. It took him a moment to get mounted and settle his wife against him before taking off for the castle. He frowned at the groan she made at his relentless pace but was heartened that at least she was alive enough to offer a complaint.

"I'm sorry, love. You can tell me what a bugger I am as soon as you are able, but I need to get you tended. Hold on, lass. 'Tis not far now."

With Merlin running behind him, their thundering hooves captured the guard's attention.

"Open the bloody gate," Ronan bellowed to the man. Ronan didn't have time to wait until they were close enough to see who he was. He had to hope they recognized him from that distance.

The gate opened just as he rode inside.

"Close it, and whatever ye do, don't let Ewan Grant inside," he ordered the confused men.

"What has happened?" Malcolm came running from where he sparred with Gabe.

"Get a healer. Bring them to the hall."

"But Brenna is the healer."

"She isn't going to be able to stitch her own wound. There must be someone else. Get Moira."

"Yes. Right."

Gabe ran off as Ronan passed down his wife to the larger warrior. By then, the rest of the guards had gathered and followed them inside.

"Lay her here." Ronan pointed to a table. He sent a maid for water and clean clothes to be made into bandages.

"The wound is too high to have hit her heart," Will said, which was what Ronan had been hoping. "You," he yelled to one of the lads. "Get a fire going in the hearth. We'll need to sear the wound. Put some water to boil."

With everyone rushing about, Ronan was left to stand there looking at his pale wife along with the other men who'd been unable to protect her.

"She was shot with her arrow. I'm sure it had been meant for me. No doubt meant to make it look like she'd shot me. Ewan would have had both of us out of the way so he could take over the clan."

"Bastard," Hugh whispered.

"Aye. I want the forest by the kirk searched. Find my uncle. Turn over every rock he may have slithered under and bring him to me."

His men hesitated momentarily, a testament to how much they cared for their mistress, as they clearly wished to stay to see to her needs. But Hugh repeated the order, and with a round of "ayes," the men rushed from the hall to capture the monster that had injured Ronan's wife.

Ewan would pay for this.

Moira hurried inside a few minutes later, carrying a basket. The maids entered at the same time, holding a steaming pot of water, and the boys by the hearth had a fire stirred to life.

Ronan stepped to the side so the older woman could work.

"Ye did well, Ronan."

"It wasn't my first time tending to an arrow wound," he said. He didn't say it was the first time he'd done so for a woman and one he cared for at that. "I hope I wasn't too rough. Instincts took over."

"She is a strong lass. This is not a mortal wound. She will be fine so long as the wound doesn't fester."

As if ensuring such a thing didn't happen, the healer dumped a fair bit of whiskey over the wound. The pain stirred Brenna to wake, and she let out a string of curses that made the healer chuckle. Ronan might have also found it amusing to hear his wife's foul oaths, but he couldn't find the humor when his wife was in obvious pain.

Ronan stood next to Brenna and held her hand while Moira stitched her up. When she was done, she added some salve and bandaged the wound. "Let's move her to her bed where she'll be more comfortable and get her changed out of this bloody gown."

Moira had spoken to the maids, but Ronan saw to changing his wife and settling her in their bed in a clean shift.

And then he sat and waited. And waited.

Chapter Twenty-Four

When Brenna opened her eyes, the first thing she saw was her husband sleeping on the chair beside their bed. His head rested on the mattress. She reached out to wake him and encourage him to get in bed, but the movement stole her breath, reminding her why she was alone in their bed.

She'd been shot with an arrow. She glanced toward the window. It looked to be late afternoon, though she wasn't sure which afternoon. Being careful not to move as much, she brushed the long, golden locks from his face to see Ronan better. He was a formidable warrior when awake, but when he slept, he took on the youthful innocence of a boy, except for the growth on his jaw—more than one day had passed since he'd seen a blade.

His eyes blinked open, and he sat up. "You're awake," he whispered.

"Aye. And so are you," she teased him.

He wiped at his face before offering her a

smile. He kissed tenderly on the back of her hand and then stood to retrieve some water. She hadn't even needed to ask, but her throat was dry.

"I'll wait until you're properly healed to give you the scolding I have prepared about stepping in front of an arrow intended for someone else. In the meantime, I will say thank you and tell you how glad I am that you survived such a foolish decision."

She laughed, though only once because doing so pulled on her wound. She smiled and placed her palm on his cheek. "I can think of better things for you to do with your mouth than scold me, husband."

"As it happens, I plan to do a fair amount of that as well." He came closer and placed a soft kiss on her lips before whispering, "I was so frightened, Bren."

"You? Frightened? My fierce soldier?" She tried to joke, but he remained stoic.

"Yes. I was even terrified. I'll have you know I didn't survive the war and travel all this way just to be alone. I won't have it. And I'm the laird, so you'll listen to me."

She smiled at his rant but saw the genuine worry in the lines between his brows.

"I'm sorry I scared you." She glanced toward the window again. "How long exactly did I scare you?" Was it the same day, or had she been abed longer than she thought?

"Since yesterday morning. But it was more than enough time to worry, I assure you. You lost a lot of blood, and Moira said you'd sleep until you needed to."

As much as she hated causing him distress, she had to admit it felt nice to have someone care so much for her wellbeing. But happiness was quickly dismissed when she remembered how she ended up under Ronan's care.

"He'd planned to shoot you," she said so quietly she worried he wouldn't hear her. It was as if speaking about Ewan out loud would bring the devil to the room.

"I know. And with one of your blue-tipped arrows."

"He intended to murder you and make it look like I was responsible. Then he would have been free to take over the clan."

"Aye. It's pretty clear what his intentions were. But he overestimated his skill with the bow. He should have taken more than just the one arrow to see it done."

Brenna shivered at the thought and winced from the pain the motion brought. Ewan had been the ogre in many of her nightmares over the years. But she'd never been so scared of him as she was now that he had set his focus on killing Ronan.

"What will we do?" she asked.

"Most of the guard is searching the woods for him and will bring him back to face justice."

Brenna wanted to inquire as to what punishment Ewan would receive. She still regretted not taking more permanent action against him when she'd had the chance. If she'd seen him hanged for his attack on her months ago, he wouldn't be a danger to Ronan now.

Her husband wouldn't have to handle what to do with his once-loved uncle.

"I didn't know he was capable of such a thing. I didn't realize he was vying for the lairdship. He'd never said anything about wanting to be chieftain before. He saved my life when we were boys. Why would he have done this if he felt I was standing in his way?"

"I can't answer. I doubt there is any good reason. I've watched him grow angrier and more vicious over the years. His hatred for me seemed to swell into something he couldn't control. I did try to be his friend," she said quietly, remembering what a colossal failure it had been. "He only saw me as the reason you left."

"Do *you* think you are the reason I left?"

She offered the slightest shrug in answer. It was only so long before a person could hear such a thing before being forced to consider it the truth.

"I have to believe you wanted to go and that I had nothing to do with your decision…" She paused.

"But?" He guessed she had more to say.

"I wonder if you might have considered staying had you been able to marry someone you like more. Perhaps you might not have wanted to leave if you could have wed Hannah."

He tucked his finger under her chin and nudged her face to look at him.

"Nay. No one would have been able to make me stay. The glory of war was the only thing I cared about then."

She nodded. That was what Geordie had always told her. She shouldn't be upset that Ronan hadn't stayed. It had been decided before he'd known her. But she'd always wondered…

Food was brought up to their room. While they were eating, Will arrived.

"Sorry, laird, but we still haven't found the

bastard. We tracked him as far as the eastern border."

"He has crossed over to Innes lands?"

"It appears so, mistress."

"I shall write to my father and tell him to keep watch for Ewan." She moved to get up, but Ronan set his hand on her knee.

"Tomorrow will be soon enough. For now, I'd rather you finish your meal and rest."

She allowed him to settle her back against the pillows. She was not one to lie about and have people serve her, but she had to admit it was most pleasant when Ronan was doting.

By the following day, however, she'd grown weary of lying around and insisted on getting up.

She finished her letter explaining the crimes Ewan was wanted for on Grant lands and sent it off with a messenger. As she was heading for the kitchens, Ronan met up with her.

"I would feel better if you didn't do too much today. I know you are a lady of action and doing, but I am a man who has a knack for worrying over his injured wife."

She wasn't up for riding, even if Ronan would have allowed such a thing. And the truth of the matter was she wouldn't be helpful in the kitchens in her state, either.

"Perhaps you would come with me to visit the Campbell family?"

"I shall carry the basket of supplies. And you'll not be holding any of the children and risk opening the wound again."

"Very well," she said because she didn't want such a thing to happen. "You will have to hold them for me."

He grunted, but his eyes told her he was not against such a thing.

***

Ronan knocked on the door to the small cottage and greeted the lad, who opened the door with a smile.

"Hello, Thomas," Brenna greeted the boy.

"Good day, mistress." He bowed to Brenna before bowing to Ronan. "My laird, please come in."

"Such good manners," he praised the boy as he entered, carrying Brenna's basket.

"What has happened to ye?" the younger boy asked while pointing to the sling that held his wife's arm to her chest.

"I was struck with an arrow."

Their mother, Sarah, gasped as she came forward.

"My lady, surely ye shouldn't be venturing out."

"I wanted to see how you were feeling."

Sarah frowned. "I am much improved and embarrassed for my behavior these last months."

Brenna put up her hand. "It is not uncommon. I'm glad you are feeling more yourself. And I still would have come to gaze upon this little one." Brenna smiled at Joey, who was awake and looking up at his mother.

Ronan watched his wife, seeing the happiness as she stroked the bairn's chubby cheeks. But as he looked closer, he saw something else. His wife wanted a babe. It shouldn't have come as a surprise. She was of childbearing age and spent time with infants and children in her role as a healer. It made sense for her to want to be a mother herself. Perhaps it was more of a surprise to find that he wasn't opposed to the idea. Ronan could see how his wife would take to the job with love and happiness.

After the last week of catching up for what they'd missed in the bed chamber, he realized Brenna could already be with child. His heart warmed over at the thought.

The baby began to fuss, and Ronan reached for the little one, hoping to help. Sarah handed over the hefty bundle to him, and Ronan smiled down at the babe, who seemed too shocked to cry as he'd intended.

Ronan spoke to him as he would to one of his men, unable to pitch his voice as his wife did when she talked to babes and small children. "You have a fine grip, lad. Soon, we'll have a practice sword in your hand, and you'll be training for the guard."

"I would like to be a warrior someday, too," Thomas said, not to be forgotten.

"Of course. I would be honored to have such strapping lads guarding my clan."

Mr. Campbell entered the cottage carrying water and greeted Ronan with a friendly smile. "You are a natural with a babe in your arms, my laird. Perhaps you'll have one of your own before long."

"Perhaps," Ronan said, turning to Brenna to gauge her reaction.

He would have thought she'd be happy about the possibility, but her smile faded before his eyes. Did she not want to have a child with him? They'd been going at each other like rabbits. Surely, she knew what could happen from such relentless activity.

The smile that came to her lips seemed forced.

Sarah and Mr. Campbell didn't take notice, but Ronan knew. Seeing her real smile made it easy for him to know the difference.

When they left the cottage to return to the castle, he took advantage of their walk.

"Is everything all right? Ye seemed sad."

She smiled at him again and shook her head.

"I'm sorry. I have suddenly run out of energy. I want to lie down for a while before the nooning."

"Of course," he said. It made sense that she could be tired. She'd only just been shot a few days ago. He knew well how long it took to recover from losing so much blood.

But as he accompanied his wife into the castle, he worried it wasn't only fatigue that had caused her reaction at the cottage. He wasn't sure what had upset her, but he would find out.

Chapter Twenty-Five

After a long nap, Brenna woke feeling more like herself and dressed to go down for the evening meal.

Ronan was already at the table speaking to his men. "Has the messenger returned from Innes?" he asked.

"Nay. Not as yet, my laird."

Perhaps they had already found Ewan and were preparing to transport him back to Strathspey. It would be lucky indeed if they had captured the fiend. It would be strange to go out anytime she wished without fearing the man.

They'd just finished speaking of the messenger when a lad entered the hall. He bowed before the high table, looking slightly nervous to have such an essential duty.

"I was sent for ye, my laird. Someone approaches the castle in a carriage."

A carriage... It could only mean a prisoner.

Brenna stood next to Ronan in the bailey as the carriage entered the courtyard and came to a stop. She recognized the Innes crest on the carriage's door. The Grant messenger was sitting atop the conveyance.

Her body tensed in preparation for seeing the man of her nightmares. This time, though, she had Ronan at her side. He would see that no danger came to her. The door was opened, and Brenna forced her gaze to remain on the occupant rather than skitter away in fear. But when a satin-slippered foot exited the carriage following a silk gown of gold and blue, Brenna's fear shifted to the possibility of a different threat. Her heart pounded, and she felt her palms go damp as the beauty came into view.

"My, little sister, you do look pale," Hannah said with her familiar frown of distaste. Then the other woman turned her gaze on Ronan. "My laird, it is so wonderful to see you well."

How did anyone make such a small word as "well" hold so much…heat?

Hannah's sparkling green eyes flared with interest as she sashayed closer to Ronan, and Brenna wished it had been Ewan.

"Whatever are you doing here?" It was only after she'd asked the question that Brenna realized it probably sounded impolite.

Hannah went on without an apparent offense.

"I was visiting Mother and Father at Innes House when the Grant messenger brought news of your mishap. Of course, I had to come immediately to assist."

A snicker escaped Brenna's lips as she pictured Hannah, rather than Countess MacIntosh, assisting someone injured or sick. Brenna stifled the laugh in a cough.

"And it is only right that I welcome the new laird home from war." Hannah's gaze worked up and down Brenna's husband, missing nothing.

Brenna stepped closer, worried Ronan's clothes might melt from his body from Hannah's thorough inspection. She recalled the last time she'd seen her sister. Five years ago, when Brenna and Ronan were married, Hannah tucked her arm into Ronan's as if he were hers.

She'd forgotten this feeling.

***

It seemed time had been kind to Hannah Innes, Lady MacIntosh. She was as beautiful as Ronan had remembered her being the day he'd married Brenna. Hannah's coy smile and sultry smirk had been alluring to Ronan when he first met her.

But now, he knew he had been blessed with a better sister. His Brenna wasn't only lovely in her way, but she was witty and brave. He didn't doubt Hannah would not have survived with Ewan all this time. And he knew without a doubt there would have been no chance of Hannah keeping her vows.

The vixen would have probably had a man in her bed before he'd made it to the Grant borders.

Brenna stepped to his side and slid her arm through his in the most territorial way. He felt his wife stiffen at Hannah's extended perusal. Of course, she had commented to undercut Brenna first. Hannah wasn't wrong. Brenna was still quite pale after her ordeal. But considering she'd been shot by an arrow just a few days ago, he was grateful for her presence next to him regardless of her pallor.

Things could have been so different. He could have lost her. The thought sent a shiver of fear up his spine. He looked down at the woman who had become so important to him quickly. He would do anything to protect her. Strike down any foe to ensure her safety.

Feeling the tension in his wife's grip at the presence of her sister, it would seem at the moment that his protection would not come from clashing swords or bruised knuckles. Instead, he would stand behind her as she stepped into battle and protect her luscious flanks.

"We've just finished our meal, but I shall have something brought out. You must be hungry after your travels."

"I would appreciate it, though remember I don't eat as much as you. I prefer to keep a trim figure."

"Of course," Brenna said, and Ronan feared for his wife's teeth. It was possible they'd be ground down to nothing before Hannah left Strathspey.

"You've come at an opportune time," Brenna went on. "I am to plan a wedding for one of my guards and his bride. You love planning such things. Perhaps you could assist me."

Hannah chuckled. "I might be able to offer some ideas, but such a meager match hardly seems worthy of such a grand affair. Could a guard and his bride be handfasted?"

How had Ronan ever thought this viper to be superior? He frowned at her response.

"Gabe is a Grant and dear to me and my wife. He has done much to keep Brenna safe while I was away fighting. He has my gratitude, and he is doing an honorable thing. For those reasons alone, he deserves a grand wedding feast."

"One could say he didn't guard her well if her injury is as serious as it seems."

"It was just an arrow," Brenna said, causing Hannah to gape.

"You were shot with an arrow?"

"Aye. But Ronan saved me."

"I had expected you to have challenges, but I'd not considered the Grants would dislike you so much as to shoot you."

Ronan wanted to defend his clan and Gabe's skills as a protector, but Ronan spotted the sticky web this woman had weaved around them. Any way he moved, he would be trapped.

"Well, to the hall to feed ye, *sister*," Ronan emphasized the last word before smiling. "You're looking rather thin."

***

Hannah was here in Brenna's home.

Brenna could hardly believe it as the woman chattered away about plans for a wedding far too elaborate for Gabe and Isabelle. But rather than say so, Brenna went along with it as if every wedding held at Strathspey was grand.

Hannah had not spared time to visit in all the years Ronan had been away, but here she was in all her glory while Brenna was...pale. It was an apt word that had described her since she was born. Brenna was always pale in comparison to Hannah's bold countenance.

"Come, sister, it grows late, and you must be tired. Let me see you to a room and bring your maid for you."

"We can have Jane see to it," Ronan said with worry creasing his brow. "You were shot recently. You should still be resting."

"Thank you for your concern, but it is nothing." Brenna brushed his worry aside despite being nearly exhausted—not just physically but emotionally. Having to be ready for verbal spears aimed at her heart grew tiring.

Ronan nodded, but the crease remained as Brenna and Hannah left for the stairs. He could likely see how weary she was.

"This way." She addressed Hannah and noticed the lustful look she spared for Ronan as they crossed the hall.

Hannah inspected every person and thing in the large room with her shrewd gaze. "A bit gloomy, but nothing some more colorful tapestries couldn't remedy," Hannah mentioned almost as if to herself.

"It is clean and filled with memories of previous lairds," Brenna defended the room. "Besides, it is full of light in the mornings. All halls are gloomy when the sun has gone down."

"And where is the lady's solar?" Hannah asked as they took the stairs.

Brenna had wanted nothing more than to dispatch her sister to a guest room for the night. But despite the late hour, she seemed expected to give a castle tour. If she'd known, she should have taken her husband's suggestion to have Jane see Hannah for the rest of the evening.

With a sigh, she showed Hannah to the solar. It was her favorite room in the castle. Or it had been until she and Ronan had made such good use of the laird's chamber. One wall was a window that let in the daylight, which one could use to read or sew. Or sit and look out at the hills, wishing a particular soldier would crest the outcropping of stone on his quest for home.

Clearing her throat, she turned back to Hannah, who was testing the fabric of the heavy drapes between her fingers with a frown. "I see you've not kept up on the latest fashions for yourself or your home."

"You know I've never been one for fashion sister. One gown is as good as any other. I feel the same about drapes."

"Do you still go about in men's clothing?" Hannah laughed, a perfect tinkling sound like she'd spent many hours practicing it.

"Shall we sit? I'll have wine brought up." She hurried to the door and asked a guard to fetch a maid to bring them the wine. If Brenna could keep Hannah's mouth filled with drink, she wouldn't have to answer her questions.

Hannah continued her inspection but sat across from Brenna when the wine arrived. Brenna fairly gulped her first glass while Hannah took delicate sips. It seemed the perfect example of their differences.

"I was sorry to hear of your earl, Hannah. It must be difficult being widowed so young." Brenna hadn't meant the comment as a sting, but Hannah's gaze narrowed as she set her glass down.

Hannah's husband had died from a fever two years ago. Brenna had sent a note of sympathy but had received no reply. Brenna assumed Hannah to have been overcome with grief as Brenna would have been if she'd received word of Ronan's demise in

France.

Hannah waved her hand dismissively. "My only regret is that I didn't beget an heir so that I might keep my place at Castle Wenlock. Instead, the earldom fell to a distant cousin. Though meager, he's seen fit to bestow an allowance."

Brenna guessed the allowance would have been enough for anyone other than Hannah, who always wanted more than what was offered.

"No matter. I won't need it much longer."

Before Brenna could inquire about that statement, Hannah pointed to the painting above the fireplace.

"Who is that? She is quite beautiful."

"The laird's mother, Deirdre MacPherson."

"Ah. I can see where Ronan gets his striking good looks."

"Yes." Brenna had never met the woman. She married the MacPherson laird shortly after Ronan's father died, so he'd grown up there with his stepbrothers and stepsister instead of here with Geordie.

What Brenna knew of her mother-in-law was only what the ladies in the kitchen had told her: Deirdre had never deigned to step inside or speak to them. Brenna thought Hannah and Deirdre were probably much alike. They cared only for themselves, so Brenna decided to get to the heart of the matter as they left the solar.

"Why are you here, sister?"

Hannah offered a feigned look of surprise but quickly gave up the ruse of shock that her intentions would be questioned.

"Very well, I had planned to come sooner

when I'd heard Ronan had returned, but I wanted to give him a moment to settle into his new role." Even the shrug of her shoulder was elegant.

"I'm to believe you came here simply to greet my husband on his return?"

Hannah stopped at the double doors of the laird's chambers in the corridor leading to the bedrooms. Her fingers traced the Grant coat of arms carved into the wood.

"I'm here to be his wife," she said as if it was expected. Perhaps it should have been. Had Hannah not been betrothed when Ronan and Geordie came to her father, she would have been married to him. Still, it was too late.

Brenna blinked and shook her head. "But *I* am his wife."

Hannah laughed, but it lacked the light, bell-like sound it had earlier. Somehow, it was darker and struck deeper into Brenna's soul.

"We all know how easy it is for the laird of a powerful clan to bend the church's rules. Why, he only need to declare me his wife, and it shall be so. Many do not even bother with the formality of an annulment."

The wedding plans seemed more precise now. She wasn't considering such extravagance for Gabe and Isabelle. She was planning for her ceremony and feast.

"But..." The only words that came to mind were the ones she'd already said. "I am his wife."

"We both know he would have wanted to wed me had I been available back then," Hannah said, her words conjuring up a memory she'd done her best to forget for all these years.

Ronan whispered to his grandfather that he'd instead marry Hannah. The disappointment at being told she was already betrothed. But that had been a long time ago, and they had… He had…

"I'm sure he planned to make the best of the situation with you. He seems to care for your health genuinely, almost as he would a sister."

"But we have lain together since his return."

"Of course, for the benefit of his people, he would want to show his virility. Did he tell you he'd been true to you while away, or was he honest? A man cannot go very long without the company of a woman. It confounds the mind and makes them go mad. And our dear Ronan does not seem addled in the least."

Brenna swallowed, feeling much like the child she'd been five years ago. She'd not known. She'd been told not to be angry, that he would have lain with other women. She'd foolishly thought it a choice he made, not a medical requirement. How silly she was. About everything.

Hannah must have seen the tears forming in Brenna's eyes, for she pulled Brenna into an embrace that tugged at her wound uncomfortably.

"Fear not, sister. You may return home to Innes House. You can return to your hunting and riding as you had before. You'll have the freedom to live out your life without the duties of a castle and wife. Oh, I wish for such freedoms as well, but alas, as eldest, Father has required me to fulfill my duties here."

Not only was she to leave Ronan, but she was also to return to her parents' home, where she'd never been a daughter they could be proud of.

She shook her head. "Nay. *This* is my home now."

Hannah pursed her perfect lips in a pitying look. "Of course, you are welcome to stay here. I only wished to spare you having to see me with him. You have feelings for him. How could you not feel a misplaced affection for a man who has offered you such kindness?"

Brenna wanted to argue, but her sister's words had a ring of truth. He had worried about her when she'd been shot, as any man would for someone who'd saved his life.

"Now, let's see you settled next door until arrangements can be made. I must make myself ready in the laird's chambers."

"We must ask Ronan what he wants." The words burst from Brenna's tongue.

Hannah's brows went up, and she settled her best smile on her pleasantly curved lips.

"You are quite brave, little sister. I think you'd want to avoid hearing him voice his selection. But let us both wait until he arrives so he can decide which of us he prefers." Hannah's gaze trailed unimpressed over Brenna, and she knew how she must look.

Pale, haggard, exhausted. Even at her best, she could not compete with Hannah's beauty. Brenna's stomach twisted at the thought of standing beside her sister while Ronan determined which of them he favored.

She'd worried Ronan would be taken from her in war all these years. She'd not been prepared for the most vicious battle of all.

Chapter Twenty-Six

It was late when Ronan returned to the castle. Soon after his wife had left with her sister, a messenger arrived with news of a woman who reported the laird of the Grants had slept in her cottage the night before.

The woman lived in a village to the north of the castle. And while Ronan knew he hadn't warmed this woman's bed, he needed to see if it had been Ewan. He was like an evil mist drifting about. But on meeting the woman and asking if the man she'd spent the night with looked like him, but with dark hair and blue eyes, she'd described the laird as a plump man, short in stature, and with little hair.

Not Ewan, and certainly not the laird of the Grants.

He passed Malcolm as he headed for the stairs. "Is my wife already settled for the night?" he asked the surly guard.

"Nay, she is waiting for you in your study.

She asked me to ensure you saw her immediately upon your return." With a frown, the man gestured toward the stairs.

"Has something happened?"

"We will know soon enough. Pray you choose correctly."

"Choose?"

"The lady awaits."

Perhaps Brenna was in pain? He knew she didn't care for the bitterness of the willow bark tea, but indeed, it was better than hurting. He entered the study expecting to have found her sleeping. He was pleased she'd wanted to wait for him, but it was late.

However, Brenna was awake and hurried toward him, closing the door behind him.

"Are you well?"

"I am…" She shook her head. "I'm not in any pain from my wound, but I am not well."

She began pacing, and Ronan reached out to take her hand. "What's amiss?"

"What's amiss is my sister did not come here to nurse my injury."

"That is good, as she is horrible at it."

"She didn't come to welcome you home, either."

Ronan was unsure why this upset Brenna so much, but he reassured her quickly. "I don't need her welcome. In truth, I hardly know her at all."

"She wishes to change that."

"What do you mean?"

"She is in your bed—our bed—waiting for you. She wants to be your wife."

"But you are my wife."

She smiled slightly. "That is what I said. But

she is sure you will want to change that."

Ronan worried his eyes might dislodge from his head. "And what do you think?"

She let out a breath and threw her hands up. "I think you want me. But then I also remember overhearing your conversation with your grandsire. You didn't wish to marry me but found my sister bonny. How Hannah was already betrothed, so you were stuck with me instead. And it makes me…"

"Doubt?" He frowned. "Bloody hell." He had forgotten he'd asked about Brenna's older, more beautiful sister. Or he'd thought her more beautiful at the time. Now, she was nothing compared to Brenna. "It seems fitting I be forced to feel what you must have felt when I didn't believe you. At least for a few moments, anyway. Long enough for me to assure you, *you* are my wife."

He swallowed. "Even if I wasn't smitten with you, Hannah reminds me of my mother." He shivered. "Not that they look alike, but their actions and the way they wield their beauty as a weapon to get their every desire. I don't want her," he said. That was the most important thing. "And I'm glad fate interceded, so I didn't end up with her."

She nodded. "Very well. I will remove her from our room so we can get ready for bed. I'm quite exhausted."

Ronan bowed. "I would happily toss her out if you wish it."

"I believe it's time I handle my sister myself." His wife brushed back her hair with one hand and stood tall as if preparing for battle.

***

Brenna's body hurt nearly everywhere as she

strode toward the room she usually shared with her husband. The wound in her shoulder throbbed. Her throat burned, and her eyes were scratchy with exhaustion. But she'd never felt better.

She felt foolish for believing her sister had any hold on Ronan, for even the short time she'd considered it. Brenna had allowed her sister to infiltrate her insecurities and weaken her from the inside out. It had been that way all her life. But no more.

After a quick conversation with Malcolm, Brenna tapped only twice on the double doors before entering. Her sister was naked and positioned in what Brenna assumed was a seductive pose on the bed.

"Oh, it is you? What do you want? Where is Ronan?"

"My husband is busy. I have sent to have your retainers awakened, and your carriage is being brought round. You'll want to get dressed, for my men will arrive in a few minutes to escort you to the bailey, clothed or not."

Hannah laughed. "What do you think you are doing?"

"I'm removing you from my home. You are no longer welcome here, and I want you to leave. This instant. Your days of controlling me with your venom are over, and I don't wish to see you any longer."

"Come, sister, you are angry, but you'll see this is for the best."

Brenna wanted to scream at her sister.

"You are a sickness, sister. Every word from your mouth is intended to penetrate and burrow under the skin where it festers and destroys. I am not angry,

Hannah. No more than I could be angry with a viper for doing what it is naturally intended to do. But as with you, I do not wish to keep a viper in my home a minute longer than I must. Get up. And get out."

"But what about the wedding? You asked me to help you." Brenna saw it as the ploy it was and shook her head.

"Out. Now!"

Seeing that her usual methods would not work in this situation, Hannah turned to another strategy. Her beautiful face pulled up in a pucker, and she sobbed tearlessly, wailing loud enough to bring her guards, causing Hannah to snatch up her robe.

"You'll want to load your trunks quickly, sister."

During the brief moment when Hannah dramatically sucked in another breath for her next round of bawling, Brenna interrupted.

"I shall pack your things." Brenna threw open the lid of the closest trunk and began tossing things in as quickly as she could grab them with her uninjured side. When all but a single gown remained, she turned toward Gabe. "If she is not dressed and leaving in the next ten minutes, you shall have my permission to carry her down to the bailey and put her in the carriage by any means necessary."

"Stop!" Hannah shouted, running to retrieve a gown Brenna had tossed in carelessly. Crying with abandon, Hannah moved on to her next technique.

"You are daft and touched with madness. It's no wonder our dear parents married you off to a murderer."

Brenna stood there looking at her sister. She thought she was truly seeing the other woman for what felt like the first time—not the poised beauty others saw when they looked at the eldest daughter of the Innes laird, but the desperate girl who was so unhappy with her life that her only relief was to wreak havoc so others would be as miserable as she. Letting out a startled breath, Brenna stepped closer and hugged her sister.

"I am so sorry your life is filled with such agony. I see it now when I look at you. Sadness nearly drips from you, unlike the tears you can't produce. There had been a time I'd envied you. I had tried to be more like you. Graceful and beautiful. But I can see past that now. I see the pain and desolation."

"Don't you dare pity me." Hannah ripped the dress from Brenna's fingers and tossed it in her trunk much in the same hapless way Brenna had. "You know nothing. *You* are in your working gowns with a husband who is not sound of body. I am grateful I was not burdened with a lame, ruined man. He is more suited for you."

In the past, Brenna may have felt each of her sister's hurtful words as a lash on her heart, but Hannah's power had faded to nothing. Hannah continued to ramble as they packed the rest of her things, clearly trying to get a rise from Brenna. She even resorted to telling Brenna she was not her full sister but a bastard born of their mother and her lover, a MacColl deserter who passed through Innes lands. Wasn't that the darkest accusation of children? To claim one's blood was tainted by the MacColl clan?

Brenna continued to pack—the woman had more things in the room than Brenna, who lived there—and while Hannah stomped about, Brenna remained calm and silent.

Hannah grew even angrier, disparaging every Grant who lived there. Her rage was good for one thing, at least: it served to hurry her along.

When her men returned to carry Hannah's trunks down to the carriage, she had a serving girl provide a basket of bread and cheese so Hannah could break her fast come morning. Hannah threw the basket back at her.

"I'd rather go hungry than eat the slop from this keep."

Ronan had come to stand next to Brenna. "She seems displeased with our hospitality."

"She is in a rant because she is so horribly unhappy with her life and wishes to lash out."

Ronan cocked a crooked smile at her. "Aye. I believe you are right."

"No! She is *not* right." Hannah came to stand before them. "What reason do *I* have to be unhappy? I can have any man I want."

Ronan tilted his head. "I believe we both know that isn't true."

Hannah shrieked and turned for the carriage, slipping in a bit of horse dung but catching herself before she fell. Muttering curses, she removed her fancy slipper and threw it at the gathering crowd. She hoisted herself into the carriage and reached for the retainer, who'd snickered.

Without so much as a wave from the window, the conveyance lurched into movement and passed through the raised gate.

"I'm proud of you, wife."

"I finally saw through the mask she wears."

He pulled her closer and whispered, "I'm sorry."

Those words, spoken with genuine sympathy, were for the loss of a sister Brenna never really had.

"I have set a few maids to change our room's bedding. Let us get some sleep for tomorrow, as there is much to do." They had a wedding to plan—a real one, Brenna hoped, that would lead to love and happiness for her guard.

With Hannah gone, Brenna breathed in and allowed the tension to fade away like a toxic mist suffocating her most of her life. She was ready to step out of the shadows.

Chapter Twenty-Seven

While Ronan had not enjoyed Hannah's visit or her cruelty, he had to admit the effects had been beneficial for his wife. Over the next few weeks, as she healed from the injuries caused by the arrow and planned a wedding for her dear friend, Ronan saw her heart and spirit mending from years of injuries inflicted by her sister's manipulations as well.

He still hated the role he played in Brenna's pain. He often found himself wishing he could return to the day they'd married so he could do things differently. He wished he could tell that fickle young man he'd been what was truly important in life. "I will always regret that you heard me ask my grandsire to marry your sister instead. I want you to know how pleased I am that my request was denied."

"I know," she said, and he heard the strength in her words. She believed him. Even better, she believed in herself. She was no longer a girl living in the shadows of her older sister but a woman who knew her worth.

He'd not realized how alluring such a thing could be. His heart quickened, and his body responded. He wished they could be alone in the forest, but they stayed within the castle walls these days to ensure Ewan couldn't cause more problems if he remained nearby.

Sitting in the hall for the noon meal was not the best time for his cock to grow hard for his wife. However, being a laird must have some benefits to offset all the responsibility, and he was about to take advantage of one such benefit when a messenger arrived.

Ronan smiled as he opened the missive from his brother, Shane, but he frowned while reading the words. The other laird was looking for Ronan's mother, who had fled the MacPherson clan with the contents of their coffers.

It made sense that Deirdre would have come to the Grants, but Ronan knew she wouldn't seek safety from Shane here. She knew where Ronan's loyalties lay. He would have seized the funds and returned them to Shane immediately.

"I'm afraid my mother is not here at Strathspey. I'll have a message ready to return to your laird shortly. Please have a meal."

The messenger bowed and hurried off to an open seat. He wished he could do something to help his brother and the MacPherson clan. While his coffers were full, they were not overflowing.

"What has brought such unhappiness to your face, husband?" Brenna asked.

"It seems my mother has emptied my brother's coffers and left the MacPherson clan in need only these few months before the weather turns."

"And you wish to help?"

"Aye. He's my brother. And the MacPhersons are as much my family as the Grants. I cannot allow them to starve. But I need to make sure I have enough for our people."

Brenna nodded. "We may not have extra, but we can adjust so there is enough to share."

Ronan looked at Brenna and wondered how he had ever believed Ewan's lies. She was nothing like his mother. Deirdre MacPherson would not have spared a single bauble to help another clan, yet Brenna wished to help, having never even met Shane and the rest of the MacPhersons.

"I will extend an offer of help if Shane needs it. He's stubborn. I know he won't accept unless there is no other way. But he won't allow his pride to cause his people harm. Let's see what we might do to help if it comes to that."

With the message to his brother written and handed over to the messenger, Ronan sat beside his wife once more.

"Don't worry, husband. Your family will be cared for," she said, seeming to know his thoughts and how to ease his worries. No one could be more perfect for him.

"I am grateful, wife, but I need to show you something in our chambers right now."

"But we are eating." Her cheeks grew pink, betraying her knowledge of what he had planned.

"Bring it with you." He stood, picking up their trenchers and strategically carrying them in front of himself as she followed him from the hall.

He heard a few snickers from the men but

couldn't care what they thought. Yes, he was mad about his wife and didn't worry much about who knew it. He'd waited for her to heal, and now that it was clear she was back to her usual self, he couldn't wait another minute to take her in his arms and show her how much he wanted her. In the room, he practically tossed their food to the small table near the window before turning to his wife and lifting her in his arms.

She laughed as he carried her to the bed and practically leaped on top of her, kissing the exposed skin of her breasts and tugging down her gown to reveal even more of that warm, creamy skin.

"I have missed you, husband."

He had missed her as well, but he'd needed to see her fully healed before seeing to their pleasure. Even when she'd assured him time and time again she was well enough for such things, he'd refrained so as not to cause her pain. But the stitches had been removed, and he'd seen for himself that the wound was no more than a pink scar. He kissed the mark, grateful that it had not been lower and took her from him.

"I will make it up to you, wife, and repay you for your patience."

"I'm not sure I will survive such a feat," she said with a laugh. "But I am willing to give it my best effort."

Ronan stroked a brown curl back from her face and kissed her slowly, silently promising all the ways he planned to pleasure her. It had not been five years, but as he removed each garment, he faced the same raging desire he'd felt the first time. "I can't ever seem to get enough of you," he told her.

She stared up into his eyes. "It is good then that we have all our lives to feast on each other."

And feast he did. He was focusing first on her lovely breasts and the rosy peaks that hardened under his attention. He placed kisses on her stomach and trailed his tongue over the juncture between her body and thigh that made her squirm. Finally, he settled between her legs, where he kissed her intimately.

She sat up, pulling herself out of his reach. "May I try that?"

At first, he didn't understand her request. Then, when he did, he thought he had to be wrong.

"You want to…?"

"The women in the kitchen spoke of it once, and I'm intrigued."

"Intrigued?" He laughed. "Far be it from me to keep your curiosity from being sated."

He allowed her to push him to his back as she mirrored his same movements, kissing his chest and moving lower. By the time her warm mouth touched him, he worried he'd spend at the sight, but he managed several good minutes of her exploration before he had to change positions again so he could slide into her.

Home.

He linked his fingers with hers as they moved together. Their gazes never shifted away from each other. Even when they reached their peak, they watched, sharing the most intimate moments. Experiencing their souls strengthened their bond.

And the love he saw in her eyes was exactly what he felt as they held each other in post-coital laziness.

He loved his wife.

He was easily as besotted as his father and stepfather had been over Ronan's mother.

Heaven help him.

***

For all the pleasure Brenna had shared with her husband, she'd never been so rattled as she was this time. She felt raw and exposed for sharing so much, but rather than being weary, she felt powerful.

Every touch and glance as they dressed seemed to sizzle between them.

Tonight, Gabe and Isabelle would marry in the hall in a modest ceremony. There were still some last-minute things to be done, but Brenna couldn't stop touching her husband, who seemed unable to let go of her.

With a growl, he opened the door and led her from their room. She expected the strange feeling to fade as they went about their day, but even as she spoke with Jane, she would catch her husband watching her, and they would share a private smile. Something had shifted. Perhaps it was the knowledge that he preferred her over even the most seductive temptress. But Brenna wasn't sure that was it. Or at least not all of it.

Isabelle arrived from the village, and Brenna led her to one of the chambers to help her get ready for the ceremony. Jane, Corinne, and Ada had also come.

"Are you nervous, Isabelle?"

The girl shrugged.

Brenna had encouraged her guard to get to know his bride so they wouldn't be complete strangers when they married, unlike she and Ronan.

"A kinder man you'll not find," Ada said.

"As his aunt, I'm sure you would not say otherwise," Corinne mentioned. "But as I am not related to him, I can attest that it is true."

Isabelle nodded with a small smile.

"I know of his kindness. The fact that I am preparing to wed him is proof of it. I wish… That is…" She rested her hand on her swollen belly, and Brenna thought she understood what the girl could not say.

"There is no sense to wish things were different. They are as they should be," Brenna said. She only realized how much she believed that after the words were out.

Wishing Ronan had never gone to France or that they'd had the chance to know each other better before they married was a useless waste of time. They were together now and happy. Nothing else mattered.

When the bride was ready, they helped her down the stairs.

Ronan was waiting for her with a charming grin on his face. He patted her hand and led her into the hall, where a sickly looking Gabe stood next to the priest. Malcolm stood on his other side, looking grim as usual.

"Did I look so wretched when we married?" he asked.

"I don't recall. I could barely meet your eye," she answered.

"I remember wondering why you agreed to marry me after you knew the truth. I can't tell you how pleased I am that you saw me as the best option."

They chuckled, but she looked up into his warm brown eyes and nodded.

"I now know it was the only option for me."

Gabe looked better once Isabelle entered the hall, and Brenna brushed a few tears away as the couple exchanged the familiar words binding them together for the rest of their lives. Brenna could only hope they would find the same happiness she and Ronan had.

Despite all the heartbreak that had come before, they were exactly where they belonged.

Brenna felt a chill of unease as everyone settled for the meal. Ewan was still out there, and until he was found, their happiness was at risk.

***

Ronan knew he was sleeping. He was even somewhat aware he was dreaming, and the soldiers he was striking down were not real, for surely, after this many, his arms would have grown heavy with fatigue.

His men lay among the dying, and he turned away, ready to fight the next threat.

He continued to raise his sword against French soldiers and raiding clans alike. Every enemy he'd ever faced came at him one after another until he was standing in a field of dead bodies across from Ewan.

It had been weeks since he'd seen the man. The bastard walked freely amongst his dreams. He looked down at his blade to see the gleaming steel had been replaced with a small wooden practice sword from his youth. One like those he and Ewan had sparred with as children.

"Do you plan to kill me, nephew?" Ewan asked.

Ronan opened his mouth to speak. To say yes because he had harmed Brenna, but no words came out. Instead, bubbles of air escaped.

He was in the lake.

He felt the joy of running into the cool water and splashing his uncle. The relief from the day's heat as the water penetrated his shirt caused the fabric to cling to his thin body—the chill of the mud oozing between his toes. Sheer happiness for a moment before everything changed, and he descended into darkness.

He fought to stand up but wasn't strong enough to escape his binds. The weight on his shoulders restraining him kept him from reaching the surface. He couldn't break free because the shadow was more powerful than him. He kicked at the weight and felt the pinch as the weight moved its grasp from his shoulders to clench his hair.

"Let me go!" Ronan screamed silently, for no breath was left in his lungs, and one couldn't scream underwater.

He continued to fight until his vision sparkled and faded. His limbs grew heavy, and he couldn't do anything but let go. Give up and float upward with the bubbles.

He lurched up in his bed, surprised he hadn't awoken Brenna. By now, she had grown used to his restlessness. He guessed it was just after dawn from the slant of the weak sunlight coming through the windows.

He waited until his breathing slowed as his mind struggled to decipher the dream's details and determine if it was a memory or a nightmare. It felt so real. Unsure, he left the bed and quietly found the clothes he'd tossed off hours ago. He found his boots and carried them downstairs. He'd barely tugged them into place before ordering the gate opened, and he was on the trail heading away from the castle, not even taking the time to saddle his horse and ride out.

He needed to see the place from his dream before the memories drifted away beyond his grasp. He chose the path that took him directly to the lake. His limp was more pronounced this morning, having not allowed his muscles to limber up. Despite the ache, he picked up his pace, suddenly in a hurry to find the truth, as if whatever he was looking for would still be there all these years later.

When he arrived at the lake, he was almost surprised to find it looked as serene as it had that day when he and Brenna had come upon it. The early morning sun glistened on water that would refresh later in the day. It would offer a brisk awakening if only he were brave enough to step in. Ronan found himself shucking the boots he'd just pulled on moments ago. He tossed off his belts, shirt, and kilt and stepped into the cool lake, pushing himself past his fear of the water.

He didn't run like he had in his memory. Instead, he took careful steps as he submerged in the dark water until he was near the center. From here, the water only came to his chest, slightly above his nipples. Gauging the depth, he realized he would have easily cleared the surface even at twelve. He'd been tall for his age and had only grown a few more inches to his current height. He'd only been two inches shorter than Ewan.

At the thought of his uncle, he recalled the look he'd given him that day when Ronan had launched himself into the pond, splashing him, laughing, and making a right nuisance of himself. Ewan had been angry and grabbed him. And then, just as he'd known all this time, his uncle—the man he'd loved as a brother—held him under the water until he'd stopped fighting. Until he'd stopped moving.

Until he'd stopped breathing.

Ewan had saved his life that day, but only after he'd nearly killed him first.

As if he'd conjured the man, Ronan looked up to see Ewan standing on the bank near the pile of Ronan's clothing and his weapons.

"You look like you've seen a ghost," Ewan taunted.

"What I've seen is the *truth*. By having the courage to step into the lake, the water has washed the lies from my eyes."

Ewan tilted his head. "What do you mean?"

"I remember what happened in this lake all those years ago."

"I pulled you from the water and saved your life. Everyone knows the story," Ewan said.

"Everyone knows the story you told them, but they don't know the truth, that my life wouldn't have been in peril had you not held me down. Had you not caused me to drown in the first place, I would have not needed rescuing."

"Your memory does you a disservice, nephew."

"You were willing to take my life back then, and again when you attempted to poison me, and when you shot my wife in error. Perhaps you'd like to come in and try to drown me now."

Ronan had height and muscle on his side this time. No longer a lanky lad, Ewan would be quickly bested. Which the man knew as well. His answer was a low chuckle. "No. It will not do. For if it is known that I killed you, I would be imprisoned or worse for such a crime against the laird. But if your wife were to do it…"

Ronan was the one to laugh this time. "Not one person in the keep would believe my wife killed me even if she was found standing over my lifeless body with a knife. You will never rule this clan."

Ewan's face betrayed his anger before the smug smile returned. "We shall see. I'm a patient man, nephew." Ewan slipped away into the trees, much as he had in Ronan's dream.

Chapter Twenty-Eight

Brenna woke alone. It wasn't uncommon to find Ronan sitting by the window if he'd suffered a terror and couldn't get back to sleep. But looking across the room, she didn't see him there, either.

She washed and dressed quickly, wanting to see him and put off her unease. Downstairs, she didn't find him in the hall, and her heat began to pound in earnest now. She was about to turn for the stables to set out looking for him when he stepped inside the hall. She nearly collapsed from the relief of seeing him whole and hearty. But as she stepped closer, she saw all was not well.

"What has happened? Your skin is chilled, and your hair is wet. Were you swimming?" Everyone knew Ronan didn't swim for fear of drowning. He bathed in the shallow stream behind the castle.

"Aye. My dreams revealed the truth, and

while I doubt I'll never be one for swimming, I realized my drowning was not without help from Ewan."

Brenna gasped. "He tried to...?"

"Aye. All this time I thought he'd saved my life." Ronan shook his head.

"He's a monster."

"I saw him today, by the lake." This was said so low she thought she'd misheard.

"He is still nearby? He's not gone from here as we had hoped." She clenched her fingers into tight fists, wishing she could face the devil that moment to put an end to this.

"He made it clear he still plans to take over the clan."

Brenna glared toward the gate, wanting to go hunt Ewan down herself. He might be larger, but she was so full of rage that she was sure she could best him.

She was distracted from her anger by a messenger she recognized as being from Cluny Castle. The message was most likely from Ronan's MacPherson brother. "Have they found your mother?"

Ronan shook his head and let out a breath. "No, my mother's destruction continues across the Highlands, it would seem. She married the MacColl laird of all people and escaped from him with all of his funds."

"Oh my. Why ever does she need so much coin?"

Ronan's gaze flickered over her, and she suddenly felt embarrassed in her common wool gown without the smallest amount of frippery. She'd not really cared how plain her gowns were until then. They but served a purpose. She didn't need anything fancy.

"I know that look, wife, and you have nothing to worry about. I'm aroused by you, not your clothes, as evident by how hard you make me while wearing men's trews."

She laughed and felt more at ease as he explained.

"Some women must purchase the charms they lack and will pay a high price for such things to distract men. While others, such as yourself, come by them naturally." He made a point to leer at her until her cheeks turned pink. "Lovely."

Suddenly, she was irritated with her gown for a different reason because it was in the way.

"Now you've gone and done it," Ronan said.

"Done what?"

"You've licked your bottom lip in that way that means you wish we were alone."

How could he have known that from such a simple gesture? Not that she cared as he bent to brush his lips over the shell of her ear.

"Come, there must be something you wish to show me in our chambers."

Brenna thought they'd need a better excuse, but not right now. She turned and followed him to their room.

***

The next day, Brenna spent much of the day with Jane and the other women taking stock of their larders and estimating their expected harvest. She knocked on the door to the study before entering to find Ronan looking over the ledgers. She placed a piece of parchment down before him. "This is what we can spare from the kitchens."

He rubbed his temple and offered her a smile. "Thank you. Ye are as giving as you are lovely."

"They are your family. I like to think you're more like the MacPhersons than the Grants."

"I hope I am not like my uncle."

She came to sit on his uninjured leg and kissed his lips. She placed her forehead against his so grateful he was the man he was.

"You are nothing like Ewan. If you were, I would have let that arrow find you."

Ronan laughed at her jest as he leaned in and placed a kiss on the scar at her collarbone.

"Does it still pain you?" he asked.

"No. It makes me angry that he is still on our lands, making his threats and keeping us from enjoying a walk or a hunt." She felt like a prisoner being forced to live behind the castle walls. She was grateful the truth was known, but with Ewan still out there, the danger was too great. It surprised her when Ronan sat back and looked her in the eyes.

"Tomorrow, we go out early to hunt and enjoy a lovely walk."

"With plenty of guards," she added.

"Aye. With plenty of guards. We will not cower away inside the keep."

"Do you hope to lure him out in the open?"

He laughed again. "You are too wise, wife."

"I only considered it because it is what I would do in your position."

The following morning promised a beautiful day. She and Ronan dressed quickly, her in her trews and he in his kilt. With a dozen warriors to offer protection, they were ready to ride out when Angus came into the bailey complaining of someone taking one of his cows.

"I think if Ewan knew how often he would need to deal with Angus' complaints, we'd not need protection for he'd realize how much work this job is and would run fast and far from it."

She smiled at his joke, though it wasn't funny. The truth of it was Ewan only wanted the power the job offered. He would have no intention of seeing to clan affairs or the responsibilities that came with being laird. "I'll stay with you."

"Nay. It is a beautiful morning. I'll not have you miss it. My men will watch over you, and I'll join you as soon as I'm done with him."

"Are you sure?"

"Yes. I want to give you a head start so I have an excuse as to why you got more rabbits than me."

She laughed as he kissed her right on the lips in front of everyone gathered in the bailey.

"Come, Angus, you're keeping me from frolicking in the forest with my wife." He waved as he ushered the old man into the hall.

She rode with the men through the gate and then announced her desire to stop at the kirkyard before hunting. One of the men held onto her horse, the others spread out searching for possible dangers, while Malcolm and Gabe stayed close to her as she gathered heather.

With her proper bundles, she meandered to the kirkyard and stopped before the newest grave that had not yet grown over with grass.

"I miss ye, Geordie. You would be pleased to know Angus is pestering Ronan about his cattle as he did you. Ronan is a fine laird. If only we could deal with Ewan, I think we could find happiness."

She placed her second bunch of heather on the small, blank stone next to Geordie's. As was common, tears pricked at her eyes, and her throat grew tight to see the stone with no name. She may have asked Ronan about his wishes, but they had yet to discuss the matter, and she hadn't the courage to bring it up as yet.

She placed a kiss to her fingers and pressed them to the cool stone.

"I'm sorry. I love ye, Marcas."

She hadn't realized Ronan had joined her until he spoke. She jumped from the surprise as much as his anger.

"Who the bloody hell is this Marcus ye love? And why did ye plant the bastard between my grandsire and my father in our clan's kirkyard?" He scowled down at the stone.

Anger surged over her in a wave so fierce she imagined her eyes must be throwing sparks as she clenched her fist, ready to strike him. Instead, she opened her mouth and let him have it.

"He was not a bastard!" she screamed. "He had a father! Though I'm sure you didn't want to be his father any more than you'd wanted to be my husband. But it didn't matter what you wanted. He was your son, you bloody arse!"

She gave his chest a right shove, not that he moved, but it made her feel slightly better to cause him some small discomfort for the pain he had just caused her.

He didn't budge or say anything. He stared at her with his mouth hanging slightly open. She probably should have stood down, but she was caught up in her anger and continued her rant. She was a mother warrior protecting her child or at least the memory of her child.

"Whatever you want to say about me and my failures, go ahead. But you will not say anything about Marcas. He was an innocent baby."

"My son?" Ronan managed to say. "This grave is for my son?"

Her brows pulled together, her chest still heaving with her anger, but she calmed slightly. "Aye."

"I had no idea. I didn't know." He looked at her in confusion, but it was she that was confused. How could he not know?

"Did you not get my letters?"

He swallowed and looked away, guilt clear on his face.

She drew a shaky breath and put an unsteady hand to her chest. She had read the truth in his eyes. Her shoulders fell in defeat. She worried she wouldn't have the strength to stand. She must have swayed, for he put his hand out to steady her, but she slapped it away.

"I fretted over every line and curve, hoping you wouldn't find my writing lacking." She tossed a hand. "When I had to write to tell you I'd lost the babe, it was nearly as difficult as the birth, but you needed to know." Her voice grew quieter, no longer able to muster the energy to yell. "You hated me so much you didn't even read my letters. When I thought I was alone in this pain, I truly was."

With that, she retrieved her horse and rode back to the castle without him.

HIS FORGOTTEN HIGHLAND BRIDE

Chapter Twenty-Nine

Ronan opened his mouth to speak, to maybe call out to his wife as she rode away from him, but he couldn't manage any words to defend himself. He was shaken to his core with shock, grief, and guilt. Even if he'd somehow found the words to speak, his wife had left him standing there alone in front of their son's grave.

The guilt he'd felt at receiving Brenna's letters was nothing compared to the weight he felt now. He'd kept her letters in his pack unread. He always worried they'd contain words that would make him long to come home. At the time, he didn't think he could bear it, for he had also wanted to come home.

But this. This was so much worse than he'd ever considered.

He turned to see her riding away. He wanted to go after her, to beg for her forgiveness, but he didn't know how to begin. Instead, he fell to his knees before his son's grave and wept for the child he never knew. He wasn't sure how long he'd sat there staring at the blank stone before Hugh came up next to him.

"I didn't know," he told his friend.

"You didn't get her letters?"

He looked up at the sky wishing he'd opened the bloody letters. Had he known, nothing would have stopped him from returning home to her. "I didn't read them."

Hugh didn't need to say anything. His silence spoke louder than any words he might have said in judgment.

"I was a fool."

"About so many things," Hugh added.

All Ronan could do was nod in agreement.

"What happened?" Ronan asked, grateful this man could provide the details he needed.

"Moira isn't certain. Everything was going along fine. Brenna only had a few months left to go. One night the entire castle was roused by her screaming. I wasn't in the room—it isn't a place for a man—but I was outside in the hall, and I will never forget the sounds of her…" He shook his head. "It haunts me still all these years later. She was clearly in a great deal of pain with the birth, and it was too soon for the babe to come. She told me months later that he'd breathed a few times as she held him, but then he was gone. And so was she for a long time after. She was there, but not."

"Alone."

"Aye. Even surrounded by all of us. Of course, Ewan used it to taunt her. He told her how disappointed you would be that she'd lost the babe. As if the lass didn't blame herself enough already."

"Just now, as I stepped up, she'd apologized. She thinks she's responsible." Ronan wanted to find Ewan and break his neck with his bare hands. But doing so wouldn't do anything to alleviate his true anger with himself.

"She was so afraid to write to you and tell you what happened because Ewan had convinced her you would want to cast her away. Geordie and the rest of us told her the opposite, but we all know the bad things are easiest for us to believe, especially when we already think them true ourselves."

And after she'd worked up the courage to write him, in the midst of her own grief, he'd not had the decency to read her letters for fear she would make him feel guilty for leaving her? As if that amount of guilt was anything in comparison to what he was feeling now. Every bit of it earned because he'd left his wife without so much as a word and not been there when she'd needed him most.

"I don't even know how to begin to make this right," he whispered more to himself as he looked down at the blank stone. "Why is it blank?" he asked the warrior.

Hugh shook his head. "I canna say. She called the babe Marcas for it was your father's middle name, but she never had the stone etched. It seemed she was waiting."

He clasped the man on the shoulder. "Thank ye, for watching over her." It was true enough the men that guarded her served her better than Ronan ever had. He was ashamed of how selfish he'd been.

Ronan rode back to the keep and handed Brimstone over to a lad to see to him. Ronan normally cared for his horse, but today he had other things to do.

Pushing his leg harder than he should, he rushed upstairs; passing his chamber, he continued to the chamber he'd first shared with Brenna when he'd arrived home. Going to the trunk at the foot of the bed, he opened it and searched until he found his knapsack.

The four letters from Brenna were neatly stacked in the bottom. He'd kept them in order, so opening the first one was easy.

Dearest husband,

I hope this letter finds you safe and healthy. As you can see, I've learned to write, as well as read. Your grandsire has been so kind with his impatient pupil.

I have some other wonderful news to share. I am with child. To be sure we know when the babe was conceived, so it's easy enough to know the bairn will arrive near the end of February.

I understand you did not wish to wed me, but I hope you are pleased to become a father. Geordie said you would be excited as he is by the news.

Please be safe. I look forward to seeing you soon.

Your wife,
Brenna Grant

The guilt he'd expected filled his chest as he took in the bold slash across the "T" at the end of her name. He felt the happiness in those lines on the page. The hope in each word. He read through the other two letters where she'd shared castle news as well as how the babe was moving and the clothes she and the ladies had started making in preparation. It was clear she was excited.

She'd asked him what he wished to name the child and suggested Marcas in honor of his father. Ronan ached knowing that she'd waited for an answer that never came.

The last letter was sent just before Christmastide. He noticed the blurry marks where the ink had smudged, as if it had been written outside in the rain. It didn't take him long to realize the drops hadn't been made by weather, but by his wife's tears.

Dear Ronan,

I've lost the babe. He was a beautiful, strong boy who held on to life for a few breaths despite his early arrival.

Geordie and Moira insist it's not my fault, that these things happen, but I should have been stronger. I should have fought harder against my body when it betrayed me and pushed our son out into the world before he was able to survive.

He was buried yesterday, and it feels as if my heart was placed in the ground with him.

I will await your confirmation before I have the name carved into the stone, in case you do not approve of the name I suggested.

I'm so sorry. Please forgive me.

His tears dripped onto the paper, some overlapping hers from years ago. She hadn't signed her name, and he crumbled to the floor from the emptiness she must have felt back then. The stone he'd seen between his father and grandfather still remained blank. Still awaiting his approval. God, how selfish he'd been. He hadn't even been able to give her that one simple thing.

He needed to remedy this wrong immediately. He left the castle and hurried to the village until he found the stonemason, practically dragging the man and his tools off to the kirkyard. He watched as the man carved the name of his child into the stone.

Marcus James Innes Grant

James was Ronan's own middle name, and he wanted the boy to have it, as well.

When the stone mason left him, he sat in the grass until the sun dipped in the western sky, telling his son all the things he wanted him to know. But especially how sorry he was that he wasn't there when Marcus came into the world and left it too soon.

It was late when he walked back to the castle. Rudy, one of his older guards, was waiting to speak to him. The man had just gotten word from his daughter who'd married a MacKenzie that Deirdre was there and planned to marry the MacKenzie laird.

He could hardly believe how quickly his mother moved around the Highlands. She'd been the wife of the MacPherson laird for many years before he left her widowed several months ago. Then he'd gotten word she'd married the MacColl laird only to run off with the contents of his coffers. He was struck down by the MacPhersons, leaving Deirdre a widow yet again.

And now she planned to marry the MacKenzie laird, no doubt planning to rob him and leave him soon enough. Shane was looking for Deirdre, and now Ronan knew where she was.

Well, Ronan would gladly help his brother recover his coin and stop Deirdre from victimizing another clan. He would stop her, not just because he despised what his mother was doing, but because it would give him a wanted distraction from facing his own wife, at least for a short time.

Ronan knew a few days wouldn't resolve anything. He'd not be able to find the words of apology to offer his wife, for no mere words could impart how sick he was with regret over what he'd done. He could give her a few days to not have to look at him.

With that thought, he gathered a few men, and after telling Malcolm and Gabe where he was going and asking them to watch over his wife, he rode out just an hour before dark. They wouldn't get far that evening, but at least he would be gone.

***

Brenna spent most of the day sitting by the window in the solar, looking out over the fields and the crofters tending them. How many hours had she spent sitting by the window in the other chamber? At least she couldn't see the kirk from this room.

Was Ronan still standing there? She couldn't bring herself to care at the moment.

She'd already cried for her baby until she'd had no tears left, but they collected in her eyes now and leaked down her cheeks. She grieved for her child, but thankfully he was in the loving arms of his grandparents, safe from his father's disinterest.

Her tears today marked her loss of a husband she'd never had. She'd been a fool over him from the first day she saw him as she'd slid down from her mount in her father's courtyard. She'd known before they were wed that he didn't want her, but she'd thought she could change his mind. That if only he'd give her a chance, she might win his love, but that was never going to happen. He hadn't cared enough about her to even read her letters. She'd poured her heart out to him, and it had been all for naught.

Another sob escaped, and she knew she needed to leave this room. She made her way to the kitchens. Once inside, she crumbled from the weight of her sorrow. But her friends gathered to help ease her pain. She remained while the late meal was served. She may have been hiding from her husband, but she wasn't ready to face him. She was angry, desolate, and ashamed in equal measure.

"You have a right to be sad and even more so to be angry, but you'll not think yourself responsible for what happened," Corrine said. "These things happen. There was nothing you could have done differently. It just was."

"I canna believe he wouldn't have read your letters. I can't wait a second to open a missive on the rare occasion I get one from my lad. How did he not go mad from not knowing what they said?" Ada shook her head.

"I expect he thought I had written to chastise him for leaving the way he did."

"As you had the right to do. It was shameful the way he slunk out of the keep under cover of darkness like a thief in the night." Jane scowled.

These women were always quick to defend her, and in the past, she had appreciated it greatly. But now, knowing Ronan better and knowing how he regretted leaving and staying away so long, she felt the need to defend him.

And defending him forced her to see things through his eyes.

"I think he wanted to come home, and had he read my letters filled with all the tales of the castle, it might have made him want to come home all the more. And he couldn't leave. It would have been torture." Regardless of why he hadn't read her letters, it meant he was just today finding out he'd had a son that was lost.

What sadness must he be dealing with?

"Excuse me," she said and left the kitchen just as Malcolm was coming toward her from the hall.

"Mistress," he said with a bow.

"Good evening, Malcolm. Do you know where my husband is?"

He pressed his lips together and gave a nod.

"Aye. He has left for the MacKenzie stronghold. He received a letter that his mother is reported to be there. He asked me to watch over you."

She pressed a hand to her chest from the surprise.

"He left?"

"Aye."

She nodded. He'd left her alone yet again.

Chapter Thirty

The next morning, Malcolm and Gabe were waiting for her when she left her chamber.

"Are you ready for your ride today, mistress?" Gabe asked, barely restraining the excitement in his voice.

They thought of escorting her to the kirkyard, as had been her habit, after all that occurred yesterday? "I don't think I can bear it," she said, her voice sounding as tired as she felt. She hadn't slept the night before as she considered what might come of her relationship with her husband.

She loved him. She knew it. And she thought she knew his feelings as well. But then he'd left her.

"Ach, but ye must," Malcolm said. "That is, you should not want to miss the beautiful summer day."

"Very well. We shall go for a ride." She looked down at her brown work dress, not caring enough to go change into proper riding attire. Or rather appropriate for her.

In the bailey, she found her horse already waiting for her. It wasn't until they were through the gate she felt the fine mist on her face and looked up to see it wasn't a lovely summer day at all. The gray skies promised more than just the light sprinkling it offered now.

She wasn't sure what her guards were up to, but she allowed them to guide her across the field toward the kirk. When they stopped and dismounted, she remained seated. She'd rather nudge Merlin into a full run away from this place that was filled with sorrow and pain. "I'm sorry. I don't think I can do this today."

"You must see something. Please."

Curiosity got the better of her, and she slid down from her tall horse and followed the two men toward the kirk. Either they were walking faster than usual or she was lagging, but they were waiting next to her son's stone as she came closer.

Gabe pointed down, and she took a few more steps so she could see what he was showing her.

She gasped at the small stone nestled next to Geordie's larger one. It had been blank. Waiting for Ronan to approve the name she'd picked for their child. A permanent reminder that he had not written back. All this time she'd thought he'd been too angry or disappointed in her to write back.

But that wasn't the case. He hadn't known. She knelt down at the marker and traced her fingers over the recently engraved letters.

Marcas James Innes Grant.

A small bundle of violets lay atop the grave. Brenna always brought heather, so she knew this had been placed there by Ronan.

"He did this," she said, quietly, already knowing the answer. "He does care."

"He does. We saw with our own eyes."

"Why did he not show me?" Her earlier anger flared to life once more.

***

Ronan, Will, and Hugh hurried along to meet up with Shane. It would still take days to get to the MacKenzies' castle where Ronan's mother was hiding.

He wasn't sure what to do when he met with her. She was the cause of so much heartache. She'd been the reason he'd not been able to trust a woman. After witnessing her deceit, Ronan expected all women to be out for their own gains.

But Brenna was different. She'd proved to be a faithful partner, even after the pain he'd caused. And every step his horse took in the opposite direction, he felt he'd done the wrong thing to leave as he had. That night as he settled onto his furs to sleep, he had so many more memories of her than he'd had in France. He could easily remember her smile and the sound of her laughter. Her quick wit, and eagerness to join with him in the most inconvenient of places.

Ronan slept restlessly. His usual dreams of the war had been bad enough, but now as he battled his demons, he was faced with Brenna's tear-streaked face, holding their silent child. He woke up screaming.

"Christ Almighty," Will said. "Ye said you made it out of the war, but I don't think that's true. I think it just follows you wherever you go."

"You have the right of it, but I wasn't troubled by the war this time. I'm thinking of Brenna and the babe. The pain..."

"Hugh said he told ye what happened," Will said, looking at the man across the fire who could apparently sleep through anything. Even Ronan's screaming and carrying on.

"Aye. I should have been there for her. I should have done so many things differently. So much time has been wasted."

"Then perhaps you should not waste anymore."

"What do you mean?"

"I mean, this journey to the MacKenzies' to stop your mother. Hugh and I and the two other guards can see to it. It seems you took advantage of the distraction to leave rather than face your wife."

"I want to call you out for saying such a thing, but I can't because I think it may be true."

Will chuckled and looked up at the stars. "She deserves to be loved."

"By a better man than me."

"Mayhap you could be that better man."

"Aye. I will do everything in my power to make sure she never has reason to be alone again."

"Starting in the morning."

Ronan laughed. "Aye. In the morning, I shall leave you to return home so I might tell my wife how much I love her so I might offer comfort as I should have years before and so I might beg her mercy for all the wrongs I've done to her."

"And she will forgive ye. It's not her nature to carry a grudge, even if she has the right to do so."

"I am glad I have ye for that."

In the silence of the night, he and Will talked about the things that haunted him.

They must have fallen asleep at some point because Ronan woke to see the other men still sleeping while their men were going about hunting to break their fast.

Ronan thought it might have been the first bit of sleep he'd had that hadn't been filled with terrors from the war. Though he hadn't slept peacefully. He still dreamed of Brenna and the babe.

He wished he hadn't left her without speaking to her. It mirrored his actions from the past. He packed up his things quickly, for the first time feeling like he was doing the right thing going home to Brenna so he might make things right. However, that might come about.

He wouldn't give up until she knew the truth—that he loved her.

Chapter Thirty-One

With Ronan away, Brenna was in charge of the clan once more. It meant she couldn't sneak away that morning as she usually did to hunt and ride. Instead, she was pulled away to deal with a squabble between two older men who should have known better.

Her patience was in short supply when the guard on the gate called out, "Rider!"

Brenna's heart gave a kick at the announcement. Had Ronan returned so soon? And if so, how would she address him? "What flag do they fly?"

The guard shook his head. "No flag, my lady. It looks to be a lone woman."

"Let her in," Brenna said, keeping her disappointment reined in. The fact that she was disappointed spoke of how much she had wished it was Ronan.

Brenna awaited the lone rider, curious to who

it could be. Hannah would never set a horse, let alone ride any long distance without a proper carriage. When the woman entered, Brenna was momentarily baffled, for she recognized the woman, though they'd never met. It was amazing Brenna had made the connection at all given how different Ronan's mother looked now compared to the painting hanging in the solar.

Deirdre was pale and ragged looking. Her perfectly coifed gold hair from the painting hung in lank clumps down her back. At Brenna's nod, Malcolm left her side to go assist the woman down from her horse before she fell. But instead of standing, the woman crumbled. Gabe hurried to assist Malcolm in gathering the woman up.

As Brenna stepped forward to offer a greeting, she noticed the dark cloak the woman wore was shiny with moisture at the shoulder. She pulled the garment away to see the vast amount of blood.

"Hurry, bring her inside and fetch Moira straight away." Brenna gave her orders, which her men followed without question.

"Who are you?" the woman asked.

Brenna realized that while she recognized the woman, Deirdre wouldn't know her. "I am Lady Grant. You may call me Brenna."

"You are married to Ronan?"

"Aye."

"Then it seems you may call me *Mother*."

Brenna should have known Ronan wouldn't have informed his mother of his marriage. Not five years ago when they'd first been wed, and not more recently, either, it seemed. What Brenna didn't know was if it was because Ronan didn't want to share the information that he was married or because he hadn't spoken to his mother in all that time.

From what Ronan had said about Deirdre, Brenna thought it could be the latter. Malcolm had told her Ronan rode for the MacKenzies to find his mother. But if she was here, where was Ronan?

Deciding there'd be plenty of time later for questions so long as the woman survived the day, she set to care for the woman's injuries first.

"If it's all the same, I shall call ye Deirdre for now. Please lie back so I can see to your wound."

Deirdre looked like she might object but instead did as Brenna ordered.

"Do not give me a dram that will put me out. I prefer to be awake."

"Very well." Brenna doubted she would wish to be awake when the wound was stitched or sealed, but that was an argument for later. First, Brenna had to examine the wound to determine the care needed.

Moira entered through the far door, and as she came closer, she sniffed.

"I was called to come help you heal someone, but ye must know I don't tend to serpents or the devil."

"Hello, Moira. I thought I'd looked on you my last. I'm sorry to say I was wrong about that." Deirdre's words were said through a tightly clamped jaw as she panted in clear pain, but still she held a certain level of authority and dignity.

Brenna might have been impressed if she hadn't already been annoyed by the posturing. She couldn't help but roll her eyes at the women.

"Perhaps we could put aside our pettiness until after the woman has stopped bleeding all over my hall like a stuck boar."

Deirdre seemed to take offense to being likened to a pig, but she kept her mouth shut and offered only a tight nod.

"What kind of wound is it?" Moira asked while still keeping her distance.

"I believe it was a dagger?" Brenna guessed and looked at Deirdre for confirmation.

"Aye. A dagger. I was…attacked while trying to escape the MacKenzie laird. He'd captured me and meant to force me into a marriage. I barely escaped my fate."

"It sounds as if it was the MacKenzie laird who escaped being shackled to a witch like you," Moira muttered loud enough to be heard by everyone.

Brenna gasped in surprise. She'd never heard Moira speak so. But then Ronan hadn't spared flowery words for his mother, either.

Deirdre reminded Brenna much of Hannah and, as such, Brenna was reluctant to believe the woman except for the fact she'd taken a dagger to the shoulder. And only after she'd inspected the wound and saw for a fact it was from a dagger.

Who stabbed her, or for what reason, was yet to be determined.

They worked on the woman for over an hour. Moira was happy to tend to the stitching after she learned Deirdre didn't wish to be knocked out with a dram.

Brenna watched briefly to ensure the woman wasn't making it intentionally more painful. She felt Deirdre's gaze on her and did her best not to cringe under the woman's thorough inspection.

"What is it?" Brenna asked when the woman

continued to stare at her.

"I would have expected Ronan would have had his pick of any laird's daughter in the Highlands. I expected he would have chosen someone more…" She let the sentence hang there as if Brenna couldn't understand her meaning. Then she cursed Moira to the devil for a particular sharp needle poke.

Brenna silently thanked Moira for taking up for her even if it wasn't the kindly thing to do.

"If ye must know, Ronan didn't choose me. Geordie did. An alliance was needed because Ewan had accidently killed one of my clansmen." Though for years now she'd wondered if it had been an accident at all. Ewan was more than capable of cold-blooded murder.

"That makes a good deal more sen— Christ, Moira! I don't need a stitch down to my liver, and don't think I don't know ye did that on purpose, you spiteful shrew."

Moira chuckled and winked at Brenna.

"Lady Brenna is a better wife than Ronan deserves, I can tell you that."

"I'm sure that isn't so," Brenna said in Ronan's defense.

Deirdre chuckled, the sound coming off sinister.

"Ah, lass, you've gone and fell in love with him, haven't you? I can see it in your eyes."

Brenna shifted under the woman's scrutiny and didn't attempt to lie, though she didn't confirm Deirdre's accusation, either.

"You lose all your power when you fall in love, lass. The moment they know you won't leave them is the moment they realize they can do whatever they want and you'll stand for it."

Brenna couldn't argue. So far, Ronan had done what he wanted and she was still there at the keep, waiting and hoping for his return. She'd felt most powerful after loving Ronan with all her heart. So perhaps the woman was wrong, and true power was only found when one gave themselves up to another person, trusting that it was safe to do so without question.

Suddenly, she felt it again as she considered her situation. Ronan had left but made it clear to Malcolm to tell her why and where he'd gone. And that he would return soon. They may have serious and painful things to discuss when he returned, but she knew he would return, and they would face it together, because he cared for her.

She laughed at the joy in knowing her place as his wife was secure even when things were strained between them. Surely, there was nothing so powerful as that knowledge. Deirdre was staring at her as if she thought Brenna daft. Perhaps she was, but Brenna simply smiled at the woman.

"I do love Ronan, but there is nothing so powerful as that."

Moira winked at her, and when Deirdre opened her mouth to no doubt say something scathing, Moira set the needle again, and Deirdre shouted another curse.

Despite Deirdre's desire to stay awake, she quickly succumbed to the pain and lapsed into unconsciousness for the duration of the stitching. Brenna thought it was probably for the best.

"What do you intend to do with her now?" Moira asked when they were washing up from the procedure.

"Ronan went to the MacKenzies' to intercept her. If he hasn't seen her, it wouldn't do to let her leave," Brenna reasoned. "But I can't very well throw her in the dungeon."

"Why not?" Moira asked as if the idea was not to be cast away too quickly.

But Brenna wouldn't treat her mother as a common criminal even if it was deserved, for the same reason she hadn't had Ewan hanged. It was for Ronan to decide their fate.

She had Deirdre moved to the tower's top floor and put two men on the door. And there she would stay until her husband returned. Brenna only hoped she wouldn't live to regret this as she had with hanging Ewan.

By the next morning, their visitor was voicing her displeasure at being held prisoner in what she described as unfit quarters. There'd been nothing close to resembling a thank-you for Brenna's efforts.

"I will have a horrid scar from that woman's wretched stitch work. I've seen fisherman's nets sewed with more skill than hers."

"We were most intent on keep ye alive," Brenna pointed out, but the woman continued to argue until finally Brenna left the room with no intention of returning.

In the kitchen, she had Jane assign a maid to take Deirdre's meals to her room.

"I'll send Lizzy up. She is being punished for leaving her work to her sister last week," Jane said. "That will teach her."

"Do you not have a maid guilty of a much more serious crime?" Brenna asked, thinking poor

Lizzy wasn't being served a just punishment.

By the evening meal, Brenna had thought to assist the maid so not to have Lizzy bear the full brunt of Deirdre's unpleasantness, but the maid did not come to the kitchens. They found Lizzy's sister, who said she hadn't seen her since before the nooning.

"I'll tan the girl's backside for abandoning her duties," Jane threatened. "In the meantime, I'll go with you to deal with that she-devil in the tower."

"I thank ye, Jane. I wish I could say I would see to it myself, but I don't think I can face the woman alone. She's quite vicious."

Jane laughed as they made their way down the corridor to Deirdre's chamber. They were still a few rooms away when they heard the yelling from inside.

"It makes you want to turn and run the other way, does it not?" Brenna asked, making Jane chuckle once more.

Auld Ephraim and Young Adam were on duty, and both looked like they'd rather be anywhere else at the moment.

"At least our guest is feeling better, aye?" Brenna said to the men.

"Ach, aye, mistress. Such a goin' on from a lady." Auld Ephraim shook his head in disgust.

They couldn't make out what she yelled from inside, but Brenna was certain she'd made out a curse or two.

"I guess we best get it over with," Brenna said, giving Adam a nod to open the door for her and Jane.

Brenna braced herself for Deirdre's displeasure but instead was greeted with a hoarse, "Thank God, you've finally come."

But when Brenna studied the woman who'd spoken, she found it wasn't her mother by marriage, but Lizzy. The lass was wearing not but a shift and had a large lump on her forehead.

"The witch knocked me out and stole my clothing."

"You've been locked in here since the noon meal?" Brenna asked but knew it was what clearly happened. Ephraim and Adam came in looking at Lizzy in surprise.

"But ye left with the tray earlier," Ephraim said. "I was sure it was ye."

The man was near as big as a horse, but his sight wasn't the best in recent years. Wearing Lizzy's cap and dress, the man would have been fooled by Deirdre. Which meant Deirdre had escaped hours ago and could be anywhere by now.

"Get every available man to search for the laird's mother."

Having her wound tended, she was likely miles from the castle. Brenna hurried back toward the steps and slipped into Ronan's study where the clan's funds were kept. The lock on the cabinet where the strongboxes were kept was broken and twisted free.

She backed out of the room and went to the smaller chamber she'd first shared with Ronan and threw open the lid of the trunk at the foot of the bed. Breathing a sigh of relief, she took in the bags of money, right where she'd left them after moving them the night before.

Deirdre might have gotten away, but Brenna made sure the woman wouldn't count the Grant coffers in with the rest of her booty.

Chapter Thirty-Two

Ronan stared up at the darkening sky and frowned.

It had rained most of the day, and now the sun was giving up to the clouds. He hadn't wanted to stop in his hurry to get back to Brenna and beg her forgiveness. But it appeared the weather was going to force him to delay his plans. When he'd realized he needed to see Brenna, he couldn't wait even the time it would have taken for him to pack all his things.

Hugh wasn't happy he was leaving without him, but Ronan wasn't traveling with treasure or livestock, so he'd not be bothered. By anyone but the weather, apparently. His horse, stalwart and sure-footed as he'd always been, could also do with a rest. He quickly removed the saddle and brushed the horse down before tucking him in close to a fir tree.

Ronan was not far from Strathspey. Another hour and a half and he would have been able to spend the night with his wife. Instead, he'd be sleeping rough in the forest another night. Using some branches to provide shelter, he lit a fire and set a snare for his meal. Soon after eating, he pulled his plaid over his head, hoping to catch some sleep to leave at first light. But rest wasn't to be had.

He'd no sooner fall asleep than the fire would pop or sizzle in the rain and startle him awake. He was nearly back to slipping off when he heard a different snap of a branch, and Brimstone snorted his unease. Ronan tossed off his plaid to see someone standing over him in the darkness. His eyes didn't have a moment to adjust before he heard a low, familiar chuckle that sent a shiver up his spine.

Ewan.

Before he could think, he took a sharp blow to the side of his head, and the darkness of the forest pressed in, blocking out everything else.

***

The storms the night before cleared off by morning. The sky was a cloudless blue, and the air was warm but not stifling. The perfect day. Or would have been if Ronan was there and they could talk things out.

Instead, Brenna visited the Campbell family, and as she was walking back to the castle before noon, she saw a group of men riding for the castle carrying the Grant banner. She picked up her pace, wanting to see Ronan. She wasn't sure how to start the conversation they needed to have, but she knew they'd have it and be stronger for it. Her gaze searched the men dismounting in the bailey, eager to see the one man she loved more than all.

Hugh, Will, Ephraim, and young Adam, the same men who had left with Ronan. Yet she didn't see her husband among them.

"My lady," Hugh greeted her.

"Hugh. It's good to have you back. Where is Ronan?"

The three men stopped in their unpacking and turned to her.

"He left a day and a half before us," Hugh said. "We didn't reach the MacKenzies before meeting up with the MacPhersons, who told us Deirdre was not at the castle. So we returned to inform Ronan his mother was still on the run."

"He had not wanted to wait another minute to see you," Adam added, and Brenna's heart would have warmed over if not for her worry.

"He should have arrived last evening," Ephraim said.

"There was a storm. Mayhap his horse lost his footing and Ronan was thrown." Brenna could feel the fear settle in as she considered her husband lying somewhere hurt and alone. "We must find him."

Turning to the stable lad who'd come for the men's horses, she instead instructed him to bring her mount. "Please hurry."

"I've never known that beast he rides to slip a foot, but we'll look for him. You should stay here," Hugh said. Malcolm and Gabe came up to meet them.

The men came up with a plan. Will ordered Hugh and a few of the others to stay back and take watch of the keep while the other men mounted fresh horses to go look for the laird.

"Is there any use in asking you to stay behind?" Will asked, unlike Hugh, who had made it sound like an order.

Brenna only cast him a look. She knew better

than to make a nuisance of herself. If she thought she would cause a distraction by going, she would have willingly stayed back even if the thought made her stomach flip. But she knew she could help.

She wouldn't hold them back.

He let out a breath. "I didn't think so. Come on, then. Let's go find him."

They rode out together. While Brenna just wanted to push on, calling her husband's name, the men had a plan, and she did her best to be patient so they could find him quickly.

Norman, the warrior known best for his tracking ability, was in front. He stopped where the three men had cut across the field.

"Only three horses."

Brenna refrained from yelling, but in truth, if Ronan had been in the field, he would have been easy enough to see. Except for a few outcroppings of rocks, it was mostly flat and unobstructed.

Skirting along the woods, they continued on. They were riding too quickly to look into the forest. She understood. Ronan wouldn't have ridden through the woods if there was an easier path. He'd been in a hurry to get home to her. And because of that, he may have been injured.

She made an impatient sound, and Gabe looked over.

"We'll find him. You've never seen a tracker like Norman. He's a spook when it comes to talking to people, but he's the best at reading prints and determining which way an animal would go."

"But it's not a stag we're looking for. It's a man who wouldn't think like a deer."

"Patience, my lady. We'll find him. We won't

stop until we do, even if we end up back at the MacKenzies's."

It turned out she didn't need to gather all that much patience. It was only an hour later that the group stopped.

Dismounting, she heard Norman say, "Here."

Pushing through the horses, Brenna couldn't help but call out, "Ronan? Is he alive?"

But when the men parted, she saw the tracker bent down by a small shelter made from branches. A dark spot on the ground indicated a past fire.

"It's new. Surely from last night. It burned out," Norman said while pointing at two logs that hadn't burned through.

"Where is he?" Brenna asked.

Norman moved to the other side of the burned wood and bent down again. At first, Brenna thought it was ash, for it was the same dark color as the place where the fire had been laid. Stepping closer, she saw it was not blackened earth, but bloodstained.

"He's injured. He stopped because he was bleeding."

"Nay. He wasna bleeding when he got off his horse over there. There are other tracks coming from deeper in the forest. Someone met him here. And then someone was dragged off. Whether it be the laird or the other person, I can't say."

Brenna could barely swallow around the lump in her throat. Her gaze met Will's pained expression as four terrifying words hissed across her lips.

"Ewan has my husband."

Chapter Thirty-Three

Ronan woke up with a start, knowing he was in danger, though he couldn't quite recall why. It didn't take him long to remember what had happened the night before. At least he hoped it was only the night before.

He couldn't be sure how long he'd been out, but it was day now. Bright sun filtered through the forest, bathing everything in bright green light that seemed to pierce directly into his aching skull.

Ronan raised his hand to shade the sun so he could take in his surroundings, not that there was much to see. His arm didn't reach his face before a chain pulled taut and dug into his wrist.

Ronan didn't know where the chain had come from, but it looked as though it had long served its purpose. It was rusted through in many places, and it appeared someone had bent the links to take up for the missing bits.

He gave the chain a good tug, expecting it to

break apart under his strength, but the chain proved stronger than it looked, for it held. The clinking of the chains must have alerted his uncle to his wakefulness, for he came around a crumbling wall with a smile on his smug face.

"Good day, nephew. Welcome to my home," he said in a lilted greeting. "Temporary as it may be."

Ronan had been on Grant lands when Ewan had found him. He probably hadn't been far away to happen by Ronan where he slept. The bit of forest where he'd stopped ran the length of a cliff where the old castle had clung until the years and weather had worn it down and Strathspey had been built.

"The ruins of Brahstraud."

"Aye. Remember how we used to play about here as lads with our wee wooden swords fighting off the English invaders?"

"I remember. It seems you had more honor back then than now." Ronan lifted the chain, making it rattle. "At least, until you were about twelve."

Ewan narrowed his gaze on Ronan.

"What happened when I was twelve?"

Ronan stared him right in the eye when he spoke, watching for some sign he was wrong.

"When you tried to drown me."

Ewan's brows went up, and his lips pulled up in a sinister grin.

"Ye finally puzzled it out, did you? That took a fair amount of time."

"Why would I have had reason to assume such a thing? We'd been friends, nay, we'd been brothers."

"Nay," Ewan sneered. "If we'd been brothers, I would have been heir because I was older than you."

"You can't truly want to run the clan. You've

never shown any great skill in leading and no interest in the duty that comes of it."

"True enough. I don't wish to be bothered by the clansmen's squabbles or whether the larders are stocked enough to get through winter. But my father was laird, and it should be *my* birthright. You moved away to the MacPhersons. Even when you were old enough to return, you chose not to. It is true it's my fault you had to wed that Innes bitch, but you just left again. And even if you had died in France, I still wouldn't have been heir. Not when that witch was carrying your babe."

Ronan was fine to let the man blabber on until nightfall, despite the pain and stiffness that had settled into his leg, but when Ewan spoke of the child Brenna was carrying, Ronan couldn't help but react.

Ewan laughed cruelly and shrugged. "I managed to take care of that."

Rage the likes Ronan had never known burned through his veins as he pulled at the chains.

"You bastard! What did you do to my child?"

"I sought a wise woman in another village who gave me an herb for such things. She warned too much would end the mother as well, but I used all of it, and while it was a close thing for a few days, your wife lived." Ewan seemed mildly disappointed as if rain had doused his plans for the day.

Ronan had chastised his wife for banishing this demon from the castle. He'd already thought himself the lowest of the low for not reading her letters and forcing her to deal with such heartache alone. But now this?

He felt the shame of his betrayal tenfold, and it manifested as anger for this monster who had caused so much pain for anyone who had the misfortune to be caught in his path. It was then Ronan heard a low moan from somewhere in the shadows. It was a woman. Ronan searched the darkness, wanting desperately to see who made the sound. Was it his wife? Did Ewan have Brenna held captive as well?

"What have you done?" Ronan asked through clenched teeth.

"Ah. Now that you should be thanking me for." Ewan left and returned with a slim woman with straggled blond hair. Not Brenna then, but his relief was short. Whoever the woman was didn't deserve this fate. She raised her head, and it took Ronan much too long to recognize her.

"Mother?"

She hadn't changed much in the years since he'd seen her last. It was seeing her in a such a state that made it difficult. He'd rarely seen his mother with a hair out of place and in the best gowns his stepfather could afford.

Seeing her now, dirty, disheveled, and clearly ill, was a shock.

The smock she wore had once been light blue, but blood stained the front from the left shoulder to her slim waist. MacKenzie had said she'd taken a dagger when fleeing his home. From the grayish cast of her skin, it seemed that injury had festered and poisoned her.

"Ronan?" his mother said in a breathy voice. A smile graced her face briefly and, in that moment, he saw the mother of his memories, the one that got whatever she wanted with that smile, fake as it might be.

"What has happened?"

She looked down and shook her head. "I only fell on a branch…" She faded off with the lie when Ewan laughed.

"The MacKenzie didn't take kindly to her plan to rob him, and she took a dagger. Your bride refused to treat her wounds."

"That's not true," Deirdre spat.

Ronan wasn't sure if he could believe anything either of them told him.

"Lady Brenna and Moira tended the wound and stitched it. It was just that your wife locked me up in a bed chamber for your return. So I escaped, and during my retreat, I was thrown from the horse, breaking the stitches."

"You need to return to Strathspey so they can see to you," he said as if this were an option. There was no way Ewan would allow his mother to ride off to the castle only to tell everyone where Ewan was hiding with the laird held his captive.

Instead of responding, she turned to Ewan. "Ye said you wouldn't hurt him." His mother pointed to Ronan's hands, which were now covered in blood where the chains had dug into his skin.

Ronan wanted to laugh. For all his mother's worldly pursuits, she was incredibly naive to think Ewan's plans wouldn't end in death for both of them.

"He caused those wounds himself," Ewan said in a soothing voice. "He will be fine. We'll use him to get the ransom as planned, and then you and I will escape to England. I'll buy you the finest jewels. Just as I promised."

His mother smiled and nodded rather wobbly. "Then let's do it soon, for I don't wish to sleep in the forest another night. I've grown chilled."

Ronan wanted to point out she was most likely fevered as the day had grown warm. Instead, he tried to reason with her. "Mother, he doesn't plan to ransom me off and leave Scotland. He wants to be laird, for whatever reason. He plans to kill me and take over the clan."

His mother looked at Ewan with the shrewdness only another liar could muster.

"He is daft," Ewan crooned. "Our plan is already underway."

"Meaning you've sent a messenger to the castle demanding a price? Who? Who did you send, uncle? Did you send a note? Do you have a pot of ink and parchment here in your castle? Or mayhap a scribe since you never took much to writing." Ronan taunted the man.

At the sharp kick to his ribs, he realized mockery probably wasn't his best plan, but he needed his mother to see the truth. And if she couldn't see it in its entirety, he would point out the smaller clues.

"Who *do* you plan to send?" Deirdre asked with wide eyes. She looked almost surprised that she hadn't considered this. "I can't sit a horse. How do you plan for us to ride off to England?"

Good. His mother was puzzling out the lies.

"God. He's telling the truth. Ye plan to kill him and take over as heir of the Grants."

"Stop your fussing, woman." Ewan's mask dropped, and the manipulating rogue was gone, leaving behind a feckless viper. His mother was in danger, and she was still observant enough to see it.

She immediately changed course. "You're right. It makes no sense that you would want such a responsibility. Emptying their coffers and fleeing to live a life of luxury with me is a much better plan."

Ronan wanted to point out how neither of the plans required Deirdre and that she was in a precarious position. Though he wouldn't call out his mother for trying to save herself, he wanted her to know who she had sided with.

"This man killed your grandson. A defenseless babe, still in the womb."

For a moment, it seemed his mother had turned away, not caring what Ronan had said. But then, with more energy than he thought she still managed, she turned back to Ewan with a dagger in hand.

A loud cry left her lips, the volume that would make even the strongest war chief proud, and she ran at Ewan, blade out.

"Mother, no!" Ronan yelled, having seen the knife Ewan held at the ready. But it was too late to change the path she was on. Her dagger was deflected, causing only a cut along Ewan's arm while his sunk deep in his mother's chest.

She dropped to the stone a few feet from Ronan. "I'm sorry, lad. Sorry for it all." She blinked. "You were never to blame for what happened."

And with that, her eyes—the color of the Highland skies in September—hazed over in death.

"It was a merciful thing," Ewan spoke, barely breaking the silence that had fallen over them when his mother's raspy breaths had stopped. "The wound to her shoulder had poisoned her blood. She'd not have lived much longer anyway."

Ronan had seen the pallor of death on many men in France, and for once Ewan was not lying. He'd known his mother was not long for this world.

But he'd not allow Ewan to pretend he'd done anything for the mercy of another human being.

Rather than argue with the lout, Ronan closed his eyes and thought of all the happy times he'd had with his wife. If he was to die, he wanted to do so thinking of Brenna. He'd never have the chance to beg her forgiveness. Perhaps he would be destined to spend eternity a restless soul. It was what he deserved.

***

It was growing dark when Brenna and the warriors came upon Brahstraud.

Will had told them tales of playing there with Ewan and Ronan as a child. It offered shelter despite it having fallen to ruin nearly a century ago. They'd left the horses behind, and moved on foot, not wanting to give Ewan any warning of their attack.

But as they crested the small rise that dropped off with a view to the ruins, they encountered another problem.

"This is the only way in," Gabe said, having investigated the entire perimeter. "Until we make it down to them, the laird's throat will be cut. 'Tis a proper defense Ewan's set up here," the man added, sounding begrudgingly impressed.

Will nodded once before casting a serious gaze on her. "We'll need an archer to take him down."

"From this distance?" Hugh asked still looking out over the ledge. "To miss will mean death for the laird. Either because Ewan will have time to respond, or because Ewan's standing too close to the laird and we could hit him by accident."

Will was still watching her, and she knew

what he would say before he spoke. "Brenna can make that shot."

Gabe and Malcolm both nodded as Hugh winced. "She'll not be hunting a wee rabbit, Will."

"I'd say a rabbit moves faster and is a smaller target than Ewan makes," Malcolm put in.

"Aye, but if she misses a rabbit, the stew may be a little thin, but no one loses their life."

It was true enough and only what Brenna had been thinking since Will had honed his gaze on her. She looked down through the narrow opening where Ewan paced on the far side of her husband.

She waited a moment to hear them discuss another plan, but when she turned back, they were all still looking at her expectantly. There was no other plan.

The foundation of the old castle clung to a cliff. Rubble from the larger towers had fallen, blocking off most of the one side. Gabe was right. This was their only chance.

She was Ronan's only chance.

"I shall not miss," she said, hoping speaking it would make it so. "We need to hurry before our light is gone."

Gabe retrieved her bow and arrows and held them out to her. She wiped her damp hands down her skirt before taking the weapon with shaking hands.

If she missed, it wouldn't only be her husband's demise. Ewan would become laird of the Grants, and many other good people would suffer.

She could not fail. Everyone was counting on her.

Chapter Thirty-Four

Ewan continued to pace and spew his ramblings of how he would rule the clan. The demented fool aspired to rule all of Scotland. He planned to go to war clan by clan, acquiring land and more soldiers until he had an army at his command.

"And then we will descend upon England while they are still caught up in their war with France, and I can make my move."

Ronan wanted to point out all the ways in which his plan would likely fail, but he didn't have the energy to argue with a lunatic. His leg was causing him a great deal of pain now, and he knew even if he had the chance to escape the chains, he'd not make it very far.

"Why have you not acknowledged how perfect my plan is?" Ewan came closer and nudged Ronan's bad leg with his foot.

"Is that why you delay? Because you're waiting for me to tell you how brilliant you are? I'm sorry, but if I'm to face my death, I can't do so with a lie upon my lips. Telling you this farce of a plan will work would be the biggest lie ever to come out of my mouth. So, if it be all the same to ye, I'll just sit here while you ramble on with your hideously flawed strategy."

This infuriated Ewan to the point of murderous rage.

Mayhap Ronan had grown tired of waiting for Ewan to kill him and wanted it done, or perhaps he'd just been foolish in the grips of hunger and exhaustion, but Ronan was surprised by how calm he was in the face of death.

In France, he'd always thought it would be the worst thing, but in the hours he'd been sitting here with his fate becoming clearer by the minute, he'd had time to prepare.

He closed his eyes, picturing Brenna's face and waited for the death blow. But instead of the sounds he expected—the grunt of effort it would take for Ewan to raise his dagger and strike him through the heart, or the rush of air escaping his throat from the shock of it—he heard a strangely soft *whoosh* and then gurgling.

Opening his eyes, he saw Ewan stagger as blood escaped the corners of his mouth. His eyes were wide in shock, and his hands came up to the arrow sticking through both sides of his neck.

The arrow, fletched with white swan's feathers, tipped blue with woad.

Brenna.

***

Brenna watched as Ewan slumped to the ground in an unmoving heap and pulled in a shaky breath.

It was over. All the fear and constant danger were finally over. Ewan was gone. He'd never threaten her or the people she cared for ever again. The knowledge was nearly dizzying.

"Nice shot, my lady," Gabe praised her. "Did ye see it?" He turned to the other men who had obviously seen the shot as well.

Will patted her on the back. "Aye, we saw." As the other men cheered, he leaned closer to whisper. "Are ye well?"

She searched for an answer, and while it had been different shooting a rabbit to feed her people than shooting a man only to end him, she was sure it had been the right thing—nay, the only thing—to be done.

"I am well," she said.

He patted her shoulder again and smiled approvingly. "Ye are a fierce warrior, Brenna Grant."

"Let's see to the laird," Hugh said, shaking them all from their short celebration.

As they scrabbled down the rubble to get to Ronan, it was clear they never would have made it in time to save him. The arrow had been the only option. She only hoped it had been loosed in time. If Ronan had been mortally wounded, it would all be for naught.

Lighter on her feet than the other men, Brenna arrived first. His eyes were closed, and his stillness sent a chill through her as her gaze scoured Ronan for blood. She saw nothing severe, but she knew some wounds bled deep in the body and were just as deadly.

"Are you injured?" she asked. "Ronan?"

The only movement came from his lips. They pulled up in a slight smile. "You saved me, wife."

"We are all here," she said, lest he think she had foolishly come alone.

"Good. I'll need them to help me stand. My leg has grown stiff."

"Is that the only thing that hurts? Your leg?"

He hesitated as if thinking to say something else, but then he finally opened his eyes to look at her. "My leg is my only physical pain."

Physical. The distinction caused Brenna to step back as the other men filled in around their laird. They were loud with their exuberance, making it easy enough for Brenna to slip back into the shadows.

Her husband didn't suffer from physical pain, but he was telling her he still hurt. Because she had lost their child.

Eventually, the men quieted down. Gabe and Malcolm announced they would go collect the horses.

"Brimstone is somewhere close," Ronan said.

Hugh offered to go look for him while Will looked down to the bodies lying on the stones.

"We shall bury my mother. As for Ewan, he shall be left here to feed the vultures and animals. He'll not sully the Grant kirkyard with his mangey corpse," Ronan said adamantly.

"I'll see to your mother," Hugh said with a nod.

With all the men otherwise busy, she and Ronan were left standing there alone. He came closer, limping heavily on his injured leg.

"You should sit."

"Nay. I must walk around to loosen it up. Will you walk with me?"

She nodded and followed along as he took an overgrown path along the cliff's edge. When they could no longer see the castle, he turned to her, his eyes filled with sadness.

"I'm so sorry," she blurted as he opened his mouth to speak. She had no idea what he might say, but she needed him to know how terribly sorry she was she had lost their babe and disappointed him.

"Whatever would you have to apologize to me for?"

"I lost the babe. I didn't realize I was with child for some time, and I didn't take care like I should have right away. I rode every morning. If I hadn't…maybe…"

"Brenna, no." He let out a breath and placed his cool hand on her cheek. "Did ye think that was the pain I suffered?" He shook his head. "Christ, can I do nothing right by you?"

He walked in a tight circle and returned to stand before her. "Before I tell you what I have learned, you need to know that from the moment I learned about our child, I did not blame ye, lass. Never. I only blamed myself for not being here when you needed me. And now…'tis clear you needed me more than I realized. Not just to mourn our loss, but to have protected you from it in the first place. Had I been here, he never would have…"

His hands curled into tight fists, and he cursed Ewan's name to the devil.

"He did it, Brenna. He poisoned ye with a potion so you would lose the babe. He couldn't risk our son being the heir. He caused you nothing but pain, and I—I brought him back to our home and judged you for tossing him out, the man who killed our child. I embraced him as family and..."

He rubbed roughly at his face, clearly dismayed. She stepped forward and took his hand, squeezing it in both of hers.

"He was clever, Ronan. He tricked many people, including your grandsire."

She breathed, noticing how much easier it was to do without the constant weight of guilt on her chest. All this time she'd been told she'd done nothing wrong, and on some level she of course knew it to be true. But now, knowing it was Ewan's doing, it seemed easier to let it drift away.

Except it seemed it stayed pretty close. For every pound of guilt she shed, it appeared her husband was taking it on himself. "Ronan?"

He looked at her, and she saw the pain and guilt pressing in on him.

"We must leave this behind us. Here in this place with the man that caused it."

"I caused it," he nearly yelled. "I wasn't here where I should have been. At your side."

"I forgive you," she whispered urgently.

He choked. "Ye can't forgive me. I haven't even come up with a way to properly apologize for all I've done to ye. From the very first day we met when I told my grandfather I didn't want to marry ye and preferred your witch of a sister, I've done every single thing wrong. You deserve better than this, Brenna."

"Then offer your apology and tell me we can leave all of this sadness behind us. I don't want to carry it into the rest of our life together. Ewan has stolen enough from us already. I want a fresh start. Together. What do you want?"

He stared at her for what felt like a long time. Eventually, he took a steadying breath and squared his shoulders.

"Brenna Grant, please forgive me for all the ways I have wronged ye. For leaving you all those years. For not reading your letters or writing you back. For not protecting you from Ewan. For treating you so horribly when I returned and not asking to hear your side of things. For leaving you a second time when it seemed impossible to move forward. For allowing even one second of doubt that I blamed you for what happened. And probably most of all for not making sure you knew how very pleased I am to have you for my wife. I promise to do better. Please forgive me."

She didn't answer right away. Brushing away all he had said without truly hearing it wouldn't have been well done. So she thought through each word he said, and then, after careful consideration, she answered as she'd expected to.

"All is forgiven husband. Let us shake off all the guilt and move forward."

He nodded slowly and looked up at the darkened sky. "I know the first thing I want to do in this new start."

She tilted her head taking in the soft smile on his face. He seemed lighter, and she was so happy to see he had done what she'd asked and cast off the guilt that would easily consume him. "What is that?" she asked, hoping he planned to kiss her as she longed for.

Instead, he took her hand in his and stared into her eyes. "I love ye, wife," he said, causing her to gasp in surprise.

As much as she dreamed of him loving her, she never thought he would. After all, he hadn't chosen her. Hadn't wanted her. But she'd asked him to shake off the things of the past, and this doubt was something keeping her tethered to that old life.

It might have been the hardest thing she'd ever done. For this insecurity had wrapped itself around her soul long before she'd even met him and had only twisted tighter when he'd left.

She closed her eyes and gathered all the strength she had. Feeling his hand in hers, she pulled from his power as well and ripped the vile weed from her very being. The force of it made her stagger, but he supported her, his arms coming around her, holding her tight.

He loved her. She opened her eyes and saw the truth there in his patient gaze. "You love me," she said.

Her words lit off a spark that ignited his smile.

"Aye, lass, with all my heart. I look forward to spending the rest of my days telling you so."

And then, finally, he kissed her.

Epilogue

The following May

Ronan paused only briefly at the door to their chamber, wincing at the sound of retching from within. It had been a common thing in the mornings over the last month. Hopefully, the bannocks and honey he brought would continue to work their magic as they did most mornings.

"Hello, love. It appears today will not be the day the sickness leaves you."

"Nay. Moira said it shouldn't last much longer."

Ronan smiled at her words. The same words she said each morning as he rubbed her back and did his best to comfort her. Though, in truth, there wasn't much he could do. He knew the helplessness he felt each morning would be nothing in comparison to when his wife delivered their child.

He would be left in the corridor while his wife

faced that battle on her own.

"Bannock?" He held up his meager offering.

"Aye," she said as if he'd offered her a ship filled with jewels.

He ripped off a bite-size piece and handed it over after dipping it in a bit of honey. As was common, the sickly green tinge seemed to lift from her skin immediately. He went to the washstand and wrung out a cool cloth to wipe her face and neck. And as was also common, it was as if she had never been ill.

He handed her a glass of watered mead, and she sipped it as if it were the sweetest nectar. It was only the fact that his wife recovered her health and energy so quickly that he eventually allowed his priority to shift from protection to desire. He smiled at her and watched as her hazel eyes flared with carnal interest.

This was yet another common thing of late. Once his wife was back to feeling herself, she became ravenous for something besides bannocks. Namely him. He had yet to sate her for more than a few hours at a time.

It didn't stop him from trying, though.

***

As they descended into the main hall for the late meal, Brenna smoothed a hand over her still-flat stomach, hoping her gown was not too badly wrinkled from her husband's attentions.

He placed a kiss to her knuckles, and their gazes held for longer than was probably acceptable.

She was mentally counting down the hours until they could claim exhaustion and go to their room. Ronan was rarely away from her, always the doting husband. She worried he attempted to make up for the past. Something they'd both decided to put aside so they could live full and happy lives moving forward.

"I do hope our son has your smile," she said, not really meaning for the words to leave her mouth.

"And I hope our daughter has your eyes and spirit."

"My spirit?" Brenna laughed and he helped her into her seat next to him on the dais. "You wish her to ride in men's clothing and be late for meeting her intended."

"If he is any kind of man, he will realize she is worth waiting for."

He kissed her then, and Brenna might have been embarrassed to be kissing him in front of their clan, but like most times when she kissed her husband, she couldn't think of what she should or shouldn't do.

No word, English or Gaelic, could adequately describe the amount of love Brenna Grant felt for her husband. It could only be communicated with a kiss.

About the Author

One very early morning, Allison B. Hanson woke up with a conversation going on in her head. It wasn't so much a dream as being forced awake by her imagination. Unable to go back to sleep, she gave in, went to the computer, and began writing. Years later it still hasn't stopped.

Allison's historical romances are filled with kilted heroes. She lives near Hershey, Pennsylvania, and enjoys candy immensely, as well as long motorcycle rides, running and reading.

Other Books by Allison B. Hanson

Clan MacPherson Series
His Secret Highland Bride

Clan MacKinlay Series
Her Accidental Highlander Husband
Her Reluctant Highlander Husband
Her Forbidden Highlander Husband

Scots and Scoundrels Series
Winning Her Duke
Discovering Her Earl
Tempting Her Viscount

Safely in Scotland Series
The Lady's Reckless Abandon
The Lady's Great Escape
The Lady's Sweet Revenge

Love Under Fire Series
Witness in the Dark
Wanted for Life
Watched From a Distance

Printed in Dunstable, United Kingdom